I0733272

FALLEN MESSENGERS BOOK FOUR

OATHBREAKER

AVA MARIE SALINGER

COPYRIGHT

Oathbreaker (Fallen Messengers #4)
Copyright © 2022 by Ava Marie Salinger.
All rights reserved.
Registered with the US Copyright Office.
Third paperback edition: 2024
ISBN: 978-1-912834-30-3

www.AMSalinger.com
shop.adstarrling.com

Edited by Right Ink On The Wall

Content note: this book contains two scenes of sexual violence that may be upsetting to some readers. These scenes do not involve the main protagonists of this series.

FALLEN MESSENGERS GLOSSARY

Aerial: An angel or demon who can control wind.

Alchemist: A human who can create new matter or manipulate existing matter into new forms. Emits a scent of powdered iron.

Aqueous: An angel or demon who can control water.

Argent Lake: Home of the Naiads.

Argonaut Agency: Organization responsible for law and order in the supernatural and magical communities. Headquarters in New York. Agents include angels, demons, and magic users.

Astrea Sea: Home of the Nereids.

Bloodsand: A black tree with red veins that grows in the Nine Hells. Created by warlocks who made pacts with the Underworld after the Fall. Can be used to summon war demons from the Nine Hells.

Blossom Silver: A silver derivative that can heal injuries caused by demonic weapons or black magic. Made by the Naiads.

Cabalista: Demonic organization. Agents include demons only. Headquarters in London.

Dark Blight: A powder black-magic users use in their rituals and which is poisonous to angels and other magic users. Made by Shadow Empire alchemists from the heart of a Dryad.

Demi: The offspring of a God of Heaven/God of the Underworld and a human or a being possessing divine powers. Can take on any appearance.

Electrum: Naturally occurring alloy of gold and silver, as well as copper and other trace elements. Used extensively by Argonaut in their weapons. Combined with steel, titanium, and Rain Silver to make their bullets.

Empyreal: The highest order of angels or demons, with powers equal to those of a Demigod.

Enchanter/Enchantress: A human who uses illusion magic. Emits a scent of cedar.

Fiery: An angel or a demon who can wield Heaven or Hell's Fire.

Fractured Soul: A human's damaged soul core, extracted from the body – a powerful source of magic.

Ghoul: An evil spirit who consumes the flesh of humans. Emits a scent of rotting meat.

Glitterfang: A pale powder white-magic users employ in their rituals and which is poisonous to demons and black-magic users. Made by Nereids.

Hexa: Guild of magic users. Agents include magic users only. Headquarters in Seattle.

Incubus: A male demon who gains power from sleeping with humans and divine entities.

Ivory Peaks: Home of the Dryads.

Khimer: A creature born of the fusion of a Reaper and a living being.

Lucifugous: A heliophobic demon who abhors light and who can control darkness.

Mage: A human who uses an arcane staff to focus their magic powers. Emits a scent of Juniper.

Magic Levels: Classification of magic users based on

their abilities, with Level Six being the weakest and Level One the strongest.

Messengers: Those belonging to the Third Sphere of Heaven and Third Hierarchy of Demons.

Moirai: The Fates. The Goddesses of Destiny.

Order of Rosen: Religious order affiliated with the Catholic Church. Agents include angels only. Headquarters in Rome.

Potomoi: A male Nymph.

Rain Silver: A liquid-silver derivative that can injure and kill demons. Made by the Nymphs.

Rain Vale: Home of the Nymphs.

Reaper: A soul collector and guide of the dead. Emits a scent of camphor.

Reaper Seed: A drug that can intoxicate most beings and which is fatal in high doses. Mined by Lucifugous demons in the Shadow Empire. Potent hallucinogen for Lucifugous demons.

Shadow Empire: Home of Ghouls, Lucifugous demons, and Dark Alchemists.

Sorcerer/Sorceress: A human born with powerful soul

core magic. Uses the energies around them to manipulate magic. Emits the scent of Valerian.

Soul Core: A living being's life force. Red for demons, white for angels, and dirty gray for humans.

Spirit Realm: Home of Pan, the Gods of the Underworld, and lesser spirits.

Stark Steel: Strongest and most magic-resistant metal on Earth. Found exclusively in the weapons and armor of the Fallen.

Succubus: A female demon who gains power from sleeping with humans and divine entities.

Terrene: An angel or demon who can control earth and its derivative metals.

The Fall: An unexplained event five hundred years ago that resulted in an army of angels and demons falling to Earth.

The Fallen: Angels or demons who fell to Earth.

The Nether: The space between Heaven, Earth, and the Nine Hells.

The Abyss: A forgotten realm beyond the Nether from where there is no escape.

War Demon: Demon soldiers created for battle. Remnants of an ancient war between Heaven and Hell. Banished to the deepest parts of the Hells.

Warlock: A human who draws power from demons and the Hells and converts it to magic. Emits a scent of sulfur.

Wizard/Witch: A human who learns to use magic through spell books, and who utilizes potions and rituals to access their soul-core magic. Emits a scent of Frankincense.

PRELUDE

Five hundred years ago, Rain Vale

The sky above the capital flickered alarmingly, the lightning flashing amidst the dark, twisted clouds highlighting the sinister formations threatening to rip apart the very heavens.

Tension knotted the shoulders of the Queen of the Nymphs as she stood upon the rooftop of the north tower of the castle, her wine-red cape flapping around her armor-covered legs and the broadsword in her hand. It was the highest elevation in Isyanore and the best vantage point from which she could gauge what was happening across the realm of forests, valleys, and lakes extending to pale peaks marching across the horizon like sentinels.

What she could see and sense did nothing to reassure her.

The elements were angry. She could tell from the fury of the wind tearing through the trees and the enraged roar of the rivers that crisscrossed the kingdom of the Nymphs. Even the land protested, the very bones of Rain Vale trembling under her feet as Nature railed against what was happening high above it, in a place few dared venture.

The Nether.

Whatever this is, it's going to tear apart the realms!

The bitter taste of fear burned Kalliste's throat as she lifted her gaze from the unnatural storm sweeping across the kingdom to the firmament once more. The disturbance in the sky could only mean one thing.

They were losing the war.

A dark premonition filled her veins. She dug her nails into her palms.

"You cannot let him defeat you, Icarus!" she mumbled to herself. "All will be lost if you do!"

"My Queen, we should get you to safety!"

Kalliste startled. She looked over her shoulder.

Galatea, the captain of the Royal Guard, fixed her with a fierce green stare from where she stood at the head of a vanguard of soldiers. Though the troops showed signs of nervousness, Kalliste knew their strength and determination would not falter in battle. Contrary to popular belief, Nymphs and Potamois were not helpless creatures in need of protection.

"There is no safe place for us in this realm or any other, Galatea," Kalliste said bitterly. "Not if that God wins!"

A muscle jumped in Galatea's jawline as she looked at the sky. Not only was she Kalliste's bodyguard, she was also her closest friend and confidante. She was aware how much the war had already cost their kingdom.

"There is still hope, my Queen." Her eyes met Kalliste's once more, conviction a bright light burning in her pupils. "The Awakener will not be so easily defeat—"

The stillness that dropped around them stole the rest of Galatea's words from her lips and the very air from the atmosphere. Kalliste's ears popped. Rain Vale grew silent, the uncanny storm ripping through it abating with a suddenness that spoke of impending doom and destruction.

Galatea drew a sharp breath. Kalliste's head whipped around, her horrified gaze following that of the captain as it locked on the sky once more. The clouds wavered and rippled high above them, drawing eerie patterns across the firmament.

The sound the heavens made as they tore open was one Kalliste would remember forever more.

Darkness throbbed along the jagged breach that hadn't been there before. It expanded rapidly, a black scar that zigzagged across the sky. Rain Vale shook and shuddered as the Nether splintered.

Dozens of chasms cleaved the land, the very bedrock of the kingdom crumbling under the aberrant forces fracturing every realm connected to the space that defined their boundaries. Large swathes of forests and vales vanished inside the gulfs that appeared out of nowhere. Birds took to the sky in panicked droves, their wings darkening the air while the animals who could not escape bellowed and shrieked in fear beneath them. The screams of the citizens of Isyanore joined those of the hapless creatures as buildings cracked and crevasses swallowed up entire streets of the capital.

The sounds of terror filling the kingdom were echoed by those of the armored figures tumbling out of the inky rift high above the land, the remains of a divine army that had fought a deadly war to save all the realms and Heaven and the Hells themselves from destruction.

Kalliste's stomach twisted at the sight of the monstruous, dark-winged fiends who fell after them.

War demons!

She called upon the wind and let it carry her off the tower.

"Your Majesty!" Galatea shouted, alarmed.

"Protect the city, Galatea!" Kalliste barked. "Leave the rest to me!"

The captain and her troops became rapidly dwindling figures atop the tower as she rose above the capital, their forlorn gazes following her. Kalliste ignored them.

She had but seconds left to act.

Her heart thumped heavily in her chest as she reached inside her armor and removed the Book of Rain. The artifact gleamed, the ornate filigree of gold and silver metal encasing the blue tome shimmering with a divine glow. Her mouth grew dry as she observed the book. It was heavy and cold in her hand and not at all like the Heavenly weapon it was meant to be.

It needed something else to become that.

Kalliste slowed her breathing and focused inward, as she had been taught to do by her grandmother, the first Queen of Rain Vale. Heat filtered through her veins, the godly energy in her soul core filling her body with enough force to rattle her teeth. The clasp holding the tome shut peeled open with a soft snap as it acknowledged the power of her bloodline.

Dazzling brilliance exploded from the artifact, so bright Kalliste had to squint. The tome vibrated violently in her grasp. She gnashed her teeth and hung on grimly.

Rain Vale trembled, the realm responding to the Heavenly forces contained within the Book of Rain. Pillars of light exploded into existence at the cardinal points of the realm, their shining tips glimmering faintly in the distance.

The artifact grew hot as it resonated with them. A pale barrier tore across the sky from the bright columns, the translucent veil barely visible except for where the light struck it at an angle. It coalesced above the capital and all around the realm, taking the brunt of the damage the tear in the Nether was causing.

The quakes shaking the land started to subside.

Awe filled Kalliste as she watched the chaos outside the protective bubble enclosing her kingdom. Though she had heard tales of what the Book of Rain could do, it was her first time seeing it in action.

A flash amidst the churning shadows darkening the sky caught her eye. Horror filled Kalliste when she realized what was about to happen.

No! She grasped the artifact in her hand and willed her intent upon it, her pulse racing. *Please! Save them!*

The shield wavered seconds before the armored angels and demons who had fought on their side of the desperate War in the Nether struck it, letting them pass without killing them.

The war demons and monsters who formed the enemy faction smashed upon the barrier with loud cracks and thuds a moment later, their screams of pain and rage rumbling across the kingdom as it obliterated them. Some slipped through the gaps where the angels and their demon allies fell.

Kalliste scowled and shot up into the air. Galatea and her troops joined her rapidly as she started felling their enemy.

The blood of the war demons and Hells' beasts rained upon Isyanore, a cursed drizzle that felt like it would stain the land forever more. Kalliste wielded her sword and the dazzling artifact in her hand with fury, bolts of light shooting from the book to dispose of those foes who escaped her attack and that of her army.

The terrible screeches tearing the sky above the capital finally faded as the last of the fiends and their monstruous accomplices met a ghastly end.

Kalliste's chest heaved where she floated high above the land, her breaths shuddering in and out of her lungs. Though she was a demigod, battling war demons and Hells' monsters was a task that would take a toll on even the strongest deity. She wiped sweat and blood from her face and had just turned to head to where

Galatea was when the Book of Rain throbbed in her hand, startling her.

Her stomach twisted as a burst of cognizance flared through her soul core. Instinct drew her gaze to the sky. The tear in the Nether was closing beyond the barrier that had protected Rain Vale, the unusual darkness within the void roiling viciously as it was forced back where it belonged.

An armored figure with one white wing intact slipped through just before it sealed shut.

Kalliste froze. She recognized the long, flowing hair and slate-blue armor of the being falling limply toward the ground.

No!

She moved, as swift as light, and caught the Guardian some thousand feet from the valley floor. Bile flooded her throat when she clocked the extensive injuries he had incurred.

The left side of his face and body were missing.

His right eye fluttered open, revealing a beautiful, sapphire iris dulled by pain and shock. "Ka…llis…te?"

"Hush, Rohengar," she whispered, sorrow a heavy weight in her chest.

They both knew the wounds he bore were fatal.

Kalliste carried the dying demigod to a low hill just outside the city. It was where the majority of those who had fallen from the Nether had crash landed, their winged bodies carving deep grooves in the land before they came to a standstill, powerful frames shuddering and barely conscious from the injuries they had borne.

Already, the citizens of Isyanore were rushing through the gates of the city to help them.

Blood burst from Rohengar's lips as she landed lightly on the hillock. Kalliste carefully lowered him to the ground, tears swarming her vision. Dirt and grass darkened beneath Rohengar as he bled, the warm, crimson flow pulsing with every beat of his dying heart and soul core.

"You used the Book of Rain," he whispered.

Kalliste wiped her cheeks and met Rohengar's sad gaze. "Yes."

A shadow swept over them. Galatea landed a short distance away and hurried over. "My Queen! Is that—?!"

Kalliste met the captain's eyes and dipped her chin wordlessly. Galatea's shoulders drooped, grief leeching the color from her face.

Light flashed at the corner of Kalliste's vision.

Rohengar had opened his right fist. Lying in his palm, blazing with Heaven's power, was a shard of light. Kalliste stared.

"The Spear of Light resonated—" Rohengar stopped and swallowed convulsively, "it resonated with the Book of Rain when you activated it…"

Kalliste's eyes rounded.

"That's what drew it here." Rohengar smiled weakly. "And me."

Understanding dawned belatedly. The Spear of Light was identical to the four pillars the Book of Rain had triggered into existence from within the heart of Rain Vale. It was one of the many reasons Rohengar had often left the Nether to visit the realm, the weapon he wielded seemingly just as hungry to taste the air of the land it had been born upon as he was.

The South Star and Guardian of the Nether placed the shard in her hand and closed his fingers atop hers. "Keep it safe, Kalliste…" A tortured gasp rattled his chest, distorting his words for a moment. "It is for the next South Star…to…wield…"

Kalliste swallowed a sob. She could feel Death's shadow racing across Rain Vale to harvest the soul of the demigod.

"Tell Icarus that I…love him…" The light faded from Rohengar's eye as he stared up at the sky. "And that I…do not…blame…him…" A soft smile curved the South Star's lips. "My only regret remains that I failed…to tell the one…I cherished with all my… heart…how I truly…felt…about…him…"

Kalliste froze as Rohengar grew still. The South Star's smile lingered long after he passed, the Guardian oblivious to the sounds of sorrow that would echo through Rain Vale for decades after the news of his demise spread across the kingdom.

CHAPTER ONE

Cassius Black cursed and pivoted on his heels. His shoulder skimmed the brick wall of the alley he entered, slowing his pace a fraction. The running man in the distance became a dim figure. Cassius scowled and accelerated.

"This would go so much faster if I could use my true strength and my wings!" he snapped into his mouthpiece.

Adrianne Hogan's voice came over the earpiece, her tone sour. "Yeah, well, that ain't happening. Strickland will have our hides if we let your identity be known."

"I hate to break it to you, babe, but his wings are not the only things that can divulge his identity," Bailey Green drawled over their comm line. "Dude's face has been plastered all over the news these past two weeks."

The sound of a scuffle followed.

"Got my guy!" the wizard announced triumphantly.

There was a fleshy sound. Someone grunted and wheezed out some colorful swearwords.

"What was that?" Adrianne asked, suspicious.

"Oh, just our suspect," Bailey replied cheerfully. "He needed reminding that he has balls."

Cassius could practically feel Adrianne scowling where she supervised their operation from the back of an Argonaut van one block away.

The gang they were after was responsible for the death of over a dozen magic users up and down the West Coast, many of them agents of Hexa. Argonaut had gathered enough evidence to prove beyond doubt that the men were trafficking Dark Blight out of the Shadow Empire and a warrant had been issued for their arrest that morning. Poisonous to angels and magic users alike, Dark Blight was a chemical banned on Earth and in all other realms bar the Hells and the Shadow Empire, where it was manufactured by alchemists from the hearts of Dryads and used in their black-magic rites.

It was Bostrof Orzkal, the former king of the Shadow Empire and Cassius's friend, who'd provided them with the final proof of the gang's culpability and a tip-off to their location. Though he flirted with the laws that governed the human world, Bostrof knew it was not his place to dispose of the criminals. Cassius was aware the outcome would have been different had the men they were after been found in the Shadow Empire. Even though that realm was technically no longer his to rule, the criminals would definitely not have survived the Lucifugous demon's wrath.

Pretending to ignore the affairs of the Shadow Empire was a lie Bostrof had perfected over the centuries, ever since he'd been forcibly relocated to Earth after the Fall. Once he'd become aware that the new ruler of his realm had turned his kingdom into a haven for dark alchemists and ghouls, Bostrof had enrolled other Lucifugous demons loyal to him to be his eyes in the Shadow Empire and the Hells.

It was because of his network of spies that Cassius and Morgan King had managed to put a stop to the trade of Reaper Seed ripping through San Francisco a few months back. A hallucinogen that had caused untold suffering among Lucifugous demons and rendered some mad from addiction, Reaper Seed had been a key ingredient in the human sacrifices that had terrorized the city that summer.

Sacrifices linked to Chester Moran, the warlock son of Tania Lancaster, a sorceress specializing in necromancy who had overseen a reign of terror across England and Europe half a century ago.

Though they had each been wicked in their own right, Tania and Chester had ultimately been the victims of manipulation by Elios, the God of Darkness who had been the mastermind behind every scheme to tear apart the Nether, including the disaster that had caused the Fall.

Elios was not only twin to Hypnos, the deity suspected of being behind the loss of memory incurred by all those who fell and many who were left behind in the fractured realms the Fall caused, he was also a half-brother to Morgan and to Victor Sloan, the men Cassius cherished most in this world.

It was during their recent battle with Elios in the Spirit Realm that Victor's suppressed powers had awakened and he had finally learned his true identity. Namely that he was Coraos, the demigod who had chosen to stand by Elios's side in the war that had torn the Nether apart.

Cassius had also recalled his own true name during the fight.

He was Icarus, the North Star and Awakener. The most powerful Guardian of the Nether and the being who had rallied an army of angels, demons, Gods, and spirits to lead the war against Elios and his dark army.

Elios's ultimate intentions had also finally become clear. He wanted to resurrect his grandfather Chaos from the Abyss, the place where the first Primordial God was banished millennia ago by an army led by his own children. A realm from where none had ever returned, the Abyss was reputed to be able to destroy all the realms by consuming them. And it was becoming clear that the Nether and its Guardians existed solely to stand between it and everything else in existence, including Heaven and the Hells.

Movement ahead brought Cassius sharply back to the present. Willis Brock, the guy he was after, had darted into a passage to his left. Cassius slowed as he approached the opening of the side alley. He hugged the wall and edged an eye around the corner. A bullet winged out of the shadows, the whizz of its passage making his ears ring.

It slammed into the wall behind him and carved a hole halfway into the concrete. Cassius narrowed his eyes at the scents he detected from the shot.

Stark Steel and Electrum. Bostrof was right. These assholes are asking to be killed!

Found exclusively in the armor and weapons of the Fallen, Stark Steel was the strongest and most magic-resistant metal on Earth. It was also the only element capable of inflicting mortal wounds on angels and demons.

It was illegal to combine Stark Steel with Electrum, a naturally occurring alloy of gold, silver, and copper. Anyone found in possession of ammunition possessing both was guaranteed a life behind bars. Since they were responsible for law and order in the otherworldly and magical communities, Argonaut was the only agency allowed to carry bullets made from the two elements. Even then, their use had to be sanctioned at the highest level of the organization before agents were permitted to carry them in public.

The sound of running footsteps reached Cassius's ears. He cursed and dashed into the passageway, heedless of danger. If push came to shove, he could always transform into his Empyreal form and take care of Brock.

It was imperative they stop these men before they caused more deaths.

Brock had already disappeared around the next bend by the time Cassius was halfway down the back lane. He took the turn at a run and heard a woman scream.

Shit!

His soul core throbbed, lending a burst of divine strength to his limbs. Bright sunlight washed over him as he shot out of the alleyway and onto a busy avenue in Belden Place.

A middle-aged woman was slowly sitting up on the sidewalk across the road, pale and visibly shaken. Passersby were rushing over to help her. A cold sweat prickled Cassius's nape when he saw the slowly spinning, revolving door behind her.

It was the entrance to a clinic.

"Adrianne, we may have a hostage situation!" he barked into his comm piece as he darted into the traffic.

"What?!"

"Brock just went into a Medicaid clinic!"

He ignored the horns blasting around him and gave her the address of the building. The woman Brock had knocked over trembled violently as gentle hands helped her to her feet.

Cassius closed in on the crowd. "Are you hurt?!"

The woman jumped at the sound of his voice and looked around, startled. "I'm—I'm alright, I think. Just shook up!"

Cassius jerked his chin toward the clinic. "Did he go in there?"

The woman swallowed and nodded. Recognition dawned in her eyes. She stared, her mouth rounding.

Someone in the crowd gasped. "You're that angel, aren't you?! The one who—"

Cassius was already headed for the revolving door.

CHAPTER TWO

A SHOT SLAMMED INTO THE LINOLEUM FLOOR INCHES from Cassius's left foot as he entered a reception area. He rocked to a stop, his gaze swinging from the bullet's impact point to the petrified receptionist behind the desk opposite him and the waiting area to his right. Anger sparked through his veins.

Brock was swinging his gun wildly at the patients crouching in their seats, faces pale as they stole petrified glances at the madman threatening them. A child started to cry. A woman sobbed.

"Stop right there or I'll shoot them!" Brock shouted, desperation lending him a crazed look.

Cassius's palms itched for the Stark Steel blade strapped to his waist.

"This place will soon be surrounded," he said calmly. "Even if you were to kill everyone in here, you would not walk out of this building alive."

His level tone did nothing to pacify the man. Brock snatched a little boy from his mother's arms, dragged him to the far end of the reception, and locked an arm around his throat. Ice skittered down Cassius's spine.

"I swear to God, I will kill this kid if you take a single step forward!" Brock spat.

He pressed the barrel of his gun to the child's temple. Cries of horror filled the reception area. The child's mother lunged forward.

"Stop!" Cassius barked.

She stumbled and fell onto her hands and knees, her sobs loud as she gazed desperately at her son.

Cassius never broke eye contact with the boy. "What's your name?"

Tears streamed down the kid's face. He stayed frozen, as if he sensed his very life depended on it.

"It's—it's Mi—Michael!" he hiccupped.

Cassius's mouth curved in a faint smile. "It's gonna be okay, Michael. Now, close your eyes."

The boy's lips parted on a gasp. His pupils widened, his gaze rising to the black and red wings that had unfurled from Cassius's back. He squeezed his eyes shut.

Brock's jaw sagged open. "You're—you're that guy! That goddamn angel everyone's talking ab—!"

Heaven's Light flooded the room, making everyone squint.

Cassius moved.

Brock choked as he found himself slammed bodily against the ceiling, his gun falling limply from his fingers and his hostage free below them. He gawped vapidly at Cassius before clawing at the fingers wrapped around his throat, clearly unable to comprehend what had just happened.

Few could grasp the movements of an Empyreal, let alone a demigod.

"You're under arrest," Cassius said coldly, the seraphic light projected from his pupils painting Brock's face a stark white. "Anything you say can and will—"

Something glinted out the corner of Cassius's eye. A blade had appeared in Brock's hand. He wrinkled his brow.

This guy really is a moron!

He was about to tell Brock the knife wasn't made of Stark Steel and would not inflict a single scratch on him when the front door exploded inward and a dark whirlwind filled the room. One that smelled green and fresh and full of the rage of a demigod.

Brock was wrenched from Cassius's grasp by Morgan.

"I've got this!" Cassius protested.

His lover did not acknowledge his words, the seraphic fire in his eyes telling Cassius he was beyond hearing him. Brock screamed as Morgan carried him through the gaping remains of the entrance, his Sword of Wind in hand and his body wreathed in black currents mixed with the iridescent green magic stemming from his Dryad lineage.

Deathly stillness descended upon the clinic in the wake of their departure. It was broken by the sounds of vehicles squealing to a violent stop outside and a cacophony of horns.

Cassius blew out a sigh, retracted his Empyreal powers, and landed lightly on his feet amidst the broken glass littering the floor. "Adrianne, we have another situation."

"I can see the situation just fine, Cassius!" Adrianne snapped in his ears. "The situation is currently carrying our suspect into the sky!"

"Fuck!" Cassius swore.

He became aware of dozens of stares.

The clinic staff and their patients were gawking at him. Cassius stiffened, expecting to see revulsion in their eyes. Instead, he read only awe and adulation.

It had been two weeks since all four agencies responsible for the otherworldly and magic users in the world had officially acknowledged everything Cassius had done behind the scenes to keep Earth safe from harm these past five hundred years. That the most feared and shunned angel on Earth had in fact been doing the dirty work of the organizations that had long lambasted his very existence had come as a shock to otherworldly and humans alike. It was the topic of conversation in every city and town across the globe, with everyone now clamoring to catch a glimpse of the champion who had saved them from the shadows innumerable times in the past.

As far as Cassius was concerned, the whole revelation thing was turning out to be a giant pain in his ass.

Unfortunately, making his heroic deeds public was the bargaining chip Morgan had used to force everyone's hand when they'd been fighting Elios and his army of war demons a few weeks back. Tired of seeing Cassius subjected to abuse he did not deserve, the demigod had threatened to abandon Earth and claim his rightful place as the heir to the Dryad kingdom throne, with Cassius as his consort.

The prospect of losing two of the most powerful otherworldly in the world when the threat of Elios's presence still cast a shadow upon the Earth was not a risk the agencies had been willing to take. Hence why the whole world was now looking at Cassius in a brand-new light. One that straddled the line between admiration and veneration too closely for his liking.

The attention the announcements had garnered upon the San Francisco branch of Argonaut meant that its director, Francis Strickland, had insisted Cassius keep a low profile for a while and not use his powers in public. Strickland had even gone as far as to reject all offers for interviews that had come his way by virtue of being Cassius's boss and had asked the angel to similarly decline the many personal requests he had received.

Not that Strickland had had to work hard to convince Cassius. The media circus surrounding the agencies' revelations was bad enough from a distance and the last thing Cassius wanted to do was be in the middle of that.

Francis is sure gonna be thrilled about this little development.

He filed that glum thought away and turned.

The little boy stood in his mother's arms, the woman bawling her eyes out as she knelt and hugged him tightly to her chest. He stared unblinkingly at Cassius over her shoulder.

Cassius walked over and squatted. "You alright?"

The boy nodded and sniffed before wiping snot on the back of his shirt sleeve. His mother turned to Cassius, her gaze full of gratitude.

"Thank—thank you!" she blubbered.

"No problem." Cassius smiled faintly and gently ruffled the boy's hair. "You were very brave."

The boy nodded, chin wobbling. "Where—" he stopped and gulped, "where did the bad man go?!"

Cassius grimaced. "Somewhere where the air is thin."

The kid blinked, confused.

"This asshole had better not drop our suspect," Adrianne grumbled in Cassius's earpiece. "People are filming this shit. I swear to God, if he lets go of him, I will *THAT SON OF A—!*"

Cassius's pulse quickened. He moved, the force of his departure leaving gasps and a violent backdraft in his wake. He was through the door and in the air in a heartbeat.

Brock was plummeting to Earth, arms and legs pinwheeling wildly even as the wind snatched his scream from his lips. Cassius cursed and shot up, the city shrinking rapidly beneath him.

Morgan dove and grabbed Brock's wrist about a mile and a half from the ground. A dark stain dampened the front of the man's trousers as he jerked to a bone-jarring stop. His eyes rolled back in his head and he fainted.

Cassius rocked up beside them and directed a glare at his lover.

"What?" Morgan shrugged innocently. "My hand slipped."

He retracted his demigod powers, his gray wings emerging from the shrinking, dark and verdant tempest that had engulfed him.

CHAPTER THREE

"Let's get him down there," Cassius said between gritted teeth. "And then you and I need to have a word."

Morgan tensed a little, guilt flashing in his eyes.

Zach Mooney and Julia Chen appeared. The demon and the angel slowed and kept abreast of them as they headed for the avenue.

"You really know how to put on a show, don't you?" Julia told Morgan acerbically.

"It wasn't a show," Morgan protested. "The asshole attacked Cassius!"

"Lest you've failed to notice, I can take of myself!" Cassius snarled.

"You okay?" Zach asked Cassius.

"Besides the fact that I'm dating an idiot, yes, I'm fine!"

Morgan winced at his words.

Zach patted Cassius on the back, his expression sympathetic. "He used to be our idiot. Now he's all yours."

Argonaut and San Francisco PD had cordoned off half the block by the time they reached the ground. They landed on the sidewalk amidst a barrage of camera clicks and flashes, everyone keen to take a snapshot of the star of the hour and the secretive hero whose identity had just been revealed. Heat warmed Cassius's face as a sea of hungry gazes scored his face and figure.

All he wanted to do was sink into a hole in the ground.

A muscle jumped in Morgan's jawline. Cassius could tell from the angel's stormy expression that he resented the people ogling his lover.

A streak of petulance had Cassius muttering, "This is all your fault."

Morgan stiffened, his gaze turning haunted for an instant as he darted a look his way. Cassius's stomach plummeted. He'd opened his mouth to apologize when a disturbance drew their attention.

Adrianne and Charlie were barging through the crowd. They ducked beneath the crime scene tape San Francisco PD had erected and closed in on their position.

"Everyone alright?" the sorceress said sharply.

"Yeah." Morgan wrinkled his nose at the stench of urine filling the vicinity. "Well, except for this guy."

Brock sagged limply in his hand, still unconscious.

Charlie fixed the stink situation with a spell that smelled of wild flowers. Though he specialized in dark illusions, the enchanter's magic had acquired a soft edge lately. Everyone in their team knew it was a result of his burgeoning relationship with Reuben Fletcher and Jasper Cobb, the angel and demon who headed the San Francisco Order of Rosen and Cabalista bureaus respectively.

Though the affair had taken everyone by surprise, they'd accepted the enchanter's choice of partners. It was a strange ménage to say the least but one that worked surprisingly well. There were even rumors circulating among the otherworldly in the city that Jasper's ill-disposed demeanor had changed and that the demon was no longer being a total asshole to his subordinates.

The only one who was still disgruntled about the entire thing was Morgan. It had become clear to Cassius that the demigod had seen himself as Charlie's mentor and was currently embracing the role of a malcontent father whose son had been snatched from under his nose by two wayward beasts.

It's a good thing we don't have kids. He'd be a total ass to their dates.

The thought had Cassius's chest tightening with a mix of emotions. Not that it would be possible for him to bear Morgan's children anyway. And besides, angels and demons were not known for their instinct to breed; unlike humans and other supernatural races, it was not in their nature to want to seed the world with their offspring.

Yet, Cassius couldn't help but brood over it sometimes.

To have the fruit of their union breathing and walking this world would be his and Morgan's ultimate declaration of love for one another. He'd often wondered what such a child would look like and if it was the godly bloodline that ran in his veins that made him ache for such an impossible dream.

Adrianne lowered her brows at Morgan. "I wasn't talking to you, jerkface!"

"May I remind you that I'm your boss," the demigod said in a hurt voice.

"My boss wouldn't deliberately let go of a suspect's arm three miles up in the air." Concern clouded the sorceress's face as she scanned the zealous crowd gawking at Cassius. She fixed him with a worried stare. "Let's get you back to the bureau before the news stations show up."

Cassius frowned. "You mean, let's get Brock and the other suspects back to the bureau."

"We can take care of them," Adrianne said dismissively. "Strickland called. He wants you and Morgan in his office, pronto."

"I'M PUTTING THE TWO OF YOU ON ADMINISTRATIVE leave as of this moment."

The director's words punched a hole in Morgan's stomach and stole the breath from his lungs. Cassius's knuckles whitened where he sat beside him.

Strickland watched them dispassionately from

behind his desk, his stare brooding above his steepled hands.

"Look," Morgan started, "if this is about what happened in Belden Place, I'll apologize—"

"It isn't," Strickland said darkly. "That was beyond the pale, but considering all the guy suffered was soiled pants, I'll let it pass. I'm not sure Adrianne will be so easy to pacify."

Cassius side-eyed Morgan with a pinched look. "She won't."

Morgan swallowed a sigh. He knew he was at fault for the incident with Brock, but he hadn't been able to help himself. Not when the man he loved was being threatened. The fact that Cassius was more than capable of looking after himself never factored into the equation. Cassius was his long-lost soulmate and Morgan was determined never to part from him again.

It was this conviction and the wealth of feelings he possessed for the beguiling demigod that had led him to blackmail the four agencies into admitting all of Cassius's secret achievements over the last five centuries. Achievements others had been recognized for, among them the current head of Cabalista and Cassius's former lover, Victor Sloan.

Though Morgan longed to blame the demon for taking the credit for bringing down Tania Lancaster and her cult of black magic users, it was Cassius who had insisted Victor assume that particular mantle of glory.

Guilt thickened Morgan's throat. He was conscious

Cassius loathed being in the limelight and the last two weeks had been the definition of that. Even Morgan hadn't anticipated the degree of attention the agencies' revelations would garner or how the whole world would suddenly become obsessed with uncovering every aspect of the life of the fallen angel they had shunned for so long.

The fact that people fawned over Cassius's beauty everywhere he went these days wasn't helping matters. The demigod's alluring looks had grown even more mesmerizing lately, the darkness that had long haunted his eyes replaced by a warmth that made him shine like the sun.

No wonder Pan thinks he's the son of the Primordial God of Light.

"What is this really about, Francis?"

Cassius's quiet words resonated in the fraught silence.

Strickland stayed quiet for a beat. He blew out a sigh and rubbed his brow.

"You never beat around the bush, do you?" he grunted.

Morgan clocked the shadows under the director's eyes and his haggard appearance. As always, Cassius had been the first to pick up on the fact that something else lay behind Strickland's statement. He'd always been more intuitive than him that way. Perhaps it was a remnant from when he'd lived as Icarus.

It was one of the many reasons why an entire army of divine beings had entrusted him with the task of leading them into battle, all those years ago.

Cassius shrugged. "We know each other too well for that kind of bullshit. Spit it out, Francis."

The glance Strickland directed at Morgan had him straightening in his seat. "The agencies are worried about a backlash concerning their recent announcements."

Cassius lowered his brows. "What kind of backlash?"

"It seems it's not only humans who are angry about what's been done to you since the Fall, Cassius. Now that they know the truth about your actions, the angels and demons who fell to Earth have started questioning their leaders' motivations in shutting you down and spreading twisted allegations about you." Strickland hesitated. "It appears whatever caused the memory loss the Fallen suffered has started to become undone. There have been angels and demons coming forward in the last week to declare your true identity as well as their own. And they've all made their outrage about your treatment clear."

Surprise widened Morgan's eyes.

It was during their recent battle in the Spirit Realm that they'd learned Cassius's real name and that of their enemy, Elios, the God of Darkness behind the Fall. The Wild God Pan, who'd sought their help to free his lover Demetrius from Elios's grasp, had also revealed his theory about why they'd recovered part of their memories. He believed it was Victor's awakening and his manifestation as the demigod Coraos that had broken part of the spell that had long suppressed their recollection of their past lives. And that that power was somehow linked to the God Hypnos, Victor and Morgan's missing half-brother and Elios's twin.

Though Morgan and Cassius had eventually told Strickland and their team the truth after they returned to Earth, they had requested the information not be made available to anyone but the people at the top of the agencies. Especially since making that information public would reveal Victor's role in the war that had caused the Fall and place him in a precarious position as the head of Cabalista.

However much he might resent Victor for having claimed Cassius in this lifetime before he himself had met the demigod, Morgan could not deny one thing. The demon was anything but evil. His actions since he'd come to Earth had proven that beyond a doubt and he had protected Cassius time and time again since the Fall, be it from the attention of the agencies or in the battles they had fought together. Had they not been competing for Cassius's heart, Morgan knew he and Victor would have been friends.

"What you're saying is you want to staunch a rebellion in the ranks before it has a chance to form?" Cassius said thoughtfully.

Strickland exhaled heavily. "Precisely. Having you out of the limelight for a while would help calm everyone's nerves."

Irritation prickled Morgan's skin. "What are we supposed to do with this leave of absence? Besides, our caseload is sky high. Our team can't manage without us!"

"That's a lie and we both know it," Strickland

retorted. He frowned at Morgan's glare. "I'll spread your caseload to the rest of Argonaut if they can't cope. Besides, I'm only asking you two to lie low for a couple of weeks, until this damn media circus dies down. Why don't you guys take a vacation?"

CHAPTER FOUR

Silence and shadows greeted Cassius when he entered his apartment. A dying, crimson light streamed through the glass wall at the far end of the open-plan living area, the setting sun turning the waters of San Francisco Bay the color of rusted blood beyond the penthouse terrace.

He listened out for the soft pitter patter of Loki's paws for an instant before he recalled the demon cat had gone to stay with Lilaia and Bostrof for the night. The imp had bonded with the Nymph and was enjoying being thoroughly spoiled by the mother-to-be. He'd also grown fascinated with her rapidly growing pregnancy bump.

The gestation period of a river spirit was different to that of a human and the child inside Lilaia would be born into this world in a matter of months. It would be the first time a Nymph would bear a child away from Rain Vale, where she would have received the care she would require in labor. Since no doorways existed between the kingdom of the Nymphs and the realms it had fractured from after the Fall, Lilaia only had her own instincts and a handful of other Nymphs who'd fallen to Earth at the same time as her to rely on.

Which meant Bostrof was an utter mess.

It wasn't every day their two species became a couple and that union resulted in a baby. Though his wife was a nature deity and they had both longed for a child for centuries, the Lucifugous demon had started to fret about whether giving birth on Earth would hinder her physical health, much to Lilaia's ire.

"If he's not careful, she's going to ban him from the delivery room," Cassius had told Morgan when they'd returned from visiting their friends a few days ago.

"It might help," Morgan had muttered. "He'll likely just get in the way. I mean, it was cute seeing a giant, grown-ass demon get all emotional at first, but now all he talks about is baby clothes and whether he's gonna have to raise the kid on his own."

Cassius dropped his keys in the bowl on the kitchen bar and shrugged out of his jacket, suddenly weary. The door shut softly behind him. Even though neither of them needed lights to see in the growing dark, Morgan flicked them on with a quiet click.

"I'm sorry."

Cassius closed his eyes briefly. He raked his hair with his hand and twisted around to face his lover, frustration overcoming his fatigue for an instant. "For what, Morgan?! There are so many reasons for you to apologize, I've lost count!"

Morgan's fingers twitched at his sides.

Cassius steeled himself. He wanted desperately to storm over and wipe away the tormented expression shadowing Morgan's face. But he knew he needed to hold his ground. He had let Morgan get away with too many things lately and it was time for him to put a stop to the demigod's behavior.

However much Morgan cherished and wanted to protect him, Cassius couldn't let him go around destroying the world for him.

"I'm sorry about today," Morgan confessed. "I should have let you bring Brock in." He faltered, his tone dropping an octave. "And I'm sorry about everything else." He met Cassius's gaze unflinchingly, his own tortured. "I thought I was doing the right thing when I asked the agencies to tell the world the truth about you. I—" His voice thickened. "I only wanted everyone to acknowledge all the good you had done. I wanted them to stop hating—"

Cassius closed the distance to Morgan, clasped his face, and pressed his mouth to his, his heart heavy with guilt while his soul burned with love.

Morgan froze. His fingers trembled as he slipped his hands over the back of Cassius's to keep them there, shoulders sagging and breath catching as he kissed him back sweetly. A sigh fluttered through Cassius. He melted against Morgan, his body seeking the demigod's heat like his lungs sought air.

It was a while before he ended the kiss. Morgan chased after his mouth for a moment before reluctantly letting go of his lips. They stood holding each other for a while, hearts thundering against one another's chests and foreheads pressed together.

"You have nothing to apologize for in that respect, Morgan." Cassius stared into the turquoise depths opposite him, his voice heavy with emotion. "I know it's a shit show right now, but in a way, I'm glad it happened." He shuddered. "The world needs to know the truth about what Elios did. We owe humanity that at least." He smiled tremulously. "Also, knowing you care that much for me makes me incredibly happy. I mean, I thought you were insane when you threatened to leave Earth, but I can't deny how it made me feel."

His cheeks and ears burned at his mumbled admission.

Morgan's fingers clenched on his back. "Have I told lately how much I adore you?"

He tilted his head and skimmed his lips across Cassius's brow.

Cassius chuckled, his heart lightening for the first time in days. "Well, you kinda show me that every night. Speaking of which, something hard is digging into me."

They looked down at Morgan's straining erection and the bulge denting Cassius's jeans.

Cassius licked his lips. "Want some help with that?"

"Do you even have to ask?" Morgan groaned.

Cassius grinned and pushed him against the kitchen bar. He dropped to his knees and looked up at Morgan from under his lashes as he carefully unzipped him, his belly clenching with lust.

Morgan's irises darkened to aquamarine as Cassius freed his cock and gave the leaking tip a languorous lick. He shuddered as Cassius kneaded and teased his aroused flesh before wrapping his lips around the head and swallowing him into the scalding depths of his mouth.

Cassius breathed through his nose as he worked Morgan's erection, his lover's shaft stretching his jaws to the limit as he took him in deep. It wasn't long before Morgan braced his legs and started punching his hips. He dropped his head back, soft grunts tumbling from his lips.

"Jesus, your mouth feels so *fucking* good!" he groaned. "My dick could happily stay inside you for hours!"

His hands found Cassius's hair. He fisted his fingers and guided Cassius to blow him like he liked it, his hisses and murmurs of encouragement making Cassius moan.

Cassius lowered a hand to the front of his jeans as he sucked Morgan hungrily. He freed his cock and started rubbing himself, his fingers frantic and wet with precum and his ass throbbing.

Their soul cores resonated with flashes of fire as they neared their climax.

"Fuck! *Yes!* I'm—*I'm coming!*"

Morgan's knees locked as he rose on his toes, his erection exploding on Cassius's tongue in a hot, sticky flood, his shout of pleasure echoing around the apartment.

CHAPTER FIVE

CASSIUS GULPED AND SWALLOWED THE SCALDING evidence of Morgan's orgasm, his spine tingling and his belly growing painfully tight as he neared the dizzying crest of his own wave. A gasp left him when Morgan hastily freed his half-hard cock from his greedy mouth and lifted him onto a bar stool. Morgan stripped them of their clothes, his eyes burning feverishly and his fingers none too gentle.

Cassius watched, heart pounding and shivers racking his body.

Morgan knelt and hooked his legs over his shoulders.

Cassius's passage contracted in anticipation as Morgan lowered his head. Pleasure slammed into him, the demigod swallowing his aching, trembling cock in one fell swoop.

"*Ah!*"

He came on the fifth suck, the lustful sounds tearing from his own throat making him flush. Morgan laved him tenderly for long seconds before finally letting go of his sensitive flesh. He spread Cassius open and tongued his hole. Stars exploded in front of Cassius's eyes when he pushed inside.

"Morgan!"

Cassius's fingers locked punishingly on the demigod's head. He gasped and shuddered, toes clenching in mid-air and glazed eyes fixed on his lover's fiery gaze where his face dipped past his balls to tease him.

He loved it when Morgan tasted him down there.

The demigod prepped him for long, torturous minutes, turning him into a whimpering mess. Then he was on his feet, his hard cock rising proudly from his trimmed pubes. He locked his hands on the back of Cassius's calves and raised Cassius's legs past his ears.

Cassius grabbed Morgan's shoulders, his mouth rounding on a shocked, *"Oh!"*

Fire flooded his face as he found himself stretched wide and intimately exposed to his lover's searing stare.

"Morgan, I—"

He swallowed the half-protest tearing up his throat at Morgan's feral expression.

"Do you want me to stop?" Morgan growled.

"N—no!" Cassius panted, his erection throbbing.

Morgan crowded him on the stool, the head of his shaft finding Cassius's quivering opening with unerring accuracy. They both gasped as he probed the soft folds. Morgan leaned in, driving Cassius's legs even higher. His breath teased the shell of Cassius's ear.

"Tell me what you want."

Cassius's heart thundered against his ribs as he met Morgan's sultry gaze. Though he would never openly admit it to him, Morgan teasing him this way drove him crazy with desire. He shuddered, so turned on he knew he would come on Morgan's first thrust.

"I want your cock inside me. I want you to fuck my *—Ah! Oh God! YESSS!*"

He convulsed around the thick rod that had just impaled him, Morgan sliding home with a practiced roll of his powerful hips. Cassius's pulsing dick bounced against Morgan's belly and smeared his release all over their skin as the demigod started pounding him.

He raked Morgan's shoulders and back with his nails as they mated with sweet savagery, Morgan's mouth finding his lips between the untamed sounds rumbling from his chest. Fire filled Cassius's veins and every inch of his body as their soul cores thumped in tandem with the waves of pleasure crashing over them, accentuating the blistering sensation to the point it was almost pain.

Morgan brought Cassius to another orgasm before he came inside him with explosive violence, his ejaculation so powerful Cassius felt it would strike the very core of him. He squeezed his eyes shut and buried his face in the crook of Morgan's neck, welcoming the sinful feeling of being filled to the brim with Morgan's seed. His heart twinged for a moment at the thought that this act would forever remain sterile.

Morgan rained tender kisses over his face as he

finally slowed his erratic thrusts, his breathing ragged. He stilled for a moment, released a shuddering breath, and unclenched his fingers from Cassius's calves, leaving marks on his skin.

Cassius blinked fuzzily. Morgan was wrapping his legs around his waist.

"Hmm, aren't you pulling—!"

His words ended on a gasp as Morgan punched forward slightly. Cassius slumped forward, his head falling limply on Morgan's shoulder.

"How the hell are you still hard?" he groaned.

Morgan chuckled, tilted his chin up with a knuckle, and nuzzled his sweat-slicked nose. "I haven't had my fill of you yet."

Cassius chewed his lip and gave his lover a stern look. "I can tell this enforced vacation we're about to take is going to involve our bed and little else."

Morgan grinned. "Would that be so bad?"

Cassius narrowed his eyes, his insides still throbbing. "You're not the one getting pummeled by a hammer drill, asshole."

Morgan blinked, shocked. He burst out laughing.

Cassius's thoughts scattered to the winds as the thick intruder still wedged deep within nudged his pleasure spot. Then Morgan carried him to the shower and proceeded to show him exactly how much he desired him.

&

M ORGAN WOKE UP WITH A START. HIS FINGERS clenched on empty sheets.

"Cassius?"

He sat up and looked blearily around the dark bedroom. The bed beside him was still warm.

They'd retired late, having only had dinner at midnight, after their marathon sex session had ended. His gaze flitted to the clock on the nightstand. It was 4.36 a.m.

Brightness bloomed on the terrace.

Alarm quickened Morgan's pulse. He jumped out of bed, grabbed his blade, and stormed over to the sliding doors. He yanked them open, only to stumble to an abrupt halt when he stepped outside.

Fear squeezed his chest.

Cassius stood naked in the middle of the patio, white wings spread open and Heaven's Light wrapped around him in a layer of crackling electricity.

"Cassius?!"

Morgan unfroze and closed the distance to the motionless demigod in a few swift strides. He slowed as he rounded him.

Cassius was staring sightlessly at the sky, his eyes ablaze with seraphic power and his face devoid of emotion. Morgan's head jerked up.

There was nothing but clouds and stars peppering the vast firmament, the twinkling dots fading in brightness as a pale band leached the darkness from the horizon.

Morgan swallowed. He raised a faltering hand, suddenly scared to touch his lover. "Cassius?"

The demigod's head swiveled around mechanically. He looked blankly at Morgan before gazing at the heavens once more. *"Something is coming, Ivmir."*

Morgan's stomach lurched at the sound of Icarus's voice.

Cassius's breath hitched. His wings fluttered agitatedly, the pale feathers sparking. Morgan's heart throbbed painfully as a liquid-silver tear trickled down his lover's left cheek.

Cassius shuddered and blinked. The radiance in his pupils and around him snapped out with a suddenness that swarmed Morgan's vision with black spots.

Cassius's wings turned black and red once more. He retracted them, awareness returning to his face. His fingers shook as he raised a hand to his cheek and touched the wetness there. His bewildered gaze collided with Morgan's before sweeping the terrace.

"What—what just happened?!"

Morgan's blood thundered in his veins. "I don't know."

He glanced at the dazzling drop on Cassius's fingertip before taking the demigod in his arms and squeezing him close, the foreboding that had taken seed inside him a bitter aftertaste on his tongue.

CHAPTER SIX

MURKY CLOUDS ROILED AROUND THEM, THICK, GRAY billows that masked the desolate expanse of the Nether.

Nildar ignored the cool drops condensing on his skin and feathers as he and Archon winged their way rapidly across miles upon miles of dull emptiness, the wind whistling eerily in their ears. Floating islands loomed out of the eternal mist around them, dark tombs once full of color and life. Bitterness twisted the Guardian's gut. He missed the chatter of the birds and creatures that used to inhabit them.

He missed many things about the old Nether.

"War demon to your right," Archon warned.

Nildar clocked the ghastly shape hanging in mid-air a short distance ahead. The war demon hovered in place, wings motionless and seemingly unaware of their presence.

Even though hundreds of years had passed since the War, he and Archon occasionally came across one of the monsters that had been left behind after the Nether tore apart. The creatures were always like this. Lifeless and gazing blankly into space.

Nildar unsheathed his holy sword. He didn't slow as they passed the monster, his blade slicing it in half in a single strike. The war demon never put up a fight, its hideous form crumbling to fiery ash without a sound.

Whatever had once powered it was long gone from this realm.

"There!" Archon said a while later, the urgency in his voice reflecting the tension thrumming through Nildar.

Rohengar's island appeared in the distance. Nildar's chest tightened as they drew closer. The precarious cliffs making up the tapered base of the floating isle were riddled with jagged cracks. Bits of rock crumbled and fell into the clouds even as they watched.

Nildar clenched his jaw. *How long has it been since we were last here?*

"Damn," Archon muttered. *"I did not think it would be in such a bad state."*

They flew over the island and arrowed toward the white palace that graced its center, their winged shadows skimming across the landscape. All that remained of the vibrant gardens and woodland that had once surrounded the residence of the South Star were the skeletal remnants of dead trees, their black trunks punctuating the dismal terrain like silent soldiers while their stark branches pointed accusingly at the sky. Even the lake that had once been full of lilies and water fowl had turned into a dirty, still bog.

Nildar's soul core throbbed the closer they grew to Rohengar's abandoned home. He didn't have to look at Archon to know that the West Star was experiencing the same sensation. The faint pulse of energy they'd detected a while back was definitely coming from Rohengar's palace.

They landed on the terrace overlooking the main gardens and folded their pale wings. Torn, gossamer curtains billowed in their wake as they hurried inside, their footsteps echoing on the once shiny floor, now dull and littered with debris. The power they'd sensed from across the Nether grew stronger as they navigated empty hallways and passed cathedral-like chambers filled with dust and the echoes of the past.

It drew them to the sacred temple at the very center of the palace.

Nildar's pulse quickened as they emerged into an open courtyard filled with dead flowers and climbing plants. They carved through the brittle brambles blocking their access to the round, domed structure that rose in the middle and finally reached the shallow steps leading to a pair of majestic, gold and silver doors.

Nildar's breath caught at the sight of the radiance throbbing through the slit-like gap at the bottom. Already, the shrubs closest to the entrance of the temple were starting to show signs of life, dark roots and stems turning green and faint buds blooming under the influence of the ethereal glow.

Archon exchanged a stunned look with him. *"It cannot be."*

Nildar clenched his jaw. *"Yet, it seems it is."*

His instincts were never wrong.

Something was happening. Something they had long hoped for but thought they would never witness.

They placed their hands on the towering panels and sent a burst of divine energy into them. The temple doors unlocked with a creak that resonated through the palace, the heavy metal protesting as they swung open for the first time in centuries.

Warmth and brightness washed over them in a bright summer wave. Greenery exploded across the courtyard, life returning to the dead plants and flowers in a flash. The island groaned as its fading vitality was slowly replenished.

Nildar's heart clenched. Archon drew a sharp breath.

Marble gleamed and water trickled in the holy space inside the temple. It was small considering its imposing entrance and bare but for the body of water in its center.

Made from the tears of the First God who breathed all life into existence, the pool shimmered and glowed like nothing else in the known universe.

A similar temple existed in the palace of every Guardian whose task it was to protect the Nether. It was the very first structure that was erected upon the island they each chose as their home. Its purpose was simple.

It housed a fragment of the soul of the Guardian it belonged to. A fragment that would be passed on to the next Guardian who would take their throne, infusing the new Star with the experience gained from a life long lived. For there had been many Guardians before them and there would be many more after they retired from their role.

The holy pool inside Rohengar's palace had been dead the last time Nildar and Archon had visited it, the silver waters dull and devoid of life. Yet it gleamed once more, the bright surface dancing with ripples from the sphere of dazzling light that skimmed its center, the globe's low hum a sweet song Nildar had thought he would never hear again.

The power it contained tasted of the life force of their fallen brother Rohengar.

Archon surreptitiously wiped away the silver tears that had slipped down his face, his eyes full of emotion. *"He has returned. After five hundred years, Rohengar walks among us once more!"*

Nildar swallowed heavily, too scared to acknowledge Archon's words. The presence of a soul fragment in Rohengar's palace could only mean one thing.

A new Guardian had indeed been born.

"We do not know that." Nildar fisted his hands, his chest so tight he felt a little sick. *"We should not come to a hasty conclusion upon this matter, Archon."* His gaze swung from Archon to the bright orb. *"After all, it is our first time witnessing this phenomenon. This may very well be a different South Star."*

Archon stiffened, his expression at once angry and miserable.

Nildar sighed and touched his arm.

"We always hoped and prayed that he might return to us one day," he said gently. *"But the Fates do not work that way, Archon. They are fickle."*

Archon furrowed his brow.

"This soul fragment is imbued with Rohengar's divine energy," he said stubbornly. *"You will know if it is him, Nildar. Only you can locate where the physical form bound to this soul fragment resides."*

Nildar faltered. Archon was right. His powers as the East Star meant he could see the past and the future of any soul he touched.

Well, any soul but his.

Icarus's face flashed before Nildar's eyes. Instead of the rage and bitterness he used to feel whenever the North Star came to mind, he only experienced regret and melancholy. He had had plenty of time to reflect upon what had happened during the ghastly war that had transformed the Nether from a realm full of life and the purest light of Heaven to a place that reeked of darkness and despair.

Nildar was conscious that Archon had still not forgiven Icarus for what he did that day. And that he still blamed him for Rohengar's death. But Nildar knew the truth. What had transpired on the day the Nether tore was not the fault of their brothers.

Though both Icarus and Rohengar had acted recklessly out of love for the one they held closest to their heart, the being ultimately responsible for the disaster that had befallen all the realms between Heaven and the Hells was still out there.

Elios, the God of Darkness, first grandchild of Chaos and twin of Hypnos.

Archon shifted impatiently.

Nildar pursed his lips as he gazed upon his brother's restless mien. *Four millennia old and he still behaves like a child at times like this.*

He moved toward the holy pool before Archon could drag him there, the loose clothing he wore rustling softly as he sat on the raised edge of the basin. He extended a hand to the blazing soul fragment hovering above the shiny surface and faltered for an instant, his fingers stopping a hairbreadth short of touching the sphere. Fear, an emotion he rarely experienced, lifted the hair on his arms and nape.

He and Archon had lived a suspended existence these last five hundred years, mostly locked out of the realms they had once guarded and forced to endure a new reality in the Nether. The hands of time had started to move again and he was suddenly scared about where it would take them.

Does the path ahead lead to our salvation or our damnation?

"Nildar?"

Archon's voice stiffened Nildar's resolve. He took a shallow breath, clamped down on his dread, and touched the orb.

Cognizance blasted through him. He startled.

Wait! This—this soul fragment has—!

Images flashed before his eyes, freezing his thoughts. His focus shifted from what he was sensing at the tips of his fingers to the visions unfolding before him.

He saw a city of man on the verge of destruction. He saw monsters from the Hells swarming its streets and attacking its fleeing citizens. He saw angels and demons engaged in a battle against the ghastly creatures on land and in the air. And then, he saw them.

Two armored beings glowing with divine energy high above the metropolis, pale wings spread open as they hovered in place.

One was Icarus in his demigod form.

The other was a man he did not recognize.

Nildar's pulse stuttered. In the stranger's right gauntlet was a weapon he and Archon had long thought broken and lost.

How—how is that possible?! We saw it shatter with our own eyes!

The visions drew to a close. Nildar's breath shuddered out of him as he lifted his hand from the brilliant, warm sphere of the newborn Guardian's soul fragment.

"*Is it him?*" Archon asked tensely. "*Is it Rohengar?!*"

Nildar hesitated, the stranger he had glimpsed flitting before his eyes. "*I...do not know.*" He swallowed and frowned. "*I sense two entities in this soul fragment, Archon.*"

Archon jerked back. "*What?!*" He stared at the dazzling sphere as if it had grown horns. "*That cannot be right. We have singular souls!*"

Unease prickled Nildar's scalp as he studied the orb.

"I cannot be positive without seeing this new Guardian up close. He is physically different from Rohengar, for certain." He paused. *"But his soul is most definitely not like ours."*

Archon narrowed his eyes. *"Where is he?"*

Nildar met the West Star's gaze steadily. *"Earth."*

Archon's expression grew ugly.

"Icarus!" he hissed.

They'd known for centuries that Icarus had survived the tear in the Nether despite falling through it; his soul orb still burned brightly in his palace to the north. It had never faltered in all this time and had even survived a blow from Archon's holy weapon, on the day the West Star had stormed the temple in a drunken rage and Nildar had had to drag him kicking and screaming out of the holy chamber.

"Come, let us make haste." Archon turned on his heels and stormed out of Rohengar's temple. *"We have much to prepare if we want to try and reach Earth before the next solstice!"*

Nildar swallowed a sigh. He knew there would be no arguing with Archon. Not when he was in this mood.

Let us all hope you survive his wrath, Icarus.

CHAPTER SEVEN

Gauzy curtains billowed around Elios where he stood naked on the terrace of his penthouse. Lights were coming on across the city spread out below him, their brightness masking the radiance of the stars popping into existence across the firmament. He probed the darkening expanse with his sharp gaze, his godly senses detecting what lay beyond. A faint smile played on his lips at what he perceived.

"And so it begins," he murmured.

Though faint, the pulse of energy coming from the direction of the Nether was unmistakable. A new South Star had been born. One whose final awakening he had long awaited.

His smile turned cruel.

There was a reason he was always one step ahead of that blasted Icarus and Ivmir, as well as the agencies that governed the otherworldly who had fallen to Earth. Unbeknown to most who mattered, the Moirai, the Goddesses of Destiny, had been chained in one of the Hells and forced to do his bidding for the past thousand years.

It's a good thing I command two of the Fates. Without them, my plans to resurrect our grandfather would have been in vain. An unpleasant reminder made him furrow his brow. *Pity Atropos and my other sisters escaped my grasp. But I doubt they survived their providence.*

The army he had amassed since the Fall meant he would soon be in a position to restore Chaos from the Abyss. His schemes had hit some irritating snags along the way, what with the feeble humans he'd controlled falling to his nemesis, but he could almost taste victory.

The cracks his puppets had inflicted in his enemy's defenses would shatter when push came to shove.

A visceral hatred surged through the veins of the male form Elios had possessed as Icarus's face rose before his eyes. He gnashed his teeth.

I will rip out the North Star's heart myself and eat it in front of his lover.

His loathing for Icarus had only grown with the passage of time. The Guardian of Light had always been adored by Heaven and all the Gods and demigods. Whereas he, Elios, had been shunned for his powers of darkness. But there was more to his animosity than just jealousy. He and Icarus were diametric opposites. Had always been. Darkness and Light were not meant to co-exist.

A noise behind him had him looking over his shoulder.

The three women on his bed writhed on the sheets, cords of throbbing shadows moving sinuously across their naked bodies behind the gossamer drapes of the giant four poster.

One, the CEO of a rival company who had made her dislike for him inherently clear, boasted milky skin, silky, blonde hair that tumbled past her waist, and bright blue eyes. To his surprise, she had been a virgin.

The second woman had honey-colored skin, dark eyes, and wavy, chestnut hair that teased her full breasts. Her only sin was that she was the bastard daughter of a Sheikh who had opposed one of his business ventures in the Middle East.

As for the woman with the colorful afro hair, ebony flesh, and obsidian eyes, she was the fifth wife of a visiting African prince who'd just happened to cross his line of sight at a party a few nights ago.

The three women kissed and rubbed up frantically against one another, fingers busy on nipples and clits despite being complete strangers, their drugged minds seeking more of the devastating climaxes they had already endured at his hands.

Elios smiled indulgently and clicked his fingers.

Several of the black bands thickened into phallic shapes. They slipped inside the women's mouths and pussies and asses, plundering them with powerful thrusts that made them mewl for more. They jerked and shivered and panted and moaned on the sweat-stained sheets, hands desperately spreading themselves even wider for the dark cocks fucking their orifices, their juices mixing with the black semen oozing out of their holes.

Elios's dick throbbed. He licked his lips and went

back inside, his hand dropping to his shaft to give himself a few brisk rubs.

Sex was hardly new to him. Yet, it wasn't the act of fucking or getting a hand job or even being sucked dry that brought him pleasure. Though they didn't know it yet, the women on his bed would soon perish, their bodies succumbing to the corrupt energy seeping into their blood from his dark seed. Every climax poisoned them further, the ropes of darkness teasing their skin similarly spreading his venom into their flesh.

It was their deaths that would bring him the ultimate orgasm, the intense gratification he would endure lasting for hours. Were he not a God, it would drain the body he had adopted of life.

The inky bands he commanded locked the women's arms and legs in place as he approached the bed, leaving livid marks on their flesh. They didn't protest when the shackles yanked them forward in turns, pulling their bodies at angles that would normally have broken their limbs and spines, their glazed eyes burning with lust as he stood at the bottom of the bed and fucked them everywhere they could be fucked, his fingers locked punishingly in their hair and around their throats.

Grunts left him as he ejaculated again and again, filling the women's bodies to the brim with his poisonous emission, making them choke on floods of black semen. Though he enjoyed the pleasure his human form experienced from his multiple releases, it paled in comparison to what was still to come.

As the hours whiled away, so did the women's life

force, while his hunger grew exponentially. By the time night turned to dawn, one of his minions had crept inside the bedroom and disposed of his victims' still-warm bodies, gaze averted from Elios where he shuddered on the bed, the cloak of darkness around him thick with the stench of death and the dark pleasure of a God.

It was almost midday by the time Elios finally emerged from the dizzying ecstasy the women's demise had brought him to. An errant thought came to him as he padded into the ensuite to wash off the sweat and semen drying on his skin.

I wonder what it would be like to fuck the new Guardian.

His spent cock stirred as he stepped under the shower. He smiled.

Maybe I should give it a try. See if his ass is as tight as it looks.

His dick thickened with fresh arousal. He shivered and decided to give his human form another well-deserved release, the bands of darkness that had robbed the women who had occupied his bed of life kneading and rubbing his aching flesh until he came on a deep groan under the soaking hot spray.

CHAPTER EIGHT

I AM OFFICIALLY LOSING MY MIND.

Theophile Serrano stared at himself in the narrow mirror above the sink, the light from the streetlamp outside the second-floor studio apartment the only illumination in the gloomy bathroom. His face was pale, the lack of sleep he'd been suffering lately apparent in the shadows under his eyes and his gaunt expression. He leaned in and peered at his pupils.

"Well, at least the crazy light is gone," he muttered.

He'd woken up from a short nap to find his flat in Spitalfields shining like the sun. It had taken him a couple of seconds to realize the dazzling beams sweeping the room erratically were coming from his own eyes. Past experience had taught him that if he squeezed them shut for a couple of minutes, the dreadful rays would eventually die down. And so he had, his heart thumping with fear while he waited for the heat throbbing through his belly to subside.

He now knew the unexplained fever that

occasionally gripped his body out of nowhere to be a warning sign. One that heralded the insane things that had been happening to him since he'd come to London. Like his eyes projecting an ungodly radiance or the monsters he'd glimpsed in the back alleys of the capital. He wasn't sure if it was insomnia that was causing him to have these delusions or the pressure of his new job. He just knew something wasn't right.

Theo dropped his forehead against the cool glass and closed his eyes, a familiar ache squeezing his heart.

I sure wish I could talk to you, mom.

His mother Renata had passed away the year before. She'd died peacefully in her sleep, with a smile on her face. Theo knew how much she'd missed his father. An inspector in the Bourgogne-Franche-Comté Gendarmarie, Jacques Serrano had died of a heart attack on the day he'd retired from an illustrious career spanning forty-five years in the service of the city of Dijon.

Renata Serrano had never recovered from his loss. Though she'd stayed the bright and positive woman Theo had always known her to be in the three years that followed his death, she could not hide the shadows in her eyes.

Theo still recalled vividly the conversation they'd had the night she died.

She'd looked up at him across the dining table and flashed him a dazzling smile. "You're going to be okay, Theo. Believe in yourself. And trust in your instincts."

Theo had blinked at her, confused. "Ma?"

They'd been talking about his college grades and where he should apply for a job.

Renata had remained silent for a moment, a faraway look on her face.

"You *will* be okay," she'd repeated in a strange voice underscored with an edge of steel.

She'd startled a little before resuming their conversation, as if nothing had happened. That incident had lingered in Theo's mind months after she'd passed on.

Would she have thought me crazy? If I were able to tell her what I've been feeling and seeing since I came to this city?

Somehow, Theo suspected Renata would have understood. She had been a deeply religious woman when she was alive and a believer in the esoteric and the mystical. He grimaced a little. Considering they lived in a world where angels and demons walked among mere mortals, that wasn't too hard to do.

It was her death that had finally prompted him to pursue his ambitions. Though he'd initially been aiming for a position in Paris, he'd wanted to work in the City of London for as long as he could remember. And he'd finally landed a dream opportunity there a month ago.

The offer from *Sion* had come out of the blue and nearly shocked him senseless. An investment bank whose new CEO had propelled it to dizzying heights of success that had seen it grace the front cover of all the major business publications around the world in the past ten years, *Sion* was the cream of the crop for any young investment banker wanting to make a name for himself. Never in a million years had Theo thought he would one day get to work with the man most business graduates would sell a kidney to even land an interview with.

After facing countless rejections from firms in the British capital, he'd started to come to terms with the fact that the city was not quite within his reach yet. He'd applied to a talent pool database in London on a whim, thinking he would be unlikely to see anything useful come out of it. When his cell phone had rung four weeks ago and Hugo Frost, the CEO of *Sion* himself, had told him he had seen his details and wanted to hire him as his P.A., Theo had almost disconnected the call, thinking it was a prank.

Frost had chuckled when Theo had stammered out his thanks several times over during their call. "No need to apologize. It's not every day I ring someone to tell them I'm offering them a job. And before you ask why I chose you, the answer is simple. Your talents have long been overlooked, Theophile. And I'm not a man to miss talent that could be useful for my business."

Theo had flushed at his compliment. Hugo Frost was not just the richest investment banker in the world right now, he was also broodingly handsome, his dark, piercing gaze radiating a latent sexual energy even on the covers of the magazines he graced. Rumors of him dating supermodels, actresses, and heiresses were rife and he was often seen out with a beautiful woman.

Not that Theo would ever admit to his future boss

that he'd been stalking him on social media. Though he'd long suspected his parents had known his sexual preferences, he had yet to officially come out of the closet. And Hugo Frost was definitely the kind of man he could envisage giving his V card to.

"I'll have my secretary contact you with details of the contract," Frost had told him at the end of their call. "And don't worry about your relocation costs. *Sion* will pay for that."

In the end, the only thing Theo had refused was the swanky apartment the bank had rented for him when he'd arrived in London. The salary he would be receiving meant he would soon be able to afford a decent place himself. In the meantime, he'd used his meager servings to get a flat as close to his work as he could.

Though old and bare but for a metal bed, a couch, and a table with two chairs, the studio in Spitalfields was enough for his needs right now. Besides, he barely had any spare time as Frost's P.A., his new boss commanding his every waking moment from the very first day he'd entered the cathedral-like lobby of the glass and marble building housing *Sion*, near Cannon Street station. Frost was a perfectionist through and through and expected the same of his employees. But though he was a hard taskmaster, he was patient and never unkind.

Today was Theo's first day off in over a week and he'd spent most of it cleaning his place and food shopping before catching up on some much-needed Z's.

A buzzing noise had him peeking out of the bathroom. He headed over to where he'd left his phone atop the crate he was using as a makeshift nightstand. Frost had sent him a text message.

Don't be late.

Theo smiled faintly. He might be in total awe of the man he was now working for, but there was no denying that Frost took care of his employees. There was a reception tonight for the men and women who had recently joined *Sion*. It was being held at a posh hotel near the Royal Exchange.

Heat flooded Theo's cheeks. He couldn't help but feel that Frost was holding the party just for him. He'd glimpsed the stares his boss occasionally cast his way when he thought Theo wasn't looking. Stares that had Theo's cock throbbing and his belly tightening with lust. Since he'd never heard of Frost having a man as a partner, he put it all down to his imagination.

He slapped his flushed face a couple of times and eyed the rack of clothes next to the window with a decisive frown. The only things he'd spent money on since he'd come to London were his suits and work shoes. The clothes maketh the man, as his father used to say. It helped that *Sion* employees got a discount at several stores in the capital.

Theo headed into the bathroom and showered away his fatigue. His pulse quickened at the thought of seeing Frost again, all thoughts of the strangeness growing inside him and the weird incidents that had plagued his every step since he'd arrived in the city forgotten for now.

CHAPTER NINE

A COLD WIND BUFFETED CASSIUS THE MOMENT HE stepped out of the private jet. Drops of icy rain fell from the darkening sky and landed on his face, cooling his skin.

The smell of ozone tainting the air above London heralded a late autumnal storm.

"Great," Morgan grumbled behind him. "I'd forgotten how fucking depressing the weather in England is."

Cassius cast an accusing frown at him over his shoulder. "It was your idea to come here."

Morgan made a face. "Yeah, well, I knew you were pining after him."

Cassius stiffened slightly. It was true he hadn't been able to stop thinking about Victor's protracted silence since the demon had left San Francisco after the affair with Pan and the Spirit Realm. What he hadn't expected when he'd woken up from a restless sleep late that morning was that Morgan would suggest they take a trip to London to talk to him.

"It's only going to eat at you the longer you leave it," Morgan had argued in the face of Cassius's shocked look. "Better to take that thorn out and make a clean cut of it."

Cassius didn't doubt that Morgan would prefer it if he never saw Victor again. But they both knew this was something that could never happen. The bond that bound them to their past and the War in the Nether meant they had to face the future together, whatever it might bring and however it strained their relationships.

Cassius hadn't argued too strongly with Morgan over breakfast and had fallen into a contemplative silence while the demigod booked them a private flight to London for that evening. Since he was still very much the focus of the world's attention, Morgan had unilaterally decided a public flight was out of the question. And Strickland would definitely have had something pointed to say if they'd flown across the Atlantic using their wings.

Truth be told, Cassius wanted to see Victor. The demon was his oldest friend on Earth and he missed him.

There was something else. Something that had to do with the state he'd woken up from in the middle of last night, naked on his terrace and a silver tear cooling on his face.

The fear he'd read in Morgan's eyes when he'd taken

him in his arms had startled Cassius. And the way the demigod had held on tightly to him for the rest of the night only made his heart ache. He knew Morgan was terrified of losing him again. It was the reason he was so overbearingly protective, despite the fact that Cassius could more than hold his own in battle. The incident with Brock was just the latest example.

Still, a singular conviction had lingered inside Cassius when he'd awoken from the dream-like state Morgan had found him in. Something was drawing him to the east. Something that made his soul core throb with an echo of memory.

He hadn't told Morgan whom he'd dreamt of in the few fitful hours of sleep he'd had after that incident. That he'd seen Rohengar like he'd never recalled him before. That he'd caught a glimpse of what must have been their past, with the South Star smiling and laughing beside him and two other blurry figures, and had sensed a brotherhood forged in the very fires of Heaven.

The sin of Rohengar's death still weighed heavily on Cassius's conscience. From what Pan had hinted, the other two Guardians who remained trapped in the Nether had likely never forgiven him for the actions that led to the South Star's death.

Morgan ran a hand through his hair, oblivious to the flight attendant peering at them with starstruck eyes. "How about we get out of this freezing rain and find our ride?"

Since the attendant was a woman, she hadn't

become the object of his ire like a man would have done during their cross-Atlantic flight.

Cassius swallowed a sigh. *He's like a territorial mutt in that respect.*

They cleared security without a hitch, their Argonaut IDs helping speed up the process even after the immigration guys did several doubletakes at the sight of Cassius. Morgan carried their case while Cassius searched for their rental car; they hadn't packed a lot, having only planned to be in London for a week.

They were soon on their way into the city, the evening traffic in the Docklands remarkably light considering it was a weekend. Though they could both drive on the left-hand side, it made more sense for Cassius to get behind the wheel since he'd only moved from London a few months ago.

"Why don't you give Lilaia a call?" Cassius glanced at Morgan. "We promised Loki we'd ring."

"You spoil that imp too much," Morgan grunted as he dug his cell out of his pocket.

Lilaia answered after the second ring.

"Oh, hey," the Nymph greeted him with a tired smile. "You guys got there okay?"

"Yeah, we did. How's the pest?"

Loki appeared on the screen in his true form, his sing-song voice high with excitement. "Cassius?!" The imp stiffened when he saw Morgan, the brightness rapidly fading from his red eyes and his arrowhead-tipped tail swinging in irritation. "Oh. It's *you*. The lesser half of my masters."

Lilaia muffled a snort behind her hand.

Morgan scowled. "You little—!"

"Hi, Loki," Cassius said hurriedly.

He chatted with Loki and Lilaia for a short while and ended the call with the promise to bring them all sorts of goodies from London.

Morgan gazed broodingly out the window at the passing landscape while Cassius headed past Canary Wharf and took the Rotherhithe Tunnel. They got out in a secure car park in Bermondsey some twenty minutes later.

Morgan looked around with a frown while Cassius got their case out of the trunk. "I thought your place was in Whitechapel."

"I moved here before I left London."

What Cassius didn't tell Morgan was that working for Cabalista had meant he'd had a generous salary, more than the other agencies had ever paid him. He'd initially been upset with Victor when he'd seen his first paycheck, only to realize most Cabalista demons who took on the kind of jobs he did earned the same. Though Victor had showered him with gifts and attention when they'd been a couple, he'd always treated him professionally at work and had never let their relationship interfere with matters of import.

Morgan's eyes widened slightly when they got out of the lift and entered an apartment on the sixth floor of a Grade II-listed, converted granary overlooking the River Thames. "This is nice."

He scanned the modern, open-plan space with its exposed beams, brickwork, and steel supports. Double doors opened out onto a north-facing terrace at the far end and the granite worktops in the kitchen gleamed under the spotlights bathing the island separating it from the dining area.

Morgan indicated the corridor to his right. "Is the bedroom this way?"

"Yeah."

Cassius was still staring at the spot Morgan had disappeared from when he returned.

"What?"

Cassius arched an eyebrow. "I'm surprised you didn't suggest we test the bed."

The corner of Morgan's mouth tilted in a smirk. "Is that code for you wanna have sex?"

Cassius ignored the stirring in his groin and gave his lover a stern look. "Is sex all you think about?"

"No. What I always think about is your cock and your ass. And my cock *inside* your—*ouch!*"

He chuckled and rubbed the spot on his ribs where Cassius had punched him lightly.

"You're incorrigible!" Cassius huffed. "Come on, we're heading out."

Morgan sobered. "I thought we were gonna meet with him tomorrow. Besides, doesn't he live out in the sticks or something?"

"Highgate isn't the sticks, Morgan," Cassius said, exasperated. "And knowing Victor, he's probably still at Cabalista." His tone softened at the tightness in his lover's face. "How about we grab dinner after? I know a great place not far from there."

But Victor wasn't at the Cabalista headquarters in

Finsbury when they got there. According to the demon manning the front desk, he'd gone to a business function in the City. A strange foreboding stirred inside Cassius as he and Morgan stepped out of the building.

Storm clouds were gathering above them, sparks of electricity lighting up the dark mantle forming across the heavens. Morgan followed his gaze, his face equally troubled.

CHAPTER TEN

THEO SCANNED THE NARROW STREET HE WAS NAVIGATING
with a faint frown, his feet avoiding the puddles from
the recent light shower with ease. He was beginning to
regret his decision to walk from his apartment to the
hotel.

Brick Lane should have been full of life at this hour.
Yet the place was oddly deserted. The few people he'd
crossed paths with hurried along, expressions strained
and anxious gazes flitting to the shadows gathering
around them, as if they were being chased by
something.

Theo could hardly blame them. There was a heavy
feeling in the air, like the city had fallen under an
oppressive spell. It didn't help that odd flickers were
brightening the turbulent clouds gathering over the
capital.

He shivered. *It's just a storm.*

Theo rubbed his arms briskly and shook off the
unease prickling his skin. Thunder boomed above

him, making him jump. A fat drop of rain struck his nose.

"Shit!"

He hastened his steps and headed for a shortcut he'd taken dozens of times before, hoping he would make cover before the skies opened. The path appeared on his right, a narrow rectangle of gloom wedged between a pawn shop and a liquor store. He ducked into it and made it some twenty feet before he realized that all wasn't right around him. Theo slowed and lowered his brows, puzzled.

Since when did this lane have so many side alleys?

He stopped in his tracks, his gaze sweeping the shadowy openings of passages he could not recall.

I must have made a wrong turn.

He twisted on his heels to retrace his steps, only to rock to an abrupt halt. A solid wall of fog obscured his path. He blinked.

"Where the hell did that come from?!" he mumbled.

His voice bounced against the walls around him, echoey and distorted. An inexplicable dread started to churn his stomach. He whirled around and staggered to a stop.

The same, thick mist was rolling toward him from the opposite direction, pale currents twisting in eldritch shapes as they closed in on his position.

Heat flared inside Theo, startling him. His eyes widened. He pressed a hand to his belly.

No! Not now!

Brightness lit the alleyway in a flash, painting everything a dazzling white. He blinked when it snapped out just as suddenly as it had appeared, dark spots swarming his vision in its stead.

Theo froze. His hands were glowing.

Alarm quickened his pulse as he stared at the shimmer infusing his skin. He touched himself awkwardly, fingers trembling. His flesh felt warm. Warmer than it should be.

Was that—was that me?!

The flash came again. Fear brought a flood of bile to the back of Theo's throat as his entire body lit up for an instant, the unholy radiance emanating from him piercing the material of his suit as if it weren't there.

Instead of fading like it had done in the past, the heat inside him was building up. Beams of light erupted from his eyes before he could catch his breath. They brightened the fog surrounding him as he spun around in a panic, encircling him in an incandescent wall of white clouds.

Shit!

Theo pressed his hands to his face. The rays shrank to thin shafts that pierced the gaps between his luminous fingers. He clenched his jaw as the uncanny radiance throbbed in tandem with his pounding pulse.

Theo squeezed his eyes shut and prayed that whatever the hell was going on would soon stop. He didn't particularly like standing there exposed and unable to see who or what could attack him.

His brain stuttered at that errant thought. *Wait. Why did I just think that?!*

Silence dropped around him like a hammer, locking his legs in place and making his stomach plummet with an impending sense of doom. Theo started to hyperventilate, his breaths loud and erratic in his ears as he strained them, too scared to open his eyes just yet. Gone was the traffic from Commercial Street and the familiar hubbub of the markets that crowded the back lanes of Spitalfields.

It was as if someone had ripped him from the heart of London and transported him to another world.

Sweat beaded his forehead. The fever gripping his belly grew worse.

The heat that surged inside him with his next heartbeat had him gasping and bending over, tears springing to his eyes as they snapped open of their own volition. He was dimly aware that the bright streams projecting from his pupils had muted to a controlled glow. He fell to one knee, the pain twisting his insides bringing a scream to his throat.

Theo bit his lip hard and muffled the sound.

Light flashed in his peripheral vision. He looked up slowly, head heavy from the agony now carving his skull and nausea making his stomach roil. His breath caught.

Static was sparking the air around him. Theo blinked, his vision clearing as he rapidly batted away his tears.

The mist crackled with electricity. It shifted, the bands of whiteness writhing in distorted shapes before they started to coalesce. Two opposing, rippling mirrors appeared in the fog.

The hairs rose on the back of Theo's neck. He'd

experienced this phenomenon before. Except it had happened randomly and come out of thin air.

The mirrors grew translucent. Dark shapes drifted into view on the other side of the reflective surfaces. Theo's heart hammered wildly against his ribs.

The monsters he'd glimpsed before were back.

The creatures' shapes grew more distinct, their grotesque bodies becoming crisp and focused. Theo's eyes widened. Contrary to the few times he'd witnessed the horrifying beasts before, this was the most detailed vision he'd ever had of them. It was as if he were looking through a limpid doorway into their realm.

Hellish landscapes materialized behind the monsters. Ozone and the putrid stench of sulfur filled Theo's nostrils. He gagged and choked. Realization struck him like a hammer blow, robbing him of what little breath he had left.

This isn't just a vision!

Theo stumbled back onto his ass, terror a cold, heavy pit in his stomach.

The monsters' heads snapped around at the sudden movement. Obsidian eyes locked on him across the glasslike barriers, the creatures' pupils widening and constricting as they registered his presence.

A low growl sounded to Theo's right. He tore his gaze from the diabolic creatures studying him with bone-deep hunger from the other side of the mirrors and directed it to where the sound had come from. Shadows stirred in a narrow alley some fifteen feet away. The growl came again. Crimson eyes flashed in the gloom. The foul reek grew stronger.

A giant, hound-like beast some four feet tall emerged from the passage, its fangs dripping with drool and its wicked claws clinking on stone.

Theo climbed awkwardly to his feet and started to run. He slipped through the gap between the mirror-like doorways just as a clawed hand shot out of one of them. It missed him by a hairbreadth, the monster it belonged to screeching in annoyance as it failed to cut him.

Theo gulped acrid fog as he pelted blindly along the lane. Rain started to fall again, thick drops that rapidly turned into a deluge. It drenched him in seconds, plastering his hair to his head and dispersing the heavy mist.

Familiar buildings started to take shape around him.

Relief clogged Theo's throat. *Thank God!*

He stole a look over his shoulder and immediately wished he hadn't.

Monsters were stepping out of two rippling portals at the far end of the alley. The creatures looked around, heads rising to sniff the air curiously before they snapped their jaws ravenously at whatever they smelled. Their dreadful gazes found him with unerring accuracy.

Theo's shoe caught a gap in the cobblestones. He tripped and went down hard. Fire bloomed on his palms and knees as he scraped his skin raw. His chin struck the ground with a loud crack, snapping his teeth together and almost cutting his tongue in half.

He lay stunned on his front for a couple of seconds. Coldness seeped into his bones from the rain pounding his back and the dirty puddles beneath him. He pushed up awkwardly onto all fours and shook his head dazedly, his ears ringing and his chin throbbing.

Something roared behind him. Theo whirled around, lost his balance, and landed on his back. The beast from the alley sprang, its monstrous jaws widening to engulf his throat as it dropped toward him, its claws aimed at his eyes and gut.

No!

He opened his mouth to scream. But it wasn't a sound of terror that left him. Instead, someone spoke in his voice. Someone who sounded infinitely calmer than he was in that blood-curdling moment. Someone whose presence emerged from the very heart of him and filled him with an otherworldly awareness that spoke of a life long lived. A sweet, balmy wave warmed his chilled bones and charged him with the most incredible energy.

"Suspend."

Theo found himself raising his right hand. Light bloomed on his fingertips.

Time slowed. He watched breathlessly as the rain froze, the water stilling inches from his face casting his reflection a myriad times over in bright, glistening drops. The fear that had immobilized him faded as fire filled his blood.

The monster snarled, crimson eyes glowing with

hate where it floated in mid-air some four feet above him, its body paralyzed by the unearthly force Theo was projecting.

"Return to your realm, oh beast who does not belong," he said in the voice of the being filling his soul like summer itself. *"Dimensional Gate."*

The air between him and the monster shivered, forming the outline of another portal. It moved, swallowing the creature whole and cutting off the latter's scream of rage abruptly.

A wave of lassitude washed over Theo as the beast vanished from his sight. Time unfroze. Rainfall pelted his face and body once more. He thought he heard screeches and roars coming from the direction where the two mirror-like portals had appeared, farther down the alley.

I hope we got those creatures too!

His vision blurred. Theo blinked, his consciousness flickering as he thudded heavily onto his back under the downpour, his chest heaving with his breaths.

His heart throbbed with a sudden, painful sense of loss, rousing him as effectively as a bucket of icy water. Theo gasped and sat up with a jerk. A name he didn't know bubbled up his throat.

"Co...raos..."

He was only half aware that he'd risen to his feet. He walked past the shoe he'd lost and staggered out of the alley and into the brightly lit streets of London, oblivious to the stares his ruined suit and bloodied limbs earned him, his legs guiding him unerringly toward where he needed to be.

CHAPTER ELEVEN

Victor Sloan leaned his elbows atop the stone balustrade of a balcony and gazed out into the night. A light drizzle was falling across London, bringing with it the earthy smell of ozone. The raindrops sizzled and evaporated before they could strike him, his Fiery powers keeping them at bay and stopping him from getting soaked.

Loud voices interspersed with shrill laughter and the clink of champagne flutes filtered through the glass doors behind him. The irritating sounds were thankfully drowned out by the rumble of traffic coming from the busy intersection below, which was the principal reason he'd come out here in the first place.

Victor tipped his glass and downed his whiskey, the expensive alcohol burning a smooth path down his throat. He furrowed his brow faintly.

I need to have a word with Rosemary about the invitations she accepts on my behalf.

The devoted face of his middle-aged secretary swam before his eyes. Victor sighed. There was no way he could tell her off. Not when she treated him like a son. It didn't matter that he had over a thousand years on her.

Most humans would have balked at the idea of working directly with the head of Cabalista. Although there were plenty of humans in the admin departments of all their regional offices, none had ever applied to be the personal secretary of a bureau lead. Rosemary Barnett was the exception. She'd been in Victor's employ for coming up to ten years now and managed his schedule with a steely hand worthy of a demon prince.

Victor still recalled her interview like it was yesterday. When he'd asked her why she thought she was the right person for the job, she'd looked him straight in the eye and said, "Well, for one thing, I'm not interested in the snake in your pants. That ship sailed years ago, along with my ovaries."

Victor had just about managed to keep a straight face while his HR manager had choked on a glass of water and his second-in-command had let out an unladylike snort.

Rosemary had politely ignored the two demons and smiled at Victor. "Also, I'm a fiend when it comes to organizing the shit out of things."

He was aware Rosemary had deliberately fooled him into thinking this party was being held by a Cabalista benefactor. Hugo Frost was somebody who'd expressed a keen interest in donating money to the demonic organization, but he wasn't officially signed up as a patron yet. There was a lot of paperwork involved when a private enterprise such as *Sion* wished to become a backer for an otherworldly organization. The whole thing needed to go before a board of representatives from various government departments, as well as the other agencies.

Truth be told, Rosemary had no doubt picked up on his dismal mood since he'd returned from San Francisco. She'd become his secretary when he and Cassius had still been together and she knew how much Victor missed his former lover. She pined for the angel just as badly and often reminisced about him.

Victor hadn't told Rosemary or anyone in Cabalista his true name or the role he had played in bringing about the Fall that had caused so much misery for the human world. The agency heads had all agreed it wouldn't be in anyone's interest if that fact were made public.

Still, it didn't detract from the guilt that had eaten away at his soul ever since he'd recalled who he was, during the battle in the Spirit Realm. A guilt that made him question everything he had felt for Cassius during their time together on Earth.

Was his love for the angel just a remnant of his past obsession with the demigod he had once been? Had he *ever* truly loved Cassius or Icarus? Or was he just fixated on possessing him, like a collector did a prized painting?

There was one thing Victor could not deny.

Morgan loved Cassius. Truly. Absolutely. Irrevocably.

He had proven this in more ways than Victor had ever shown Cassius in the decades they'd been together. The pair of them had their squabbles and the Dryad demigod was a stubborn asshole, but he would burn the world down for Cassius. And he would abandon it in a heartbeat if it meant Cassius's happiness, just like he'd threatened to do before they'd gone to the Spirit Realm to face Elios.

"Fuck." A low chuckle left Victor despite the pain threatening to rip his chest apart. "You win, you irritating bastard."

He pressed the cold glass to his forehead and closed his eyes, defeat a heavy mantle weighing his shoulders down.

It didn't help that he now knew Morgan to be his half-brother.

Siblings, huh? Shame all I want to do is punch that annoying fucker in the face.

The demigod he had once been would have wanted him to tear Cassius from his brother's hold and make him his by any means. But he couldn't do that. Not again. A cold conviction replaced the bitter taste of loss on his tongue.

He would never betray Cassius or Icarus again for as long as he lived, even if it meant his death.

Victor opened his eyes and gazed blindly at the bright cityscape through the cut glass of his crystal tumbler. *I guess I better start answering his messages.*

He'd deliberately been avoiding Cassius's texts and

voicemails since he'd returned to London. Not just because he was still devastated by all he had learned after their recent battle. But because, deep down inside, he'd known this day was coming.

The day he would finally let Cassius go.

He'd reluctantly allowed the angel to leave London months ago, convinced he would one day win his heart. But he knew that was impossible now. And he wouldn't stand in the way of Cassius's happiness. Not when the demigod's heart and soul so clearly belonged to Morgan.

A bright flare shot up through the darkness to the east, the light distorted through the crystal. Victor lowered his glass, unsure if he'd imagined it.

The flare came again. The rain intensified.

He straightened and frowned. *Is that some kind of spotlight?*

A sound distracted him.

Victor turned, catching the scent of the succubus before he saw her. The blonde stepped out of the shadows near the doors, her red lips matching the color of her gown, her face and body flawless in the glow of the city lights.

"Sonia."

The woman smiled and dipped her head, teeth bright in the gloom. "Victor."

The succubus was the other reason he'd come out on the balcony. He'd once had a tryst with her, decades before he'd gotten together with Cassius. Though the sex had been phenomenal and they'd fucked almost non-stop for an entire week, he hadn't been interested enough to keep in touch. Succubae were not known for being faithful lovers or forming long-term relationships.

Victor had crossed paths with her again recently, at one of the many business functions he had to attend in his role as the head of Cabalista. The woman had stalked him at virtually every party he'd been at since, eager to rekindle their past physical encounter.

Sonia's pupils flared crimson as she closed the distance to him, her body moving with lithe grace while her carnal scent thickened the air, promising sexual pleasures no man could imagine.

She stopped in front of him, tilted her chin to meet his gaze, and ran a crimson, manicured nail down his chest and past his abs. "You're a hard demon to pin down, Sloan."

Victor grabbed her wrist before she could graze his crotch. "I thought I made it clear I wasn't interested in reliving the past."

Annoyance flashed on Sonia's face at his steady tone. She wiped it away with a smirk and rose on her toes. Sultry heat warmed Victor's skin as she brought her lips to his ear and let loose her succubus powers, her pupils pulsing vermilion.

"You know I can shapeshift, right? I'll be whoever you want me to be." She brushed her lips across the side of his neck and licked his skin, her voice dropping to a husky whisper. "I'm more than happy to go on all fours and let you pound me in the ass, like you did Cass—"

A gasp left her as Victor grabbed her arm and

wrenched it behind her back. She hissed, her glamor fading for an instant to reveal her horned form.

"Do not take his name in vain, Sonia," Victor said in a low voice full of fury. "I will not tolerate it!"

The succubus bared her teeth.

"Am I interrupting?" someone drawled.

Victor's head snapped to his left.

Hugo Frost stood watching them with a slightly bemused expression, the noise of the party loud through the partly open doors behind him. Victor stared. He hadn't heard the man come out onto the balcony.

He straightened and relaxed his hold on Sonia. The succubus yanked her arm free and glared at him. She stormed past Frost and disappeared into the crowd in the function room.

"Was that your date?" Frost said.

"No."

Frost watched him thoughtfully for a moment before coming over and extending a hand, his rugged face creasing in an affable smile. "I don't think we've officially met yet. I'm Hugo Frost."

"I know who you are," Victor said neutrally. "Victor Sloan."

He shook Frost's hand.

Frost's smile widened. "And I know who *you* are."

Victor blinked. The man's fingers were icy cold where they wrapped around his hand.

"I've been a fan of yours for a long time," Frost explained at his guarded expression. "You know, Fiery demon and all that."

Victor relaxed. His phone buzzed in the inside pocket of his suit before he could come up with a polite reply.

"Excuse me."

He let go of Frost's hand and reached for his cell. He stilled when he saw the message from Cassius on the screen, his heart lurching painfully.

I'm in London.

Frost raised an eyebrow. "Bad news?"

Victor shook his head. "No. Good news." He smiled, his body growing light and his breathing easier than it had been for weeks. "In fact, it's the best kind. I'm sorry, I should take this."

"I'll take my leave," Frost murmured.

Victor started typing out a reply and nodded distractedly while his host headed back inside the function room.

Where are you?

The angel messaged back immediately. *We're at The Cock and Crown. Wanna join us for a drink?*

Victor made a face. *We?*

Morgan's with you?

Yes. We should talk.

Victor pursed his lips and hesitated before responding. *I'm on my way. That asshole had better not be kissing you in public when I get there.*

Cassius's reply had him chuckling. *Don't worry, I already punched him for doing that.*

CHAPTER TWELVE

Victor put his cell away and headed back inside the hotel. He nodded briskly at the few acquaintances who approached him while he made swiftly for the exit, too much in a rush to exchange polite conversation.

He had no doubt Rosemary and his second-in-command would have words to say about his lack of interaction with Frost, but he couldn't find it in himself to give a damn right now.

He was coming down the marble staircase dominating the foyer when a commotion near the entrance drew his eyes. A young man in a tattered suit had stumbled through the front doors of the hotel. He was soaked to the skin, his curly, chestnut hair plastered to his head, and he walked with a limp where he'd lost a shoe. Victor's gaze skimmed the stranger's grazed knees and hands before moving back to his arresting face.

The guy was sinfully good looking despite his

shabby state, his graceful build only adding to his refined features and golden skin. He staggered blindly across the floor, oblivious to the surprised guests scattering in his path, the cuts on his foot leaving bloody trails in the puddles forming around him.

Victor looked away. *Shame he's intoxicated.*

Something hot and painful throbbed deep inside his body then. He blinked, startled.

What the hell was that?!

His gaze found the stranger unerringly, his instincts telling him the guy was the reason for what he'd just felt. His pulse quickened.

"Excuse me." A male employee had left the concierge desk and was crossing the foyer toward the stranger, expression pinched. "I'm afraid you might be in the wrong place, sir."

He grabbed the guy's arm.

The stranger looked blankly from the concierge's hand to his face. "Where is he?"

Victor's scalp prickled at the slight musical lilt underscoring his French accent. *Is he an otherworldly?*

"Are you drunk, sir?" the concierge snapped.

The stranger ignored his question and brushed his hand away like it was nothing. "I need to find him."

He took two steps and almost tripped when the concierge grabbed his shoulder and yanked him back. Irritation surged through Victor. He hurried down the last few steps.

"Can't you see he's hurt?" he snapped at the concierge. "He might have hit his head."

The stranger froze. A pair of mesmerizing, green

eyes swiveled around and locked on Victor. Recognition flared on the man's face.

Victor's heart stuttered at the bone-deep longing he read in the viridescent depths. Time slowed. The foyer faded around him, until only he and the stranger remained.

He found himself unable to tear his gaze from the man's eyes. "Do I—?" Victor stopped and swallowed. "Do I know you?!"

The guy smiled tremulously, tears obscuring his vivid irises. The name that fell from his bloodless lips brought Victor to his senses in a flash.

"*Coraos...*"

Shock rooted Victor's feet to the ground as the man shrugged off the concierge's hand and crossed the floor toward him, his limp more evident as he hurried over. His pupils flared with golden brightness.

An alarmed voice rose behind Victor, shattering the intimate moment. "Theo?!"

Victor unfroze and looked over his shoulder. Frost was coming down the stairs rapidly, concern clouding his face. He rushed past Victor and grasped the stranger's arms.

Victor blinked. The pale glow had faded from the guy's pupils.

"What happened to you?" Frost said urgently, his gaze scanning the stranger's unkempt appearance.

A blank expression swept all emotion from the latter's features.

Unease flitted through Victor.

It was as if a light had gone out behind the stranger's eyes.

"Do you know him, sir?" the concierge asked Frost uneasily.

"Yes," Frost replied curtly. "He's my P.A." He took the guy called Theo by the elbow. "Come. Let's get you to the suite and out of those wet clothes."

He guided him gently to an elevator. Victor watched the two men head inside the cabin wordlessly, his heart still hammering against his ribs.

Did I imagine it? Did he really say my true name just now?!

Frost placed a proprietary hand on the small of Theo's back. The sight of it irritated Victor for some reason. Theo's gaze landed on Victor as the metal doors started closing on him and his boss. Victor's chest tightened when he glimpsed the haunted look deep in his green eyes.

He was gone the next second. The elevator started to rise.

A sinking feeling swept through Victor as he watched the numbers change in the digital panel above it. The cabin stopped on the sixth floor and stayed there. He ran a hand through his hair and scowled at the floor for long seconds, unable to suppress the strange frustration churning his insides. He stiffened.

"Shit!"

He'd forgotten all about his meeting with Cassius and Morgan.

Victor ignored the heaviness in his chest and headed rapidly for the valet desk. He had his keys in hand and a leg inside his Aston Martin when heat thumped painfully through his soul core once more. His gaze gravitated to the hotel. Theo's face swam before his eyes.

He whirled around with a curse. "Put it back in the garage!"

Victor threw his car keys at the surprised parking attendant and messaged Cassius quickly as he stormed back inside the building.

It took the front desk a good five minutes to tell him which guest suite Hugo Frost had reserved for his use. By the time Victor exited the elevator on the sixth floor of the hotel, the bad feeling churning his gut had intensified.

Something was happening. Something he hadn't quite grasped yet but that was sending all his alarm bells into hyperdrive. And it had everything to do with the two men he had last seen heading up to this floor.

The suite was at the end of the south corridor. Thick carpet swallowed the sound of Victor's footsteps as he headed down it. A gilded door came into view, fake gold and silver gleaming slightly in the low lighting. He stopped in front of it and raised a hand to knock. His knuckles froze an inch from the wood at the sound of a low moan.

A man's weak cry reached him next. "No! I—I don't want this! *St—stop!*"

A pulse of corruption washed through the door and raised the hairs on Victor's flesh. Recognition drenched him in a cold sweat.

Fuck!

The last time he'd felt that power had been in the Spirit Realm.

Flames bloomed around him as he unsheathed his dagger and unleashed his Fiery powers. He grabbed the door handle and ripped it off, the metal melting in his grip.

Victor took a step back, kicked the door down, and stormed inside, the fire wrapping around him and the broadsword he now wielded growing inky black as he assumed his demigod form, his dark wings snapping open with a loud crack. The sight that met his eyes had him drawing a sharp breath and stumbling to a stop.

CHAPTER THIRTEEN

THEO WAS DREAMING. IN HIS DREAM, FROST WAS undressing him, fingers ice cold and none too kind on his flushed skin where he lay pliantly on a bed that smelled of fresh linen. He looked around dazedly, his head spinning so badly it felt like it would fall off his neck at any given moment.

The room swam into focus. They were in a hotel suite.

A sense of wrongness prickled Theo's skin. His knees and hands felt sore, like he'd grazed them. He didn't think he'd feel pain in a dream.

Memories flitted through his mind with his next breath. An alleyway full of monsters. Rain pounding his hot body. An otherworldly presence deep within him. A presence he could no longer sense. The images danced fitfully before his eyes, a broken video playing over and over again.

His thoughts scattered as Frost tugged his pants and briefs down his legs and dropped them on the floor. A shiver of awareness raced down Theo's spine at the way Frost studied his naked cock.

"You're even prettier than I thought you'd be."

Theo's dick sprang to attention. There was no mistaking the interest in Frost's eyes or the bulge denting the front of his trousers. Lust tightened Theo's belly, the vague apprehension in the pit of his stomach fading. Whatever this was, he didn't want it to end. Not if it was leading where he thought it would.

"Oh!"

He jerked and gasped as Frost ran a knuckle up his hardening shaft, surprise rounding his eyes at how real his touch felt. Pain shot through his dick the next instant. Theo winced and throttled a moan.

Frost had pinched the tip of his cock. His boss smirked. "Naughty boy. Who told you you could get wet without my permission?"

Theo squirmed and bit his lip, the sight of his leaking precum on Frost's skin making his blood sizzle and his hole twitch. His breath caught. Frost let him go and reached down to unzip himself.

Theo swallowed and licked his lips at his first full view of Frost's dick. *Oh God! He's just as long and thick as I thought he'd be!*

Something dark moved sinuously on Frost's raging erection.

Theo blinked. Whatever it was had gone.

There was movement to the left. Theo's jaw fell open. A gorgeous blonde in a red dress stepped out of the shadows next to the ensuite. The woman's pupils glowed crimson. Horns flickered on and off above her head. Theo stared, too shocked to utter a word.

Is she—is she a succubus?!

She was moving weirdly, as if someone was controlling her body. Her nails dug into her palms and her mouth twisted in a rictus. Tendons strained in her neck as she turned her head and glared at Frost.

Frost's pupils flared with an emotion Theo had never seen before. One that made a sliver of dread coil through his gut.

Frost tilted his head to the side. "You really are a powerful demon, Sonia. No wonder you're drawn to Victor."

He gave his dick a few brisk rubs and smiled.

Dark lines exploded across the woman's skin, the inky cracks snaking across her flesh giving it a parchment-like appearance. She grimaced and gnashed her teeth. Her expression grew slack a moment later, the red light in her pupils dimming.

"Strip," Frost said in a callous tone Theo had never heard before.

She obeyed wordlessly, her dress slipping down her body and pooling around her legs. She stepped out of the silken folds, still in her red stilettos.

Theo gulped. Even though he had no interest in women, he could not deny how exquisite she was. Sonia was tall and voluptuous, with high breasts, perfect pink nipples, and legs that went on for miles. Her blonde hair fell to her mid back in glossy waves and her pussy was shaved.

"Come," Frost ordered.

Sonia moved and stopped in front of him. Theo's boss pressed a hand on her shoulder. Her legs folded easily as he pushed her to her knees.

"Open your mouth."

Theo's heart pounded against his ribs as Sonia complied, her glistening lips parting with a soft pop. Frost pushed the tip of his cock through them. She swallowed his dick with a faint hiss. Frost ignored the sound and punched in to the hilt. Sonia grunted. Then she started to blow him, her head moving mechanically up and down as she coated his shaft with her drool and lipstick, her face glazed.

Theo stared, his own dick throbbing. His skin felt tight and his belly hot. He wasn't sure if it was desire or dread he was feeling. All of this seemed so real he wanted to pinch himself to see if it was really a dream.

Frost looked over and held out a hand to him. Theo hesitated before climbing awkwardly off the bed. Never in a million years could he have imagined this scene. It was filthy and sinful and should have scared him senseless. But he couldn't stop the yearning twisting his insides.

He wanted Frost to fuck him, just like he was fucking the mouth of the woman on her knees.

Frost took Theo's hand and pulled him in, his superior smile telling Theo he'd read his mind. He snaked his fingers around the back of Theo's nape, jerked him close, and kissed him.

Theo's senses stuttered as Frost slipped his tongue inside his mouth. His cock pulsed and his breath hitched, need clashing with fear. Frost wrapped his other hand around Theo's straining erection and started stroking him.

Theo's mind went blank, pleasure taking over his senses.

He hummed and moaned at the exquisite feeling of Frost's fingers on his shaft, his flesh so hot he barely noticed Frost's cold skin, his hips rocking of their own volition.

The succubus gagged and choked as Frost plundered her mouth with hard thrusts. Theo clutched Frost's shoulders and closed his eyes, losing himself in the rawness of the moment. The sounds of wet cocks and fingers and lips and tongues melded together in a surreal fantasy that filled his ears with the melody of feral sex.

Tension tightened his body as the first wave of his orgasm washed over him. It slipped away when something bitter snaked down his throat. Theo blinked. He stiffened, goosebumps swarming his flesh.

Frost's eyes had gone black from edge to edge, the expression on his face savage as he continued kissing him with effortless mastery, his tongue lashing Theo's hard. Theo gagged as another sliver of acrid liquid shot down his gullet.

He pressed his hands against Frost's chest and wrenched his mouth free. "What—what is that?!"

Theo wiped his lips and stared at the sticky, black fluid on the back of his hand. A ringing filled his ears. He felt sick all of a sudden.

He gasped as Frost let go of his cock and pushed

him down on the bed. Theo bounced on the edge, his pulse now thrumming with fear.

Frost pulled out of Sonia's mouth, dragged her unceremoniously to her feet, and turned her around. He fixed her hips with one hand, parted her ass with the other, and impaled her back passage with his cock. The succubus rose on her toes, pupils dilating and a choked-off sound of pain tearing from her throat.

Ice skittered across Theo's skin. His erection grew limp.

What—what's happening?!

An evil chuckle left Frost at the sight of Theo's deflating cock. He twisted his fingers in the succubus's hair and forced her to bend over. A few pale strands ripped from her scalp as she resisted.

"Why don't you service Theo, Sonia? He looks like he's struggling."

Theo watched numbly as Sonia grasped his thighs and wrapped her lips around the head of his shaft, as powerless to resist Frost as he was. He cursed when she swallowed him all the way to the back of her throat, the velvety heat of her mouth scalding his sensitive organ.

He'd never had anyone touch his cock before, let alone blow him.

Sonia started sucking him with low moans. Theo's dick pulsed and began to harden again despite his terror, his body responding to the skillful motion of the succubus's lips and tongue.

"Do you like her mouth?"

Theo's head snapped up at the question. He froze.

Frost's obsidian eyes were locked on him as he thrust hard and fast, pounding Sonia's ass with enough force to make her grunt around Theo's cock and her heels rise off the floor. Slivers of darkness were poking the air around him, the currents seemingly rising from his very flesh.

A chilly sensation snaked over Theo's shaft, distracting him. Horror drenched him in a cold sweat as he looked down. He couldn't stop the incoherent sound that tumbled from his lips.

Sonia was slowly turning blue. A black liquid gushed from her mouth and nose. Her eyes had rolled back in her head, her tears leaving streaks of mascara on her cheeks.

Theo felt some of the inky fluid enter his cock. A sliver trickled down under his balls and tried to penetrate his ass. Terror clenched his belly.

"No! I—I don't want this! *St—stop!*"

He started to struggle, his hands finding Sonia's face to wrench her mouth from his dick. The black liquid stung his skin.

Darkness erupted around Frost. It thickened, forming a cloak that shivered in an unseen wind. Heat bloomed in the very core of Theo's body.

Someone kicked the door down and entered the suite.

CHAPTER FOURTEEN

VICTOR'S BEWILDERED GAZE SHIFTED FROM THE terrified, naked young man on the bed to the dusky-faced succubus with her mouth on his crotch, a horrible, black fluid pouring out of her lips and nostrils.

Sonia?!

Fury filled his veins at the sight of the monster fucking her in the ass. *"Elios!"*

The God of Darkness grinned viciously and sprang back, his black erection disappearing amidst the mantle of corruption blanketing him. He was wearing Hugo Frost's face.

Victor scowled. *Dammit! Don't tell me he's been in London all this time!*

He reached for the core of his power, flames roaring and Stark Steel sword vibrating in his hand.

Sonia collapsed at Theo's feet. Theo stayed frozen for a moment before moving from the bed. He dropped to his knees, turned the succubus onto her side, and cleared the fluid clogging her mouth with trembling fingers. Relief shot through Victor when he heard Sonia draw a raspy breath.

The succubus was still alive, barely.

"This is a surprise." Elios smirked where he floated in the middle of the room in his ghoulish form. *"I'd hoped I would at least get to plunder his body before he awakened."* His obsidian gaze flitted to Theo. *"He's a virgin, you know. And gay to boot. I bet his ass is exquisite compared to an untouched woman's pussy. I would have enjoyed tearing him open."*

Theo blanched.

Elios lowered his brows at Victor, his tone growing wintry and a daunting aura flaring around him. *"Now, tell me, how did you find us?"*

Confusion shot through Victor. He glanced at Theo. *Awaken? What does he mean by—?!*

Divine energy throbbed the air. Theo screamed and doubled over. Victor's eyes rounded. A radiant light was pulsing from Theo's abdomen.

Dread brought a sour taste to his mouth. "What did you—?"

"—do to him?"

The voice that rang around the suite drowned out the rest of Victor's words and jolted him and Elios alike. It was fire and summer and a power that was barely under control.

Theo had risen to his feet. His irises had shifted to an arresting sapphire and his pupils blazed with gold-white seraphic light.

"What did you do to this child, Elios?"

He stepped forward, the fear that had robbed his face of color replaced by a focused expression, as if he were trying to peel away the shadows around Elios.

The God of Darkness moved back agitatedly.

"*No!*" he ground out. "*This is not what is meant to happen! The Moirai didn't tell me you would return too!*"

Coldness clutched Victor's gut, Theo momentarily forgotten. "*The Moirai?!*" Understanding dawned in a flash. "You mean, you've had the *Fates* under your control all this time?!"

The pent-up rage he felt for the God who'd made him betray Icarus burst forth in a storm of black fire as he finally realized why their enemy had always been one step ahead of them. Victor moved, fury a red mist darkening his vision.

Elios exploded into a thousand inky strands as Victor swung his blade. The sword passed harmlessly through the vanishing shadows. Victor roared and attacked again and again.

Elios avoided all his strikes.

"*You should give up, Coraos,*" he sneered. "*Our powers are too alike for yours to have much of an effect on me. And, lest you forget, I am a God, little brother!*"

Icy fingers found Victor's throat. He grunted as Elios bound his wings and body with dark bands and ripped his sword from his grip.

Shit! I really wish Cassius and Morgan were here right now. I don't think I can take this guy on my own!

"*You should have done what I told you to do,*" Elios spat. He brought Victor so close mere inches separated their faces. *"You should have killed Ivmir so Icarus would lose his mind and destroy the Nether!"*

Horror squeezed Victor's heart at Elios's words, the dark God's corrupt scent filling his nostrils with the musty stench of death as he tried to draw air through his windpipe.

What?! Kill Morgan?! But—

Agonizing pain gripped his skull. He cried out and doubled over.

Another memory escaped the seal on his mind. It seared his senses and made him blink back tears.

It was from the War in the Nether.

Victor saw himself fighting Ivmir while Icarus and his brothers engaged Elios. He saw his black-fire-wreathed blade slice through Ivmir's armor and carve his flesh, the poison Elios had infused the weapon with leaving a jagged wound on the demigod's chest. He heard Icarus's shout of horror and witnessed the Awakener hurrying over to them, his battle temporarily forgotten in his panic.

He saw Elios strike Rohengar down and felt the Nether tremble as Nildar and Archon howled in fury and pain. He saw Icarus falter and twist around in mid-air, terror leaching all color from his face as he watched both Rohengar and Ivmir fall. Then there was brightness and pain and a scream that threatened to split the very universe in half.

Dread and remorse rendered Victor slack with shock as he returned to his senses. *Oh God! What did I do?!*

"Release him!"

The suite trembled. Blinding radiance filled the air, along with the scent of summer and the wrath of Heaven. Victor gasped, Elios's hold on him disappearing. He shot back to a safe distance and rubbed his throat, his flames a dull roar in his ears as he raised an arm to shield his eyes. The sight that greeted him when he peered through the gaps between his fingers had his stomach plummeting.

White wings flared from Theo's naked back, golden light fluttering amidst the brilliant feathers. He was lowering his arm from behind his head, as if he'd just cast something.

Elios grunted.

Victor's eyes rounded, his gaze finding the God of Darkness.

A gossamer spear of light had pierced Elios where his soul core should have been. He gripped it and hissed when it seared his flesh. A roar of fury left the dark God as he ripped the weapon out of his spectral form. He stared incredulously as it scattered into a million bright motes in his grasp.

"*No!*" Elios mumbled. His voice gained in strength. "*This cannot be!*" he snarled. "*I destroyed it with my own hands!*"

His black gaze burned with rage as he glared at Theo. He lifted an arm toward the young man and flexed his fingers.

Theo gasped and fell to the ground, bright wings snapping out of existence. The glow radiating from his eyes and belly shuddered and writhed, sending erratic pulses of divine energy across the room.

Bile rose in Victor's throat. He darted across the suite, landed beside Theo, and took him in his arms. Theo's skin was cold and clammy to touch. Victor's furious gaze locked on Elios.

"What the fuck did you do to him, asshole?!"

Elios sneered. *"I'm just forcing him to embrace what he truly is. Unfortunately, it doesn't bode well for this world."* He vanished in a burst of shadows and a clap of thunder, his mocking laughter fading to an echo. *"Enjoy the show, Coraos!"*

Victor gritted his teeth. Frustration gnawed at his gut as he vacillated between trying to follow the foul odor of corruption Elios had left behind and staying with the man in his arms, the God's threat ringing in his ears.

A hand pressed gently against his chest, startling him. He looked down into striking eyes that flickered from a mesmerizing sapphire to a dazzling green he could easily drown in.

Seraphic pupils fixed him in bright beams of power. *"Take care of this child, Coraos."*

Victor shuddered, a vestige of memory drifting through his mind. He knew this man. Had known him for a long time.

A tender smile lit Theo's face. He raised steady fingers to Victor's trembling lips and cheek. Victor stiffened at the wetness on his face. He hadn't realized he'd been crying or that he was shaking so uncontrollably.

Theo's expression sobered. *"Hold on tight."*

It was the only warning Victor got before Theo

went supernova in his hold, his powers scorching Victor's senses as they blasted out from his soul core. Victor gasped, the brilliance emanating from the flesh and eyes of the man in his arms searing his retina for a second before he squinted.

Theo arched, back bowing upward and jaw locked rigid. The bright beams from his pupils merged into a dazzling ray that pierced the ceiling. The scream that tore from his throat made Victor's ears throb and put his teeth on edge. He hugged him closer.

Glass shattered somewhere in the suite.

Victor ignored the sounds of chaos tearing through the suite and held on grimly to the awakening otherworldly in his arms, Elios's words finally making sense. Tremors shook the building. Distant screams reached him from elsewhere in the hotel.

The air ripped somewhere close by.

The blaze pouring out from Theo snapped out with a suddenness that made Victor's vision swim with black dots. He blinked them away in time to see talons arcing toward his face.

CHAPTER FIFTEEN

MORGAN SCANNED THE TAVERN THEY'D JUST ENTERED. "This place is kinda quaint."

"The food's good and the patrons mostly keep to themselves," Cassius said.

The Cock and Crown was a few streets over from the Cabalista headquarters, not far from Liverpool Street Station and Shoreditch. It was a typical, old-fashioned alehouse set in a Grade-II listed building down a crooked alley. In centuries past, the establishment would have been slap bang in the middle of one of London's notorious red-light districts.

Curious gazes followed them as they made their way through the dim interior and across creaky, wooden floors to an empty table near the back. Though recognition flared on several faces, no one gawked or made an attempt to come over.

He's right. They don't look like the kind of people who'll ask for an autograph.

Morgan lifted a menu from the condiment stand as they sat down. "What do you recommend?"

"Their steak and ale pie is nice."

Morgan stilled and stared at Cassius, a sudden thought bursting through his mind.

His lover narrowed his eyes slightly. "What?"

"I just realized something," Morgan said bluntly. "We've never been on a date."

Cassius blinked. "Yes, we have. We go to Occulta all the time."

Morgan waved a hand dismissively. "That's just after-work drinks. Besides, we're always surrounded by those assholes."

Cassius sighed. "I'm sure our team would be thrilled to know that you refer to them with such love and affection."

"They're cockblockers, each and every one of them," Morgan grunted. "Even that Charlie."

Cassius rolled his eyes hard. "Well then, consider this our first date."

He started looking at the specials.

Morgan wrinkled his nose. He put his menu down, smiled winsomely, and ran a finger across the back of Cassius's knuckles. "So, do you come here often?"

Cassius shivered at his touch before giving him a stern look. "That's a terrible pick-up line."

Morgan's smile widened, undeterred. "How about we hook up after this and I take you somewhere I can rock your world?"

Cassius snort-laughed. He recovered, cleared his

throat, and fixed Morgan with a fake frown. "That one is a minus fifty on a scale of zero to a hundred."

A light feeling fluttered through Morgan as he studied Cassius. This was the most relaxed he'd seen the angel in weeks. Another harsh truth struck him then.

He and Cassius had been so engrossed in finding out the details of their past, they were forgetting to live in the present.

Emotion tightened his chest. *I love him so damn much!*

Morgan leaned across the table, hooked a hand at the back of Cassius's head, and pulled him in for a scorching kiss. He couldn't help himself. He had to touch the demigod right now.

Cassius melted into him for breathless seconds before punching him in the ribs.

"*Ow!*" Morgan protested. "What was that for?"

"No kissing in public, remember," Cassius snapped, his flushed cheeks telling their own story.

As if on cue, a low wolf-whistle reached them from across the room.

A slow grin split Morgan's mouth. "Does this mean I can kiss you *there* and everywhere when we get home?"

He waggled his eyebrows and made a suggestive motion with his fingers.

Cassius's face grew redder. "You're incorrigible!"

Morgan chuckled. He went to the bar to get drinks and put their order through and returned to the table to find Cassius smiling faintly at his phone.

"What?"

"I messaged Victor. He's on his way."

Morgan placed their glasses on the table with a bit more force than was necessary. "Great."

Cassius fixed him with a pointed stare.

Morgan sighed. "I'll be on my best behavior, I promise." He took a sip of his beer. "Even though the worst cockblocker of them all will soon be here," he added under his breath.

Cassius's expression grew pinched. Their meals had just arrived when his cell buzzed. He checked his messages and frowned faintly.

"What?" Morgan said.

"He says he's gonna be late."

Morgan suppressed a smirk behind his glass. They tucked into their food.

"You're right." He raised an eyebrow after he'd swallowed a couple of bites. "This really is nice."

He looked up to find Cassius frozen in his seat. The demigod was staring out the window, his face blank but for the seraphic light brightening his pupils, his fork held aloft.

Morgan stiffened and followed his gaze, senses going into hyperdrive. "Cassius?"

Cassius put the fork down and stood up slowly, his hands fisting at his sides. He furrowed his brow. "Something is coming."

Dread coiled through Morgan at his lover's words.

They were the same ones he'd said that very morning.

The blast that rocked the city had lights and glass

exploding around them and the building trembling violently. Morgan jumped to his feet as screams broke out across the tavern, his inky wings snapping open and the Sword of Wind appearing in his hand. His crown of dark wind and oak formed on his head, sending Dryad magic dancing amidst the black currents.

Cassius had already assumed his demigod form, his white wings and the light crackling around him and on his holy blade the only source of illumination in the room. They rushed outside, the patrons scattering to make way for them.

Horns blasted the air as they ran out of the alley. The sounds were followed by a cacophony of crashes. They staggered to a stop on the curb overlooking a main junction. Morgan stared, his pulse racing.

London had gone dark. The traffic in the streets converging onto the intersection had come to an abrupt halt, headlights off and batteries dead. Many had bumped into the back of the vehicle ahead of them, while others had veered into lamp posts and smashed into stationary cars.

Morgan's fingers tightened on his sword. "Is it an EMP pulse?!"

Cassius shook his head, his face grim. "No. I'm pretty sure that was divine power."

Morgan glanced at him. The seraphic glow in Cassius's eyes had intensified, a sign that Icarus was conscious.

Light flared to the south. A bright beam shot up and pierced the dark clouds covering the heavens. The formations started to spin turbulently around it even as they watched.

This time, Morgan detected the godlike energy that saturated the air. "What's going on, Cassius?!"

"I don't know!" Cassius snapped his wings open and rose. "But I think we need to be where that light's coming from!"

Morgan followed as he took to the sky. They cleared the buildings with a few powerful beats of their wings and steadied themselves on an eddy as they assessed the landscape around them.

Other winged forms were rising into the air across the capital, the soul cores of the angels and demons who lived there similarly responding to whatever that light was.

It went out with a suddenness that made Morgan draw a sharp breath and had his vision swimming for a second.

"Fuck!" Cassius swore.

Morgan followed his gaze. His stomach dropped.

The sky was turning red where the clouds twisted and gyrated into a descending funnel.

The power of the Hells washed across London.

CHAPTER SIXTEEN

Cassius's heart thundered violently against his ribs as he and Morgan shot over Liverpool Street Station. He could taste the panic engulfing the dark city below. Though London was mostly full of humans, even they would be able to sense the uncanny nature of what was happening.

For one thing, the crimson haze spreading across the firmament was a surefire sign that all was not well in their world.

Cassius and Morgan slipped between two high rises and arrowed toward where they'd seen the bright beam cut through the clouds, the hue from above painting their wings in shades of vermilion. It didn't take them long to reach a junction near Bank tube station and the Royal Exchange.

People were screaming and running out of a swanky hotel overlooking the intersection. Cassius narrowed his eyes. It was where the sulfurous taint of the Hells was the strongest.

Radiant light pulsed through a smashed-up window on the sixth floor.

"There!" Cassius barked.

He and Morgan dove. They snapped their wings closed seconds before they arrowed through the jagged opening and rocked to a halt in mid-air. Dread curdled Cassius's gut.

A portal had opened in the middle of a hotel suite. Hellbeasts, lesser demons, and monsters were pouring out of it.

Victor was fighting them, his flames raging around his dark demigod form and his face locked in a furious scowl as he blocked the creatures from leaving the room and heading farther inside the building. Cassius's gaze dropped to the naked figure wrapped in a bedsheet the Fiery held protectively in one arm, his charge hampering his movements somewhat.

Time slowed.

Cassius's soul core throbbed with a strong wave of cognizance as he looked upon the face of an unconscious young man. Though the stranger's features were unfamiliar, his nature wasn't.

Morgan darted in front of him and blocked an attack. "Watch out!"

Victor's crimson pupils flared when he clocked their presence. "Cassius! Morgan! Over here!"

Cassius gritted his teeth. He could ask all the questions he wanted afterward. Right now, he needed to focus on the battle at hand. He and Morgan carved their way through the hordes blocking their path and soon reached Victor.

"I'm glad to see you!" the demon said, relieved.

They shifted position until they stood back-to-back in a defensive circle. Hells' monsters snarled and snapped their fangs inches from their blades, their hateful eyes straying to the light around Cassius.

"What the hell happened?" Morgan asked Victor. "And who's *this* guy?!"

He cocked his head at the unconscious figure.

The demon's reply had ice filling Cassius's veins. Morgan's jaw clenched so hard Cassius wouldn't have been surprised if he broke a tooth.

"Elios is here, in London." Victor glanced at the comatose man in his embrace, the expression that flashed in his crimson eyes catching Cassius off guard. "He did something to him. Something that's awakened his divine powers and somehow brought these monsters here through a portal."

Cassius lowered his brows. "This isn't the only doorway his powers have opened."

"What?" Morgan said, shocked.

"Cassius is right," Victor said darkly. "I can feel it too. The taint of the Hells is coming from all over London."

Cassius's gaze swept the monsters surrounding them, urgency quickening his pulse. "We need to finish this and close those portals before more monsters invade the city!"

Surprise widened Morgan and Victor's eyes.

"You can close these portals?" Victor asked.

"Like the rifts in San Francisco?" Morgan said, hope underscoring his voice.

Cassius dipped his head. "Yes. Icarus the Awakener can." He frowned. "I'm going to unleash Heaven's Light. You guys think you can take this horde out so I can get to that doorway?"

A savage expression darkened Victor's face. "Yes."

"Bring it," Morgan growled.

Cassius looked over at the man in Victor's hold. "Give him to me. I'll take care of him so you can move easy."

Victor hesitated, his gaze shifting from Cassius to the man in his arms.

Cassius bit back a soft smile despite the gravity of their situation. *I wonder if he knows what kind of face he's making right now.*

"I won't drop him, I promise."

Victor reluctantly passed the lifeless figure over. "His name is Theo."

Theo's body was surprisingly light. Emotion clogged Cassius's throat when their flesh touched. He instinctively hugged the unconscious man closer. His soul was telling him he knew this warmth.

Cassius took a deep breath and furrowed his brow. Fire filled his veins. He gripped his sword and Theo tightly. Brightness detonated across the room as he let loose Heaven's Light.

The monsters screamed, the radiance blinding them at the same time it charred their skin and flesh.

Cassius moved, Victor and Morgan defending his blind spots. The floor cracked and the walls crumbled as the formidable power of three demigods drenched the air. The building started to shake in its very foundations.

It took mere seconds to cross the suite, Victor and Morgan's ferocious attacks felling dozens of beasts where they stood. Black flames and dark wind infused with Dryad magic buffeted Cassius's body as he wielded his blade to help them carve out a path to the doorway.

This is the way it should have been, all those years ago. Cassius swallowed past the sudden lump in his throat as he glanced at Morgan and Victor's blazing expressions. *This is how we could have won the war against Elios. With Ivmir and Coraos and my brothers at my side!*

He became conscious of a presence and looked down to see Theo's eyelids flutter open. Cassius's breath stuttered. Pupils brimming with seraphic light gazed unblinkingly at him. A gentle smile touched Theo's lips.

The scent of summer washed over Cassius.

He breathed it in, savored its sweetness, clutched its heat to his soul. Icarus's emotions danced through his heart, so full of love and regret he feared it would shatter. Theo's eyelids trembled and closed, his divine presence fading as he lost consciousness again.

The portal came into view.

The Sword of Wind carved through the air and monsters alike on a green wave of Dryad magic ahead of him.

"Whatever you're gonna do, do it now!" Morgan shouted.

Victor's black flames and blade felled the last hellbeasts.

Cassius stepped up to the mirror-like doorway and stabbed the center with his sword without a moment's hesitation, the weight of the man in his arms a precious reminder of who he was and what he could do. He drew on his powers and twisted the blade, Icarus's heartbeat loud in his ears.

Heaven's light poured out of him. It focused into a dazzling beam that sent bright ripples across the surface of the portal. An unholy sound tore the air as it started to warp and disintegrate.

The monsters still standing screeched, their bodies distorting violently into hellish shapes as they were sucked back inside the gate. Even the remains of their dead vanished with faint whooshing sounds until all that was left was gore and the havoc they had wreaked. The portal snapped closed with a pop, leaving a faint, crimson afterglow that soon faded.

The deathly silence that dropped around them was broken by the sounds of distant sirens and their own, harsh breathing.

CHAPTER SEVENTEEN

Cassius turned and looked Morgan and Victor over worriedly. "Are you okay?"

"Never better," Victor grunted as he retracted his demigod powers.

Morgan arched an eyebrow. "Do you even have to ask?"

Relief shuddered through Cassius. There was movement to his left. They whirled around, their hands clenching on the handles of their blades.

"Victor!"

A female demon flashed into view outside all that remained of the outer wall of the sixth-floor hotel suite, gray wings keeping her aloft and a Stark Steel blade coated with blood in her hand.

Victor sagged, shoulders visibly relaxing. "Delphine. Am I glad to see you."

"I would have been here sooner if it wasn't for—"

Delphine Mercier's eyes rounded on a gasp as she registered Cassius and Morgan's presence.

Cassius smiled weakly at Victor's second-in-command. "Hey, Del."

Delphine's face crumpled. She shot across the room and launched herself at him, almost taking him to the ground. Her arms closed around his chest so tightly she nearly cracked his ribs.

"I missed you, you damn angel!" she choked out in the crook of his neck.

Cassius winced and patted her lightly on the back, his throat tight. "I missed you too, Del."

Delphine had been Victor's right-hand woman for almost as long as he'd been on Earth, her steadfast loyalty to the Fiery demon unbroken since the Fall. Many had speculated that she and Victor were lovers. But Cassius knew the truth.

Victor had saved Delphine from a fate worse than death itself after the Fall. Badly injured by the War in the Nether, the once-powerful Aqueous demon had fallen prey to potent human magic, her wings too damaged to allow her to escape the traps of the magic users who'd preyed on her. She'd been destined for a royal slave market when Victor had come upon the convoy carrying her caged, lifeless form, her wings cruelly clipped by those who had captured her. From what Victor and the team of otherworldly he'd assembled shortly after he landed on Earth had gleaned, several wounded angels and demons had already been traded to the highest bidders across the continent, their bodies meant for sex while their flesh was cut open and their blood utilized in ungodly experiments meant to augment human magic.

Victor had freed each and every one of them in the first few years of the Fall, earning himself the reputation of savior and the undying trust of all otherworldly.

It had taken Cassius months to gain Delphine's trust when he'd first started going out with Victor. Like all the Fallen, her mistrust of him had run deep. Once Delphine had accepted him, the rest of Cabalista had readily followed. And she'd made sure to discreetly punish anyone who ever dared say anything unpleasant about Victor and Cassius's relationship from that moment forth.

"I'm afraid we don't have time for a reunion right now," Victor interrupted briskly. "Other portals have opened across London."

"I know." Delphine let go of Cassius, her expression grim. "I'm in touch with Jacob. We're coordinating forces to locate them. Hexa is helping evacuate the humans in those parts of the city."

Jacob Marsh was the Terrene angel in charge of the local Order of Rosen bureau. Rumor had it that he and Delphine had had a fling in the past.

"Cassius can close the portals." Victor took his cell out and lobbed it at Cassius. "Have everyone relay the locations of the gates to my phone."

Delphine startled. "He can close the portals?" She scrutinized Cassius as if seeing him for the first time, her gaze sweeping his fair hair and white wings critically. "So, this is your demigod form, huh?" Her mouth quirked up in a grin. "I've seen the pictures, but you're even prettier in person."

"Flirting, really?" Morgan grumbled.

Delphine narrowed her eyes at him. "Julia was right. You're a total sourpuss when it comes to Cassius."

Morgan grew suspicious. "Wait. You know Julia?"

Delphine arched an arrogant eyebrow. "We've been friends for ages."

"How come she never mentioned you?"

Delphine snorted. "Probably because her boss is an asshole?"

Victor sighed. "Can we reserve the diatribe for later?"

Morgan ignored him and turned to Cassius. "I'm staying with you."

Cassius pursed his lips at the demigod's mulish tone. Morgan would burn London down if he were to suggest they separate right now.

He passed Theo carefully over to Victor. "Keep him safe."

"I know." Victor lifted Theo in his arms and inspected his pale face with a troubled expression. "Is he gonna be okay?"

"Yes." Cassius ignored the unease knotting his belly as he observed Theo's lifeless form. "He has to be."

Victor stiffened at his words.

"Who's that guy?" Delphine asked Morgan.

Morgan grimaced and rubbed the back of his neck. "A demigod, we think."

Delphine stared at Theo. "Wow. You guys are multiplying like bunnies."

Cassius avoided looking at Victor. He doubted the

demon had told Delphine about his identity as Coraos yet.

Screams rent the air in the street outside.

Cassius extended his wings and took flight. "Come on, we've got work to do!"

He took a last look at Theo over his shoulder as he and Morgan flew out of the hotel, a sense of loss twisting his insides.

It took two hours to locate and close the dozen portals that had opened across the city. Though most of the monsters and beasts who had invaded the capital were forced back into the Hells, some were too far away from their doorways and escaped into the sewers to avoid the teams of angels and demons scouring the streets and hunting them down.

At the last count, there had been nine human fatalities and dozens of injured. The only thing that had stopped those figures from quadrupling was the quick thinking and coordination of Argonaut, Cabalista, the Order of Rosen, and Hexa. Unlike other cities where the four agencies were often at each other's throats, the bureaus in London enjoyed a convivial relationship, much like San Francisco.

Cassius was aware Victor had had a major role to play in establishing those partnerships in the British capital, just like he'd been instrumental to ending the Hundred Year War that had followed the Fall, when humans had fought the otherworldly they blamed for destroying their cities and taking thousands of innocent lives.

A thin sheen of sweat beaded his forehead as he

rose above the capital from where he'd just sealed off the last gate in Camden Town. Securing the portals was taxing his soul core, more so than closing the rifts the God of Darkness had created in Ivory Peaks and the Spirit Realm had done. He suspected it was because he didn't have the Eternity Key or the Ring of Death to channel into.

An unnamed dread swirled inside him. It had been slowly building for the past few minutes, like icy fingers crawling across his mind. His gaze gravitated to the red-rimmed clouds still spinning in the dark sky.

Morgan picked up on the apprehension quickening his pulse. "What is it?"

Cassius swallowed and licked his lips. "There's something…there."

Morgan tensed before following his gaze to the heavens. "Is it another gate?"

Cassius shook his head. "No." His knuckles whitened on his holy blade. Resolve hardened his heart. Whatever this was, he needed to see it through. "Let's go check it out."

Lights started blinking on across London as they rose on a cool updraft, the silence stemming from the lack of traffic still eerie. Lightning scored the clouds when they entered the turbulent billows moments later.

The vapor that condensed on Cassius's hair and feathers carried the scent of ozone. His unease deepened.

Morgan pointed at a spot a quarter of a mile up and to their right. "There!"

Cassius's eyes rounded.

It was some kind of black hole. One that was expanding and shrinking continuously, as if it were unstable. Flashes sparked across it, the jagged reflections momentarily brightening the clouds.

Understanding dawned belatedly.

"That isn't lightning. It's divine power!"

Morgan startled at his words. "What?!"

Cassius's heart raced. "Something's trying to come through!"

He shot up toward the phenomenon, Morgan on his tail.

By the time they rocked to a halt beneath the black hole, their skin and armor were covered in a thick layer of dew. A spot of brightness flashed on the other side of the dark portal. It grew rapidly before splitting in two.

Cassius made out a pair of winged shapes as the gateway shuddered and started collapsing in on itself. He froze, his soul core trembling with violent awareness.

Morgan cursed and shifted defensively in front of Cassius. Even he could taste the bloodlust in the air.

The two figures bearing down on them became defined.

The one in the lead was huge and covered from head to toe in a rich, copper armor, the color matching his long, red hair, tawny eyes, and the giant war hammer in his hand. The figure a couple of beats behind him was more slender and bore a green Stark Steel suit that reflected his jade eyes and complemented his waist-long, brown pony tail and the bow and quiver on his back.

Their pupils shone with seraphic light and divine energy crackled on their white feathers as they worked their wings in powerful beats.

"Oh shit," Morgan mumbled. "Is that—?!"

"Archon and Nildar," Cassius whispered from bloodless lips.

He stared dazedly at his brothers and fellow Guardians. They were just as he recalled them from his memory of the War in the Nether.

How?! There's no doorway between Earth and that realm!

Morgan did not doubt Cassius's assertion. His grip tightened on the Sword of Wind, his demigod powers making the air tremble as he drew on his soul core.

"I don't think they're happy to see you!"

The black hole whined and started to close faster.

Archon accelerated, murder in his eyes.

"*Stop!*" Nildar shouted behind him. "*We will not make it!*"

"*We will!*" Archon growled.

Cassius snapped out of his stupor. Though he'd been right to fear what he'd been sensing, he couldn't stand back and watch the disaster before him unfold.

"You won't!" he yelled through the doorway. "You'll be squashed like a bug!"

The black hole halved in size, as if to reaffirm his statement.

Fear squeezed Cassius's chest at Archon's stubborn expression. *Shit! He's not listening!*

He took a deep breath, Icarus's presence exploding inside him. *"Desist, Archon! I order you as the Awakener!"*

The red-haired demigod pulled back at his roar, body instinctively obeying the command. Loss, hurt, regret, and rage boiled across his face.

Rage won.

Archon's scream of fury echoed in Cassius's ears long after he and Nildar vanished from view.

"Oathbreaker!"

CHAPTER EIGHTEEN

Cassius a steaming, porcelain cup.

"Thanks, Rose." Cassius took it gratefully and smiled at the secretary. "You haven't aged a day since I last saw you."

"Oh, stop it, you flirt," she chuckled. Her expression cooled fractionally as she looked over at Morgan. "Coffee, was it?"

Morgan accepted the drink she thrust in his hand with a grimace.

Victor sighed. It was clear Rosemary regarded Morgan as the Lothario who had stolen Cassius from his arms and was hellbent on treating him as such.

They'd reconvened at the Cabalista headquarters. Though it was late, the building was abuzz with activity. There were still monsters and hellbeasts on the loose and all Cabalista agents had been called in to help track them down.

Victor had put Delphine in charge of coordinating

their efforts with the other agencies. Rosemary had already arrived at the headquarters when he'd showed up there with Theo; the secretary didn't live far from Finsbury and had correctly surmised that this was one of the safest places to be in the city right now. She hadn't questioned him about Theo or why he was wrapped in a bedsheet.

A headache throbbed between Victor's temples as he took a sip of his coffee.

He had just gotten off a fraught conference call with the prime minister, the mayor, and the directors of the capital's Argonaut, Hexa, and Order of Rosen bureaus. He'd already scheduled a separate meeting with the heads of all three organizations in the morning. His headache intensified as the faces of Amal Kazmi, Ren Guiying, and Henrik Viken rose before his eyes.

They're sure to have sour words for me.

The other agencies' chiefs had grown wary of him ever since they'd found out his true identity. Victor wasn't sure if he'd ever be able to regain their trust.

"Could you leave us, Rosemary?" he said presently.

His secretary bobbed her head, her gaze lingering on Cassius as she left the room. An uneasy silence descended when the door closed behind her.

Victor studied Cassius and Morgan with a faint frown. "Tell me exactly what happened up there."

Cassius had briefly mentioned the black hole in the sky and his and Morgan's shocking encounter with Archon and Nildar upon their arrival at the Cabalista headquarters.

He recounted it all again in more detail.

Apprehension coiled through Victor. "Are you sure it was them?"

"It was them, alright," Morgan grunted. "Even an insensitive knucklehead like me could tell what they were."

Victor made a face.

"What?" Morgan snapped.

"Nothing. I'm just surprised to hear you acknowledge your deficiencies."

Morgan bristled at that.

"Stop it." Cassius's pupils flared with brightness for a second. "We have enough to worry about without you two going at it like this is some kind of cockfight."

They backed down under his glare.

Morgan gave Victor the sour you-got-us-in-trouble look of a younger sibling. Victor found himself clamping down on the childish urge to flip a middle finger at the demigod.

There was no doubt about it. They were brothers alright.

"So, Archon called you Oathbreaker?" Victor asked Cassius.

"Yeah." Cassius pinched the bridge of his nose and sighed. "They blame me for Rohengar's death, after all." His tone grew curt. "What happened in that hotel suite, Victor?"

Victor sobered. Those awful moments still felt like a nightmare, one he very much wanted to escape from. He ran a hand through his hair and hesitated before finally relating the events that had led him to face Elios and all that the God of Darkness had revealed during their fight.

"He's Hugo Frost?!" Morgan said, shocked.

Cassius stared. "You know him?"

"I have shares in *Sion*," Morgan replied distractedly.

Cassius met Victor's gaze, a muscle jumping in his cheek. "He said he's controlling the *Fates*?"

Victor dipped his head, the rage he'd felt at that bombshell revelation reflected in Cassius's whitening knuckles. "I don't think he meant to tell me that secret. It kinda slipped out."

"Shit." Morgan's hands curled into fists on his lap. "No wonder that asshole always has the upper hand!"

"I think he's had the Moirai under his thumb for some time," Victor muttered. "Probably even before the War in the Nether. Or at least two of them anyway. Bostrof did say his spy had come across Atropos in the Hells."

"I think you might be right." Cassius's voice hardened, his wrath almost palpable. He glanced at a door tucked in the far corner of the office. "What did he do to Theo?"

The door led to a private apartment Victor kept at the headquarters for those days when he couldn't return home. He'd put Theo in his bedroom when he'd arrived at Cabalista. The young man had not stirred since he'd fallen unconscious at the hotel, his deep slumber a source of concern for them all.

It hadn't taken long for Victor to find out the name of Frost's P.A. and run a background check on him. Theophile Serrano's records were spotless. The guy didn't even have a speeding ticket to his name. As for his family, they had never had any involvement with the otherworldly or magic, which made his awakening all the more bewildering.

Victor focused back on the present. "Elios said he'd forced Theo to embrace who he truly is."

Lines creased Morgan's brow. "Forced him? How?" His puzzled gaze swung between Victor and Cassius. "And who is he, exactly? I mean, I know we believe him to be a demigod, but which—"

"Rohengar," Cassius said numbly, staring at his hands.

Morgan drew a sharp breath.

Victor's stomach dropped. Though shock reverberated through his core, a part of him wasn't completely surprised.

That explains why I felt I knew him!

Cassius looked up and met their stunned gazes. "Theo is Rohengar. I'm sure of it."

The rage had faded from his face. In its stead was an agony Victor felt in his bones. Morgan reached over and clasped Cassius's trembling fingers, his lover's pain reflected in his eyes.

The gesture should have irritated Victor. Except it didn't. His heart pounded heavily as he waited for Cassius to speak, too intent on the subject at hand to explore why seeing Cassius and Morgan together no longer drove a hot knife through his chest.

"Rohengar's reincarnated soul resides inside Theo." Cassius licked his lips. "But it's not just him I felt in Theo's soul core."

Morgan recoiled. "What?"

Victor's mouth went dry.

"The human called Theo is there too. Their spirits have—merged, somehow." Cassius waved a vague hand. "Since it's Theo's body, he shares a portion of the fused soul core. I've never sensed anything like it before."

He lapsed into silence, his expression so brittle Victor wanted to go over and give him a reassuring hug. He rose and went to the drinks cabinet instead. Cassius and Morgan accepted the whiskey he poured them wordlessly.

This was the kind of news they needed to digest with a stiff drink.

"Elios said Theo's awakening is a danger to Earth." Victor wiped his lips with the back of his hand, the alcohol scorching a hot path down his throat. He met Cassius and Morgan's stares, his tone grim. "I think he meant what happened with those portals. Sonia, the succubus Elios forced to service him and Theo, said he'd slipped her some kind of poison to control her. It was in his semen and saliva. I think that's how Elios subjugated Theo's soul core."

Morgan made a disgusted expression.

"Wait." The color drained from Cassius's face. "Did —did Elios—?!"

He stopped, unable to voice his fear.

Victor shook his head. "No, he didn't force himself on Theo. I think he's been giving him the poison in other ways."

He didn't elaborate on the fact that Elios had fully intended to have sex with Theo tonight. He would have succeeded had Victor not crashed the God of Darkness's sick orgy. The thought of Elios violating Theo sent fire surging through Victor's veins.

The memory that had resurfaced during his clash with Elios danced before him then. He paled, his knuckles whitening on his glass.

"What is it?" Cassius asked worriedly.

Victor's stomach clenched. *I have to tell them. It's the only way I can absolve myself of my hateful crimes.*

He met Morgan's tense stare squarely. "Do you still have that scar on your chest?"

Morgan flinched. "What?! How do you—?!"

"Because I recovered another memory when I was fighting Elios tonight," Victor confessed bitterly. "The poison Elios uses is in his very blood. He reinforced my sword with it during the War in the Nether. I—" He stopped and swallowed. "I'm the one who gave you that scar, Morgan."

Cassius sucked in air. Morgan went deathly still.

"I'm sorry." Regret choked Victor's throat. "I know I've said it before, but I am truly sorry for all that I did to you two."

Silence met his words. Then Cassius was on his feet.

He walked over and hugged Victor, startling him. "I know, Victor. So stop torturing yourself."

Victor hesitated before squeezing him back tightly. Cassius's embrace was as warm and as comforting as it had always been.

"Hey, what about my complaints?" Morgan protested.

"You think the same too," Cassius retorted. "Don't deny it." He let go of Victor, his ears reddening slightly. "Besides, you know I find that scar sexy."

Morgan blinked. He glowered at Victor. "All is forgiven, asshole."

"Wow," Victor muttered. "You really do think with your crotch, don't you?"

Morgan gritted his teeth.

"How about we call it a night?' Cassius said hastily. "It's late. We should get some rest and figure things out in the morning."

"Alright," Victor said.

"Sure," Morgan grunted.

Cassius and Morgan headed for the door.

"There's one more thing you should know."

They stopped and turned.

"The one who killed Rohengar was Elios," Victor said quietly.

CHAPTER NINETEEN

Theo came to slowly. He moaned and winced.

His entire body ached, like he'd been hit by a truck. He lay still for a moment, nausea clenching his stomach. The surface beneath him was soft but firm. Sheets rustled as he finally shifted.

Fire licked his cock at the friction on his aching flesh.

Theo jolted upright, his heartbeat loud in his ears and his dick painfully tight, the heavy feeling threatening to drag him down once more into darkness evaporating like mist under a harsh sun.

He was lying on a bed, in a dark room. The sky outside the bay window to his left was inky and devoid of stars. He squinted at his surroundings. Details slowly emerged from the gloom as his eyes adapted to the lack of light.

Indigo and gold dominated the wallpaper and elegant furnishings around him. The architecture was

Victorian and had been perfectly restored to its original splendor.

Theo didn't recognize any of it. *Where the hell am I?!*

Memories flashed before his vision. Horror widened his eyes. He gagged and pressed a hand to his mouth. Bile rose in his throat as he choked back a scream of denial.

That wasn't a dream! It—it really happened! Hugo did that to me and that woman!

All the desire he'd ever felt for Frost had vanished, his lust replaced by revulsion and loathing. Theo's cock pulsed, distracting him from the unfamiliar anger stirring his blood.

His heart stuttered when he looked down.

He had a raging erection. He flushed, realizing his cum had already drenched the dark blue satin covering his lower body, the size of the stain a telltale sign he'd come several times in his sleep.

He twisted the sheet in his hands and hugged it to him as he folded his knees to his chest, mortification bringing a flood of heat to his face.

"It's not your fault."

Theo froze, his head snapping around.

A man stepped out of the shadows next to the door. He was tall and had rich, blond hair. The dark, open-neck shirt he wore showcased his broad shoulders and powerful chest, and his chic trousers made his legs look like they went on for miles.

Theo raked the stranger's body with his gaze, powerless to stop himself. The cut of the clothes was definitely outside his price range. His breath stuttered as he registered the man's arresting face and met his piercing blue eyes.

The stranger stayed motionless, like a predator watching his prey.

An uncanny heat fluttered to life deep inside Theo. He shivered and licked his lips. Another memory returned. He blinked and gasped.

"You're the guy who kicked the door down!" he blurted out half accusingly.

The stranger's lips quirked in a smile that went straight to Theo's cock. "You remember."

His voice was deep and husky. It started doing all kinds of crazy things to Theo's pulse.

What's wrong with me?!

"I—" Theo flushed and tried not to squirm, his arousal derailing his train of thought. "Yes, a little bit." He tensed and clenched his fists. "The lady who was there. Is she okay?!"

The stranger stared for a heartbeat. He twisted around and pressed a fist to his mouth, shoulders quaking.

Theo lowered his brows, concern giving way to irritation. "Are you laughing?"

The guy swallowed a snort and turned back to face him.

"I'm sorry," he said steadily, his mirth plain to see in the crinkles around his eyes. "It's just—I don't think anyone's ever called Sonia a lady before."

Theo bristled. "Just because she's a sex worker doesn't mean she shouldn't be addressed in a respectful manner."

This time, the stranger didn't even bother masking his laughter. He clutched his belly, his masculine peals ringing around the room and sending those weird shivers dancing through Theo once more.

The guy finally stopped laughing and straightened.

"Again, I apologize," he managed in a strangled voice, wiping his eyes. "Sonia isn't a sex worker. She's a succubus and one of the best actuaries in the city."

Theo gaped, the name finally ringing a bell. "Sonia? Wait! *That was Sonia Clark?!*"

The stranger nodded, still amused. Theo stared, stunned. He'd heard of the actuary. His belly twinged with another pulse of heat. Theo gripped his head as more memories resurfaced, jagged pieces of a puzzle that threatened to split his skull open.

"What—what happened in that suite?" He looked blindly at the stranger. "Who are you?" His gaze swept the bedroom, panic clogging his throat. "Am I still dreaming? The alley. Those monsters! What Hugo—" He stopped and swallowed convulsively. "What Hugo did to Sonia and me! Was any of it real?!"

His voice disintegrated into a low sob, much to his shock and distress.

The stranger cursed and closed the distance to the bed, his amusement fading as rapidly as it had appeared. Theo tensed as he sat on the edge and grabbed his hands.

"Don't!" the man said harshly. "What happened to you wasn't your fault or Sonia's. It's Elios who's to blame. This was all his doing."

The name he spoke sent a shudder through Theo. "Elios?"

The stranger faltered.

"My name is Victor Sloan," he confessed after a moment. "I rescued you from the hotel. There's a lot we need to talk about—"

"Victor Sloan?!" Theo gasped. "As in, the demon who heads Cabalista?!"

Blood pounded in his ears as he studied the stranger's face closely.

He'd only ever seen pictures of the Fiery demon. His reputation preceded him wherever he went, his otherworldly powers and his influence on world affairs the stuff of legend.

Oh wow. He's even more gorgeous in the flesh. Theo swallowed. *I can't believe I'm sitting naked in Victor Sloan's bed!*

Victor's lips twitched.

Horror filled Theo at the realization he'd said those last words out loud.

"I'm sorry," he whispered, mortified.

VICTOR CURSED INWARDLY. *THIS KID IS DANGEROUS.*

Seeing Theo nude and all vulnerable in his bed was doing things to his dick he wouldn't have thought possible a day ago. Never mind what smelling his arousal was doing to his sanity.

He'd come in to check on Theo half an hour ago, only to find him convulsing in the throes of passion, tears of pleasure seeping from under his squeezed eyelids as he ejaculated in his sleep. Victor had stayed and watched over him, Sonia's warning fresh in his mind while his pulse raced at the illicit show that was Theo having wet dreams.

The succubus had found him when he'd been about to leave the hotel with Theo a few hours ago.

"I'm glad you're okay," Victor had told her as she'd navigated the debris-strewn foyer.

Sonia had nodded tremulously, a glitter of tears in her eyes. She'd hugged the blanket someone had put around her shoulders to her chest. Incubi and succubae were a sturdy species. Still, an encounter with someone like Elios was bound to rattle anyone.

"Who was that?" she'd asked Victor in a low voice. "That—that thing disguised as Frost?!"

"That was Elios."

Sonia had blanched at his words.

Along with confessing the truth about Cassius's role in averting multiple disasters over the centuries, the agencies that governed the otherworldly had also revealed the identity of the God of Darkness responsible for the War in the Nether and the Fall.

"Shit." Sonia had squeezed her eyes shut for a moment before looking at Theo. "What about this guy? He's obviously not human."

Victor had glanced at the unconscious man in his arms. "I don't know what he is yet."

Sonia had shivered. Resolve had filled her eyes. That was when she'd told him about the poison Elios had used to subdue her and Theo.

"There's something you need to know. That toxin? It has a powerful aphrodisiac effect."

Victor had stiffened at her words. "What?!"

A look of pity had flashed across Sonia's face as she'd studied Theo. "I can deal with it fine with my powers. But him? He's gonna suffer. You have to help him."

CHAPTER TWENTY

"ARE—ARE YOU ANGRY WITH ME?"

Theo's dejected voice drew Victor to the present. His eyes were even more mesmerizing than Victor recalled and the way his slender body trembled tugged at every protective instinct he possessed.

"I'm not." Victor tipped Theo's chin gently with a knuckle. "Like I said, none of this is your fault, Theo."

He realized his mistake immediately.

Touching Theo had been a bad move. Because his heat was searing Victor's skin and making his cock swell.

Theo blinked, oblivious to the hot feeling simmering in Victor's gut.

"You know my name," he breathed.

Victor masked his burgeoning desire behind a faint frown.

It was bad enough that he'd spent half an hour watching Theo have wet dreams like some kind of perverted stalker. He couldn't believe the crazy feelings he was suddenly experiencing for him.

Maybe I'm the one who took that damn aphrodisiac!

"It wasn't hard to find out, considering who I am."

Theo flinched. "Wait. You ran a background check on me?!"

An impish urge to tease Theo swept over Victor.

He arched an eyebrow. "I even know about that hard drive on your computer from three years ago. The one with all the porn videos?"

Theo paled, mouth rounding into a horrified O.

"I'm kidding," Victor said hurriedly, now feeling like an utter cad.

Theo narrowed his eyes, annoyance darkening his irises and bringing some color back to his face. He squirmed the next instant and pressed his thighs together.

Victor's pulse quickened. His gaze dropped to Theo's crotch. "We should do something about that."

"I—" Theo chewed his lip and covered his groin demurely with one hand. "I'm sorry. I don't know what's the matter with me!"

His ears reddened with embarrassment.

Victor stared, his mouth dry. All he wanted to do was wrench Theo's hand away from his erection, pull the sheet off him, and stare at his cock to see if it was as pretty as he recalled.

Shit! I am losing my goddamn mind!

Victor took a steadying breath and clamped down on his raging libido. "Eli—Frost gave you something that acts like a love potion. That's why you're the way you are right now."

Confusion clouded Theo's face. "A love potion?"

Victor nodded. "Yes. An aphrodisiac to be precise. Sonia told me about it before I left the hotel. It was some kind of black liquid."

Theo's pupils dilated. He started to shake, terror raising goosebumps on his skin.

"Oh God! I remember! He made me swallow it! It—" He shuddered. "It even slipped in—*inside* me!"

He hugged his legs to his chest and squeezed his eyes shut, his body shrinking on the bed.

Victor froze. "Inside you?" Fury and fear tightened his throat. "Where inside you?!" He grabbed Theo's shoulders, causing his eyes to snap open. "Tell me!"

Theo stiffened at his tone, bewildered. "Oh!"

His pupils widened when he clocked the aura of hellfire surrounding Victor.

Victor shuddered, his heart slamming against his ribs. It took all of his willpower to suppress the storm raging inside him. The haze died down, orange glows sparking out with faint sizzles.

He couldn't believe he'd just lost his composure.

What the hell's wrong with me? Why do I care so much what happens to this kid?!

Theo licked his lips and finally answered Victor's question. "When Sonia was su—sucking me. Some of it entered my—my penis."

His voice faded to a chagrined whisper.

"Anywhere else?" Victor asked, trying his best to keep his voice steady.

Theo faltered.

Victor narrowed his eyes. "Theo?"

Theo wriggled and crossed one foot over the over, his toes clenching on his flesh. "Some of it tried to get inside my bu—my butt. But I don't think it did."

Sweet Jesus, thank you!

Victor closed his eyes, a ragged sigh of relief tumbling from his lips. He recalled what Elios had said about Theo being a virgin. The fact that Elios hadn't managed to violate Theo so intimately made a feral feeling course through him. His belly spasmed with a pulse of heat.

Relief turned into raging desire.

Victor clenched his teeth, confused and angry at the unwanted emotions threatening to rob him of his self-control. He'd still been pining for Cassius just days ago. Yet, something fundamental had shifted inside him the moment he'd laid eyes on Theo. He could feel it deep within him, in his very soul.

A voice danced through his mind then. One he hadn't heard since his awakening in the Spirit Realm.

Theo is ours...

Shock reverberated through Victor's very bones as Coraos's affirmation rattled around his skull. He repeated the words slowly. Tasted them. Savored their meaning.

The truth struck him like a freight train, making his breath catch.

Is this what Cassius and Morgan felt when they met in the past and again in this life? Is this what it means to be soulmates? This fever that feels like it will never be quenched? This need to own and be owned?!

"Hmm, Victor?" Theo mumbled.

Victor opened his eyes and met Theo's viridescent gaze, the awareness of their connection scorching his mind and heart. A fierce feeling of possession tightened his chest.

Mine. Whatever Theo is, he belongs to me.

Victor took a shaky breath, hiding his swelling emotions behind a gruff tone. "The only way to get that poison to wear off is for you to come until it's out of your system."

Theo opened and closed his mouth soundlessly. "Wh—*what?!*"

"Let me help you."

Theo looked like his eyes were about to roll back in his head. "You—you can't!"

He pushed Victor away weakly and avoided his gaze, embarrassment painting red flags on his cheekbones.

Victor wrapped his hands firmly around Theo's wrists and leaned in close, blood pounding in his skull. He wanted so badly to touch Theo he was willing to sell his soul to the Reaper God himself to make it a reality.

"The orgasms I'll give you will get rid of it faster."

Theo shivered as Victor's breath and his sinful words tickled his ear. He tilted his head unconsciously to the side. Need gripped Victor in its fiery clutches. He pressed his mouth to the side of Theo's neck.

Theo's taste exploded on his tongue.

Victor shuddered. *Sweet, like candy.*

He groaned hungrily and nipped Theo's skin with his teeth.

"*Oh!*" Theo jerked and stiffened.

He trembled violently against him.

The musky scent that filled Victor's nostrils told him Theo had just come.

Fuck. He fought down the animal urge to push Theo down on the bed, spread his thighs open, and take him. *This kid's gonna be the death of me!*

Victor reined himself in and managed to regain some semblance of control over his burning lust, his dick so hard it ached.

He pressed a soft kiss to the love bite he'd made on Theo's neck and raised his head. "So sensitive."

Theo flushed at his teasing tone, his irises dark with pleasure and his chest heaving with his pants. His gaze dropped to Victor's mouth.

He licked his lips. "Ki—kiss me!"

Victor blinked at the command. He swallowed a grin. His little virgin was braver than he'd given him credit for.

"Not until you let me see you."

Theo chewed his lip at his retort, passion clashing with hesitation on his face, his cheeks a glorious pink.

I wonder if he's the same color down there.

Victor rapidly suppressed that torrid image, lest it wreck his fragile self-control. Satin rustled as Theo released the sheet he'd been clutching to his chest.

Victor's breath caught.

Theo was beautiful. He'd glimpsed his charms in the

hotel suite and when he'd carried him in his arms, but now that he was in front of him he could see how bewitching he truly was.

Theo sucked in air as Victor trailed a hand lightly across his collar bone and down his chest.

"You're exquisite," Victor mumbled.

Theo shivered. He twitched and moaned as Victor raked a stiff, brown nipple gently with his nails.

"*Hmm!*"

Victor danced his hand across Theo's softly defined, trembling abs to where the satin sheet rested on his leaking erection. He hooked a finger on the edge and lifted it off, exposing Theo's trembling cock. Theo squirmed and closed his thighs.

"Don't."

Theo froze at Victor's quiet command. He faltered before dropping his knees open, his taut belly contracting on a shudder.

Victor's breathing grew uneven as he feasted his eyes on Theo's honey-colored shaft and his smooth balls.

He looked up, thrilled. "You wax?"

Theo faltered before dipping his head, not meeting his gaze. Victor took hold of his chin and forced Theo to look at him.

"You're lovely," he said roughly. "Every inch of you is so pretty I could weep."

Theo stilled and stared, his irises darkening with incredulity.

"Now, let me give you your reward."

Victor angled his head and crushed his mouth to Theo's.

Theo gasped and clutched his shoulders, his response immediate and so hot and sweet it made Victor shiver with need. Theo's eyes fluttered closed. He hummed and moaned as Victor seduced his lips before seeking entrance inside his mouth.

Victor groaned as Theo's tongue met his shyly. He could tell he'd never been kissed this way before.

Mine to possess. Mine to take. Mine to brand.

Victor savored the truths resonating inside him and poured those emotions into their kiss. Seraphic light flashed beneath Theo's eyelids. Victor startled, his soul core throbbing painfully.

A tear that shone like a star trickled down Theo's left cheek.

"Coraos!" he mumbled brokenly. *"My Coraos!"*

He convulsed in Victor's arms and hung on for dear life, his arms looping tightly around Victor's neck as another intense climax shuddered through him.

Awareness bloomed inside Victor as Theo's hot cum splashed on his thigh. Wonder filled him.

He could taste the other half of Theo's soul. The one that belonged to Rohengar. Another truth struck him then. One that drenched his soul in sadness and regret and fresh longing.

Desire knotted his belly for the entwined beings he held in his arms.

CHAPTER TWENTY-ONE

Victor tumbled Theo down onto the bed, linked their fingers together, and locked his arms above his head. Theo gasped, Victor's weight pressing him down into the mattress.

He blinked his green eyes open, startled. "Victor?"

Victor didn't give him time to think. He ravaged his mouth over and over again until he was a whimpering mess. Then he touched him and kissed his body all over, wrenching orgasm after orgasm from his quivering cock and balls.

Theo cried out when Victor took his cum-soaked organ in his mouth. *"Ah! No! That's—!"*

His voice strangled off into an incoherent sound as he exploded at Victor's first suck.

Victor spread Theo's thighs wide and fixed them to the bed as he blew him hard and deep. Something bitter flooded his mouth when Theo came a third time on his tongue. Victor let go of his shaft with a wet pop, alarmed. He straightened and spat a black blob into his hand. It wriggled in his palm.

Victor scowled and closed his fingers. Flames bloomed, Elios's poison evaporating in a flash of hellfire.

"Victor?!" Theo panted. He was leaning up on his elbows and looking down his quivering, sweat-soaked body to where Victor knelt between his knees. Panic raised the pitch of his voice. "What was that?!"

"Elios's poison." Victor frowned and met his frightened gaze. "Don't worry. I'll get it all out of you. Every damn drop!"

Theo shuddered. Then he moaned and dropped back on the bed, his fingers sinking into Victor's hair as Victor swallowed him in the velvety depths of his throat once more, his body shuddering and twitching with renewed pleasure.

Victor dipped a hand beneath his balls and stroked the pad of a thumb across his hole. Theo stiffened.

"I need to check here too," Victor said gruffly. "Open your legs for me."

Theo hesitated. He bit his lip, hooked his hands under his knees, and stretched his thighs wide, his shyness evident in the way he avoided Victor's eyes. A ringing filled Victor's ears as his hungry gaze roamed Theo's taint and his sweet pucker.

It really is as pink as his cheeks.

He slipped two fingers in his mouth, coated them with his spit and Theo's cum, and brought them to Theo's hole.

Theo cried out at the first slick touch. Victor moved up his body and took his mouth in a searing kiss.

"It's okay," he murmured. "I won't hurt you."

Tears glimmered in Theo's eyes as he stared up at him. He sniffed and nodded shakily. Victor bit back a groan. He was coming to the realization that he possessed a sadistic streak when it came to Theo.

One day. One day I'll tease him until he cries and begs me to fuck him. But not today.

Victor suppressed his wicked urges and kissed Theo. Theo melted sweetly against him. He trembled when Victor touched his pucker again, but didn't pull away.

Victor stroked and teased the tight folds until they softened. Then he slipped the tip of one finger inside. Theo went off like a bomb, his cock pulsing out a powerful jet of cum between their bodies as he came again.

Victor swallowed Theo's cries as he writhed against his hand. Theo's movements swallowed his finger to the second knuckle. Theo gasped, his hole squeezing Victor tight.

"Victor!" he whimpered helplessly. "Victor!"

Victor inhaled raggedly and pressed a soft kiss to his brow. "Breathe, Theo."

Theo shivered and focused on inhaling and exhaling, his body as tense as a bow. Victor clenched his teeth and pushed his finger all the way in.

Theo hummed.

"Do you like that?" Victor whispered.

Theo clutched his shoulders and buried his face in the crook of Victor's neck.

"Uh-huh," he mumbled.

Victor pulled out slightly and pushed back in.

"Oh!" Theo gasped.

Victor looked into his bright green eyes and swallowed hard. "More?"

"Yes!" Theo breathed.

Victor lost track of time as he plundered Theo's ass with his finger, his cock doing press-ups against the material of his trousers. Theo groaned when Victor slipped a second finger inside, stretching him wider. His nails scored Victor's back, his pants full of passion and devoid of pain. Victor gave him a moment to adjust before hooking the tips of his fingers and seeking out the soft bump of his prostate.

Theo stiffened and arched a second later, mouth open on a soundless gasp.

"Found it." Victor nuzzled Theo's throat and probed the soft protrusion. "That's your sweet spot."

He pressed it firmly. Theo let out a guttural shout and came with explosive violence. He rode Victor's fingers wildly, his hips rocking to-and-fro instinctively, mimicking the act of sex.

It took everything Victor had not to free his own erection and plunge it inside Theo's body.

It was some time before Theo came down from his latest high. He shuddered and trembled before opening glazed eyes, his body limp on the sweat and cum-soaked sheets. Air hissed out of him as Victor carefully withdrew his fingers.

"I think the poison's worn off," Victor said, trying not to sound despondent.

"Are you—" Theo gulped, "are you sure?"

He looked accusingly at his own cock.

Victor swallowed a smile and trailed a lazy finger along his limp shaft, causing him to shudder. "Yup. You're officially dry."

Theo's gaze dropped to Victor's raging erection.

He chewed his lip. "You're not."

Victor grimaced and made to move off the bed. "I'll take care of that in the bathroom."

"No."

Victor startled and met Theo's stare.

A mutinous frown wrinkled Theo's brow. "You'll take care of it here. It's only fair that I get to watch after everything you just did to me."

Victor's eyes widened. Shock and delight wrenched an amused laugh from his throat. "You're really something, you know that?"

Theo flushed, as if he'd only just realized what he'd said.

"Alright." Victor shifted until he was kneeling on the bed between Theo's legs. His voice dropped an octave. "Make sure you watch until the end."

Theo shuddered. His eyes flared as Victor unzipped himself and tugged out his swollen cock. He sat up, mouth parting and breathing turning shallow.

Victor started stroking himself under his hungry gaze. Theo followed the motion of his fingers avidly. He licked his lips and moved a little closer. Fire throbbed through Victor's shaft as he worked himself with practiced motions, his pleasure amplified by Theo's unblinking stare.

Tension slowly wound through his thighs and his spine. It pooled inside his belly, a knot that grew harder and tighter. His breaths deepened to harsh pants.

"Can I touch you?"

Theo's question almost had Victor swallowing his tongue. He winced as he reflexively gripped his sensitive shaft tighter.

Theo looked at him from under his lashes, a determined look in his eyes despite the color staining his cheekbones. He was hard again.

"I want to finish you off."

Victor groaned at his brazen request. *This little imp!*

He hesitated before letting go of his cock. He'd be a fool to say no when Theo was being so bold.

Theo startled when Victor took his hand and brought it to his erection. "Oh!"

A shiver raced through him as he experienced Victor's heat. He clasped Victor lightly. Victor grunted, dick throbbing.

Theo's lips parted in surprise. "It got bigger!"

Victor pressed a hand over his eyes and bit back a curse.

"That's because you're touching it," he groaned.

He hissed as Theo started rubbing him. His belly contracted painfully as he looked down and saw Theo's fingers working his flesh in tentative strokes.

Theo glanced up at him. "Like this?"

Victor swallowed and nodded. He encouraged Theo

with low murmurs, teaching him how he liked to be touched. Desire turned Theo's eyes to shimmering pools of green when Victor began thrusting helplessly in his hand. He stared into Victor's eyes and watched shamelessly as Victor's breathing grew more labored and his motions urgent.

"You're close," Theo mumbled.

Victor's eyes rounded as Theo lowered his head and sucked the tip of his cock. The sinful feel of Theo's lips and mouth around his dick stiffened his spine and tipped him over the edge. He threw his head back and came on a feral shout, the tendons in his neck rigid as he gnashed his teeth and grunted, his hands locking in Theo's hair in a savage grip.

Theo choked and coughed, cum filling his mouth in an explosive spurt.

Victor grasped the back of his neck and hauled him up against his body for a scorching kiss. His dick pulsed and drenched Theo's hands with his scalding seed as he lashed their tongues together, the taste of his own cum making his soul core flare with savage heat.

Theo's pupils brightened with divine light.

Victor tumbled him down onto the bed, anchored his still-hard cock to Theo's quivering dick with one hand, and started stroking them both.

Theo moaned and shuddered as Victor took them higher and higher, his lips seeking Victor's mouth while he locked his arms and legs around him, his irises flickering from green to sapphire to green again.

"Victor! *Coraos!*"

They climaxed moments later, the pulses of fire

shooting through Victor's soul core amplifying his orgasm until his entire being blazed with ecstasy and whiteness seared his mind. The way Theo screamed beneath him told him he was experiencing the same mind-numbing rapture.

The singular truth that had rocked Victor a while back echoed through his heart as he collapsed on the bed and wrapped Theo in his arms.

Rohengar had loved him.

CHAPTER TWENTY-TWO

Morgan awoke to a dark room and an empty bed. Fear churned his gut. He sat up with a jolt, panic squeezing his chest so hard he choked.

"Cassius!"

His soul core throbbed. Rapid footsteps sounded in the corridor. Cassius appeared in the doorway of the bedroom, a glass in hand.

"I'm here." He hurried inside, his bare feet silent on the carpet. "I just went to get some water."

Relief made Morgan shudder. The bed dipped as Cassius sat on the edge. He put the glass on the nightstand and lifted a hand to Morgan's face. Morgan gripped his fingers and kissed his palm hotly.

Cassius stared, concerned. "Was it a nightmare?"

Morgan shook his head, his heart still slamming against his ribs.

"No," he mumbled. "I—I'm just so scared that I'm going to lose you again!"

His voice faded to an agonized whisper. Cassius climbed on the bed and hugged him to his chest.

"That's not gonna happen," he said adamantly. He pressed his lips to Morgan's hair. "It must be all that talk about Elios that's brought this on."

Morgan stayed silent, the dread gnawing at him slowly fading as Cassius's warmth and scent surrounded him.

"It's almost morning," Cassius murmured. "Why don't we go out on the terrace and watch the sunrise?"

Morgan glanced at the clock on the nightstand. It was 5 a.m.

"Okay."

Cassius took a blanket out of the closet and led the way outside.

They settled on a recliner. Cassius covered them both and leaned his back against Morgan's chest. His heartbeat thrummed strongly against Morgan's arms where he'd looped them around him.

Peace filled Morgan's soul. He buried his face in Cassius's hair. He wished they could stay like this forever.

"Rohengar's soul reviving must be what drew them here," Cassius said quietly.

Morgan tensed slightly. "You mean Archon and Nildar?"

Cassius nodded. "It's what was drawing me east too." He traced a pattern on Morgan's arm. "I suspect I would have ended up coming to London even if you'd decided not to bring us here."

Morgan recalled the expressions on the two Guardians' faces. "They looked pretty upset."

"They have a right to be."

"Still, it's not as if what happened was entirely your fault," Morgan grumbled.

Cassius hesitated. "I think they both know that. Nildar more so than Archon." A wry smile curved his lips. "Though I don't remember everything about my past life with them, I get the feeling Archon's always been a pretty stubborn bastard, like someone else I know."

Morgan blinked. "Wait. Do you mean me?"

Cassius grinned and looked at him over his shoulder. "Victor was right. It's sweet that you're coming to realize your shortcomings."

Morgan made a face. "Please don't mention that asshole's name."

Cassius laughed and laid back against Morgan. An easy silence fell between them once more.

"It's changed," Cassius mused. "Your relationship with him. I could sense it tonight."

Morgan pondered his words. He couldn't exactly deny them.

Fighting alongside Victor in the Spirit Realm and again tonight had reaffirmed his gut feeling about the demigod. Victor was on their side.

"It felt good," Cassius said, startling him. "The three of us, working alongside one another against Elios tonight? It felt right. Like it was meant to be." He lapsed into silence. "I wonder if that was what Elios feared all along. Our alliance."

Morgan lowered his brows. "You think he manipulated Coraos into joining his faction because he knew he would lose the War otherwise?"

"Yes," Cassius said after a pause, his voice brittle. "Elios hates me. Not only did he need to win the War so he could finally free Chaos, he knew killing you and Rohengar would break me. Making Coraos betray me and attempt to kill you was part of his plans."

Anger simmered through Morgan's gut at the thought of the God who'd wrought havoc in their lives and so many others. He unconsciously tightened his hold around Cassius.

"What does he want with Theo?"

Cassius hesitated. "That I do not know yet. But it's clear from Victor's account of what went down in that hotel suite that Elios knew what Theo is well before any of us did. It's likely the reason he recruited him in the guise of Hugo Frost." His brow knitted. "The *Fates* may very well have revealed the truth of this matter to him."

Unease flitted through Morgan. "I still can't believe Elios has been in London all this time."

"He must have possessed Frost after I left the capital." Cassius's frown deepened. "Even though he was masking his soul core, there would have come a time when I would have detected his corruption."

"I think you're right," Morgan grunted. "Victor might have sensed something untoward too, if he'd been around him for long."

Cassius choked on a snort. "Did you just defend your older brother?"

Morgan scowled. "How do you know he's older than me?!"

"Instinct, I guess. He's a bit…wiser than you."

Irritation warmed Morgan's face at Cassius's amused tone.

"No need to twist the knife," he groused. "I'm already pissed off that bastard claimed you first in this lifetime." He hugged Cassius closer. A thought came to him. He froze. "Wait. Did Victor—I mean, did Coraos and Icarus—?!"

He trailed off, too upset to voice the rest of the question. Cassius turned his head and met his distressed gaze.

"No," he said, laughter sparking in his beautiful eyes. "I'm pretty sure Ivmir was Icarus's first and only lover before the Fall."

Morgan's heart stuttered. "First?"

Cassius nodded and turned to gaze at the dark sky once more. "Pan said it himself. Guardians are ascetic creatures." He chuckled. "You must have worked real hard to charm Icarus."

Morgan's dick twitched. Icarus's form was pretty daunting. He could hardly believe he'd been his first lover. That he'd managed to work his way into the Awakener's pants must mean Icarus had been completely head over heels for him too.

A shiver skittered through him at the thought of their first time together. *I wonder what he looked like when I took him. Did he moan? Did he cling to me and cry? Did he scream my name when he came?*

Morgan swallowed at the illicit images flashing before his eyes. "Ivmir must have had balls of steel to even think about courting him."

Cassius wriggled his butt slightly. "That's not the only steely thing he had."

CHAPTER TWENTY-THREE

M ORGAN GROANED AS C ASSIUS RUBBED AGAINST HIS swelling arousal.

"I swear your dick has a life of its own." Cassius made a rueful sound and shifted around until he was kneeling between Morgan's legs on the recliner and facing him. He studied the unmistakable shape of Morgan's erection with interest. "Good morning, Little Ivmir."

Morgan cursed as Cassius traced his shaft with a finger. "Don't give it a name!"

"Why not?" Cassius grinned, clasped Morgan's dick, and leaned in to nip teasingly at his lips. "After all, *this* —" he tugged a little, drawing another curse from Morgan, "belongs to me."

Morgan hissed as Cassius started stroking him through the material of his pajamas. He clutched him to his chest and wiped the grin from his mouth with his lips. Cassius moaned and melted against him, his hand stilling as he lost himself in their kiss. Morgan jerked his hips, urging him to continue.

It wasn't long before Cassius tugged Morgan's pajamas hastily off his legs. He stripped out of his own clothes and settled back down on Morgan's lap. Goosebumps broke out across his skin as a cool breeze danced over them. He shivered.

Morgan opened his wings and cocooned them both in a warm cage of pale feathers, drawing a surprised "Oh!" from Cassius.

He nibbled at Cassius's chin.

"Little Ivmir needs your attention, Awakener," he said huskily.

Desire painted red flags on Cassius's cheekbones. He wrapped their cocks together in his hands and started working their rock-hard flesh briskly, their precum making his grip slick.

Morgan leaned his hands back and watched, hips rising to thrust through Cassius's fingers. Bolts of fire shot through his shaft at Cassius's expert ministrations. He looked up and swallowed a groan.

Cassius's expression was so hungry and full of lust Morgan feared he would devour him whole. He met Morgan's gaze, his pupils flashing white and gold with every beat of his heart, his mouth open on harsh pants.

Morgan melded their mouths together and began playing with Cassius's nipples, rubbing and twisting and tugging them until he hissed and shuddered. Their breathing grew ragged as they rode growing waves of pleasure.

"I want to come inside you," Morgan grunted. "Here, suck my fingers."

Cassius complied, lips parting to swallow two of his fingers inside the velvety depths of his mouth. His tongue lashed Morgan's digits hotly as he worked his lips up and down them.

Morgan cursed at the carnal expression brightening Cassius's face as they gazed fiercely into each other's eyes. He removed his fingers and reached down to stroke Cassius's hole. Cassius hummed and spread his legs, widening his access. Morgan bowed his head and tugged Cassius's left nipple between his teeth as he punched his fingers inside him.

"*Ah!*" Cassius gasped, the sting on his breast distracting him from the sudden penetration.

His hands flexed reflexively on their straining cocks, drawing a groan from them both. His body took over, his hips rolling instinctively as he danced up and down Morgan's fingers.

"Fuck!" Cassius buried his face in the crook of Morgan's neck. "I need your cock in me! *Now!*"

"Not yet," Morgan teased. He turned his head and kissed Cassius's sweat-slicked temple. "Not until your ass is ready."

"Stop teasing and hurry, dammit!" Cassius groaned.

Morgan chuckled. It didn't take long for him to give in to the demands of the demigod trembling and shuddering in his arms. He slipped his fingers out, grabbed Cassius's waist, and raised him above his dick.

Morgan impaled Cassius in a single thrust, his cock sliding inside his silken heat all the way to the hilt.

Cassius came with savage violence, head thrown back and body bowed, his mouth open on a silent scream. He sobbed and moaned as he convulsed in Morgan's arms, his ass gripping Morgan's shaft so hard he feared he'd bite it off.

Fire burned Morgan's soul core as Cassius's cum painted his belly and chest in hot, sticky jets. He pressed his feet on the ground, fixed Cassius's hips, and started fucking him hard and deep, the recliner rattling beneath them.

"Oh! *Ah!* Yes!" Cassius squeezed his eyes shut for a moment, his cock twitching as Morgan pounded his sweet spot. He sank his nails in Morgan's shoulders. *"There!* Jesus that feels *so good!"*

Morgan's heart slammed against his ribs as he stared into Cassius's eyes. The seraphic glow pulsing from their pupils lit up the warm, intimate space inside his wings as they made love with untamed passion, the sounds of their mating flesh smacking together an erotic song in his ears.

Something told him Ivmir and Icarus had made love just like this before, wrapped up in their wings to shield them from any curious eyes that might have spied on them, their savage mating cocooned by feathers.

Cassius shuddered. "Wait! Did you just get—*Oh God* —bigger?!"

Morgan kissed his throat. "You can take it."

And take him Cassius did, his body stretching hotly to accept Morgan's swollen girth, as if he'd been born to fit him.

They came once. Twice. Three times.

Cassius finally collapsed in Morgan's arms after their fourth mutual climax, his breathing labored and his sensitive hole pulsing from his latest convulsions.

"I–I can't anymore!" he mumbled.

Though he was hungry for more, Morgan relented. He kissed Cassius's brow and carefully pulled out. Cassius hissed and bit his lip. Color stained his face as the evidence of Morgan's orgasms trickled thickly down his thighs.

Morgan stared, a feral feeling bubbling in his blood at the sinful sight. He stroked Cassius's loose entrance gently with the pads of his fingers, drawing another tortured moan from his hoarse throat.

"Why don't I clean you up in the bath?"

"Hmm."

Cassius shivered and nodded. He clung to Morgan and rested his head languidly against his heart as Morgan lifted him and carried him inside.

It was only after they came back out into the kitchen after a long, lazy soak that they realized something was very wrong. Morgan was getting cups out of a cupboard when his soul core throbbed with an echo of Cassius's alarm. He whirled around tensely, senses on alert.

"What is it?"

Cassius was staring out the terrace doors from where he stood at the island, face pale and hand frozen on the coffee maker. Morgan followed his gaze. He blinked. His head moved mechanically toward the clock on the wall.

It was past 7.20 a.m. The sun had still not risen.

His pulse quickened as he studied the dark sky. Cassius started for the doors. He followed.

The acrid odor of sulfur reached them on a warm gust as they rocked to a stop on the terrace.

"Fuck!" Morgan mumbled.

Cassius's cell phone rang. It was Victor. He put him on speaker.

"Are you seeing what I'm seeing?" the demon asked stiffly.

"Yeah," Cassius said grimly.

Dread twisted Morgan's gut as they stared at the crimson tint saturating the stormy clouds above them and painting the capital red. Except they weren't clouds and what lay hidden beyond them wasn't the sky.

CHAPTER TWENTY-FOUR

JULIA GOT OUT OF HER SUV AND SLAMMED THE DOOR shut just as Zach slipped his Triumph into the space next to her.

The demon turned the engine off, removed his helmet, and looked over with a faint frown. "Strickland called you in too?"

Julia lowered her brows. "Yeah."

She'd been about to go to bed when she'd received an urgent voicemail from Strickland to head into the office.

Zach climbed off his motorbike. "Any idea what this is about?"

Unease prickled Julia's skin. It looked like Strickland had been equally evasive with the demon. "No."

Headlights pierced the half-gloom before they could ponder the matter further. Another car pulled into the private garage under Argonaut and parked a few bays down. It was Adrianne's Honda.

Bailey stepped out of the vehicle with the sorceress.

Zach stared. "That's one for the books. Did they kiss and make up?"

A single look at Adrianne's conflicted expression as she sauntered over told Julia everything she needed to know. "I wouldn't say make up exactly. But it looks like they made headway."

"If by headway you mean sex, it sure looks like it," Zach drawled, studying Bailey's smug face. "By the way, did you ever find out why he was in the doghouse in the first place?"

"Yeah, she finally told me last week." Julia grimaced. "Suffice to say Bailey wasn't really in the wrong. He's only human after all."

Zach gave her a puzzled look.

A powerful whine distracted Julia. An approaching engine juddered just as Adrianne and Bailey joined them. They turned and stared at the sleek, black Porsche that crept fitfully into the underground parking. A collective wince crossed everyone's faces when it almost crashed into a concrete column as it maneuvered into a spot.

A scowling Charlie got out of it. Their gazes swung from him to the Porsche and back again.

"What the hell happened to your Volvo?!" Zach blurted out.

"Don't even get me started," Charlie ground out. "This was waiting for me outside my place with a note. Those assholes decided I needed a new set of wheels all on their own. I'm tempted not to put out for a week."

Julia bit back a smile. Never in a million years could

she have imagined Reuben, Jasper, and Charlie ending up in a relationship. And the way things were progressing, she wouldn't be surprised if Charlie turned up with a ring on his finger one day.

"So, anyone know why Strickland is being so secretive?" Bailey asked as they rode the elevator to the tenth floor.

"No idea," Julia muttered. "But it has to be something sensitive since he didn't want to say anything over the phone."

They stepped out opposite the Argonaut bullpen seconds later. Though it was past midnight, several agents were on shift to man the bureau's lines and deal with any emergencies that warranted the agency's attention after hours.

Julia narrowed her eyes and slowed to a halt.

All six agents were currently standing in front of the TV on the far wall. Static filled the screen from edge to edge. Julia's unease deepened.

"What's wrong?" Bailey called out.

A sorcerer looked over with a frown. "We don't know. Everything just went offline. All the news channels. Even social media. The platforms are all showing an 'unable to access' message."

Zach took out his cell and swiped the screen.

His brow furrowed. "They're right."

"Let's go," Adrianne said curtly.

The tension tightening her face reflected Julia's growing apprehension.

They hurried over to Strickland's office, a common

thread of urgency sparking between them. Raised voices reached Julia's ears as they approached the door. Adrianne rapped her knuckles on the steel-reinforced wood.

"Come in!" Strickland barked.

They entered the room to find the director in the midst of a full-blown argument with Amal Kazmi, the head of Argonaut.

"And I'm telling you I won't be able to keep them on these shores when they find out!" Strickland snapped, his face dark.

He spared them a harried glance.

Kazmi scowled at the director from the video display on the wall. Her gaze swept over Julia and the rest of Morgan's team before focusing back on Strickland.

"They are your people, Francis. *Make* them obey your orders! We cannot afford to lose them right now!"

Adrianne exchanged a startled look with Julia. Julia's pulse quickened, her foreboding turning into gut-wrenching dread.

"What's going on?" Adrianne said in a hard voice.

As Morgan's second-in-command, she was currently heading their team.

Strickland ran a hand through his receding hair, his expression no less fraught than it had been a second ago. He closed his eyes briefly before meeting their stares. "London is gone."

His words echoed in the stunned silence that befell them. Julia's chest tightened with an unnamed fear.

"What?" Zach said leadenly.

Kazmi blew out a sigh. "You might as well show them the satellite images."

She waved a hand irritably at Strickland. He pressed a key on his computer keyboard, a muscle jumping in his jawline. Kazmi's feed shrank to fit the upper left corner of the screen. The rest of it became filled with several shots showing the same seething darkness. It flashed crimson in places.

Strickland zoomed the images out.

Julia's stomach dropped, the enormity of the disaster they were looking at surreal compared to the bright pictures filling the periphery of the video feeds. Day had broken across England. An autumnal sun brought out the richness of the changing landscape across Greater London, crisp reds and browns dotting every shade of green amidst the urban spread.

All of it stopped in the center of the capital. It was as if someone had taken a giant cookie cutter and stamped out the heart of London, replacing it with some kind of black void.

"Most of Inner London vanished off the surface of the Earth forty-five minutes ago," Strickland said in a hard voice. "This will make international news and social media headlines in the next half an hour. That's how long we've been able to freeze all satellites and land communication devices based in England to give the agencies time to come up with a coherent message that won't induce mass hysteria across the world."

"Inner London?" Charlie mumbled hoarsely. Horror

widened his eyes. "Isn't that where Cassius and Morgan—?!"

"Yes." Strickland rubbed a hand down his face. "I can't get through to either of their cell phones or anyone in the affected area, including Victor."

CHAPTER TWENTY-FIVE

ADRIANNE SAT DOWN HEAVILY IN A CHAIR, HER FACE pale. Bailey put a hand on her shoulder, his features similarly ashen. She gripped his fingers blindly.

"So, that's Camden to Lambeth, and Hammersmith to Greenwich?" Zach said matter-of-factly.

"Yes," Kazmi replied grimly. "Most of those boroughs have been affected."

Julia glanced at Zach. She wasn't fooled by his steady tone. Crimson burned in the depths of his pupils, his stillness dangerous. She could practically see the wheels spinning inside the Aqueous demon's skull. The same ones spinning inside hers.

Strickland was right.

Nothing on this Earth was going to stop them from leaving for Europe as soon as they walked out of this room.

Julia finally found her voice. "That's one hundred and twenty-three square miles of land and four million people. Those don't just vanish overnight without any warning."

Kazmi's expression grew strained.

Strickland lowered his brows. "What are you not telling us, Amal?"

She steepled her hands in front of her face and met their stares. "You obviously haven't heard what happened in London last night. I thought Cassius or Morgan might have called you, but it seems they stuck to the plan to stay quiet for now."

"What plan?" Adrianne snapped.

She had risen to her feet, the fire in her eyes reflecting the same conviction Julia could feel bonding their entire team together.

There was a reason they were the best Argonaut squad in the world. They worked with a single-minded focus that meant they had a nearly one hundred percent mission success rate. And a lot of their accomplishments were due to a simple truth.

They would lay down their lives for one another.

"There was an incident in Inner London at around 9.40 p.m. local time last night," Kazmi said levelly. "Cassius, Morgan, and Victor clashed with Elios in a hotel in the City."

Strickland swayed and grabbed his desk. "*What?!*"

A burst of seraphic and demonic energy rattled the windows. Julia and Zach had snapped their wings open, the daggers in their hands lengthening into swords.

"*Elios is in London?!*" Julia snarled.

Zach scowled and gnashed his teeth.

They'd both regained some of their memories after Cassius, Morgan, and Victor had vanquished Elios in the Spirit Realm and they now knew who had caused the Fall and wiped their past from their minds. Though Julia recalled only flashes of her previous life, she was certain she and Zach had fought alongside Icarus and Ivmir during the War in the Nether.

Kazmi remained calm in the face of their wrath. "I'm sorry I couldn't tell you earlier. We were going to make a public statement this morning, after holding a meeting with Victor and the other agency heads."

Strickland regained his composure, though his face remained gray. "Tell us what happened, Amal."

Kazmi related the little she knew. That Victor had come upon Elios disguised as a human at a reception. That a bright light had pierced the sky above London during their encounter and a dozen portals had opened around the capital, letting through monsters and beasts from different Hells. That Cassius, Morgan, and Victor had banished the creatures and closed the portals with the assistance of the otherworldly and magic users in the city.

"And Elios?" Adrianne asked stiffly.

"He vanished, according to Victor," Kazmi said.

A strained hush befell them.

"The last contact anyone had with London was at 6.30 a.m. local time today," the head of Argonaut continued. "All lines of communication went dead after that. The private jets that were en route to the capital were urgently diverted to other airports outside the city. We've lost touch not just with Victor, but with the

London directors of Argonaut, Hexa, and the Order of Rosen too."

"What *is* that thing?" Charlie was staring intently at the throbbing darkness where Inner London should have been, the trepidation on his face giving way to resolve.

Kazmi grimaced. "The otherworldly who weren't in Inner London at the time it disappeared have reported that it's some kind of…barrier."

Julia furrowed her brow. "A barrier? A barrier against what?"

"That we don't know."

"A barrier means Inner London could be beyond it, right?" Bailey said, hope brightening his eyes. He glanced around the room. "It's not as if we've seen any evidence it's been annihilated. This means everyone in it could still be alive."

Kazmi nodded tiredly. "That's the belief everyone is holding on to. The alternative is too horrifying a reality to consider." The Argonaut head looked ten years older all of a sudden. "This phenomenon doesn't appear to have anything in common with the rifts the world saw a few weeks ago or even the rare gates that exist between Earth and other realms. We don't know what we're dealing with or indeed what everyone in Inner London could be going through right at this very moment."

A steadfast light appeared on Adrianne's face. "Whatever's happening to them, they have the best people on the ground to assist them."

Julia dipped her chin. "Adrianne's right." She

indicated the red-tinged void on the screen. "All the agency bureaus are in Inner London and most of the agents who work there live close by. Not only do they have some of the best otherworldly and magic users with them, they also have three demigods."

"Four."

Kazmi's quiet statement made everyone draw a sharp breath.

"What?" Strickland mumbled.

"There are likely four demigods in Inner London," Kazmi explained. "The light that tore the heavens open above the capital was likely due to a new demigod awakening in the city. That's what Victor revealed to the local Argonaut director. He was going to tell us more at this morning's meeting."

"Fuck me," Bailey mumbled leadenly.

Julia's heart thundered against her ribs. *A fourth demigod?! Who the hell could it be?!*

The look Zach exchanged with her confirmed the same questions were racing through his mind.

Julia turned to Strickland. "Give me and Zach authority to fly over to London. Adrianne, Bailey, and Charlie can follow us by plane."

"It's already arranged," Strickland muttered.

"What?!" Kazmi snapped. "How could you do that without—?"

"We either let them go to England or they'll walk, Amal," Strickland ground out.

Kazmi glowered at Julia and the rest of them. She muttered a curse under her breath and threw her hands in the air. "Fine! Do whatever you want!"

"Dammit." Adrianne chewed her lip, her frustration clear as she gazed hotly at Julia and Zach. "What I wouldn't give for some kind of portal right now."

Julia made a face. "If it weren't for the fact that you guys would throw up on us and likely freeze to death, we'd take you along."

"We could always ask Benja—" Zach started.

Adrianne put her hand out. "Anything but the damn Reaper's portal."

"Come on, we've got somewhere to go before we fly out," Julia told Zach.

Zach stared. "Where are we going?"

Julia turned on her heels, a grim frown darkening her brow. "We have to pick up a parcel."

CHAPTER TWENTY-SIX

THEO'S HEART POUNDED IN HIS THROAT AS HE STARED AT the crimson-dyed clouds churning the firmament. He'd slipped out of Victor's apartment and past his secretary Rosemary to come to the rooftop of the Cabalista headquarters so he could confirm what he'd just heard for himself.

That Inner London was no longer on Earth.

The stench of sulfur was everywhere, the city dark and frighteningly quiet but for the occasional sirens that tore the air. Theo could feel the collective hysteria bubbling beneath the uncanny silence nonetheless. The same hysteria building inside him.

He'd woken up a couple of hours ago to a room full of shadows and fresh sheets beneath his body. He vaguely recalled Victor taking him to the shower and washing him clean before dressing him in a pair of his pajamas and tucking him back in his bed.

The demon had been standing at the window and

talking to someone on his phone when he'd come to. "Are you seeing what I'm seeing?"

His tone had stiffened Theo's spine and had him sitting up. It was nothing like the teasing inflection he'd taken with him when they'd been making out a few hours ago.

Victor had twisted on his heels, as if he'd sensed Theo's stare. Theo's heart had fluttered at the smoldering crimson in his pupils. It no longer surprised him. If anything, it thrilled him.

The demon's eyes had been that way when he'd been making love to Theo, the color flaring bright enough to burn whenever he'd climaxed, his hot and tender touch a sharp contrast to Frost's icy and callous manhandling.

"I'll meet you guys at the Tower," Victor had said brusquely before ending the call. He'd come over to the bed, his gaze still locked on Theo's. The mattress had dipped slightly when he'd sat on the edge. "How do you feel?"

Theo had shivered, Victor caressing his cheek with his knuckles. For some insane reason, he'd wanted to grasp his hand and never let go.

"I'm—" Theo had paused and swallowed nervously. "I'm okay, I think." He'd cast a worried glance at the inky blackness beyond the window. "Why is it so dark?"

Victor's face had tightened at his question. "I don't know. I'm going to head out and see what's going on."

Fear had clutched Theo's gut in an icy hold, his

instincts screaming that something was very wrong. "Victor?"

Victor had surprised him by drawing him into his arms and pressing a soft kiss to his brow. "I'll explain everything when I get back. Just promise me you won't go anywhere."

Theo had nodded tremulously, the demon's scent making his pulse quicken with desire.

Victor had drawn back and given him a lopsided smile that made Theo suspect he knew exactly what he'd been thinking just then. Heat had prickled his skin when Victor had pinched the cuff of his pajama sleeve and rubbed it between his fingers.

"My clothes are too big for you," the demon had mused.

"Well, you *are* bigger than me."

Theo had flushed realizing what he'd just said. He'd tried real hard not to glance at Victor's crotch, the images of him eagerly touching and sucking the demon's cock making his cheeks burn.

"Keep looking at me like that and I won't be responsible for my actions," Victor had groaned.

Theo had bitten his lip. Victor had swooped down and kissed him, seemingly as helpless to resist the maddening pull between them as he was. Theo's mind had gone blank for a moment before he'd melted in the demon's arms, his breath shuddering out of him as Victor sought out his tongue.

Victor had wrenched his mouth from Theo's lips moments later and cursed. "Fuck! The things you do to me!"

He'd shuddered against Theo and pressed their foreheads together, hellfire licking the air around him while he'd gnashed his teeth and fought his arousal. Wonderment had filled Theo then.

The flames had sizzled softly against his flesh yet not burned him.

That he could make a powerful demon like Victor almost lose control had made Theo's belly clench on a wave of lust.

Alas, their desires had been cut short by the shrill ring of Victor's cell. He'd surprised Theo once more by kissing him heatedly for several seconds before rising from the bed and taking the call.

"Hi, Delphine. Yes, I'm aware. I'm heading out to meet Cassius and Morgan. I'll liaise with you after."

Victor had fixed Theo with a piercing stare. "Don't go anywhere."

Then he'd vanished.

Theo had eventually come out of the bedroom and explored the apartment, his gaze straying uncomfortably to the unnatural darkness outside the windows. A door at the end of the corridor had led him to a large, masculine office. Theo had rocked to a halt when he'd realized exactly where he was.

He'd forgotten that Victor had told him he'd brought him to the Cabalista headquarters after the incident at the hotel last night.

The outer door had opened and a middle-aged woman with a shock of silver hair had come in while he'd stood frozen in the middle of the room. Alarm had stiffened her stance for a moment before her face had relaxed in warm lines.

"Good morning, Theo."

She'd introduced herself as Victor's secretary, promised him breakfast and a change of clothes, and shepherded him back inside Victor's apartment. Since he'd lost his cell phone either in the alleyway in Spitalfields or at the hotel, Theo had been unable to check the news to see if there was an explanation for why London was still so dark. There was no TV in Victor's apartment and no landline either. What there was plenty of was books.

An hour spent twiddling his thumbs and trying to garner some interest in a tome on magic had finally seen him creeping back into Victor's office and attempting to explore the rest of the building.

It was when he'd sneaked the outer door open a crack that he'd overheard Rosemary talking to a couple of demons.

"We don't know how long we'll have power and a local network signal for," the secretary had said briskly, her face pale and devoid of the cheer she'd shown Theo earlier. "We should check the back-up generators and make sure we have enough comms devices for everyone."

"What about the people outside?" one of the demons had asked.

"There are humans clamoring to get inside all the agencies' bureaus in the City," the other demon had explained.

Rosemary had sighed. "I don't blame them. The first

place I thought to come when that light pierced the sky last night and I heard all the screaming was this very building." She'd paused, her brow wrinkling. "Let them in. We have enough space to accommodate at least five to six hundred people in our offices and the basement. The rest will have to find shelter in the Underground, like we planned. Have the prime minister and the cabinet made it to the bunker yet?"

"Yes. They got there ten minutes ago."

Theo had blinked, confused. *The prime minister and the cabinet?!*

Rosemary's next words had caused ice to skitter down his spine.

"Is it true? That we're no longer on Earth?"

Her expression had grown pinched as she'd looked between the two demons.

"It seems like it," the first one had replied reluctantly as he exchanged a glance with his companion. "We've lost communication with the outside world and no one can get past that barrier. The whole of Inner London seems to have relocated somewhere else overnight."

Rosemary had closed her eyes briefly.

"I'm just glad we have Victor, Cassius, and the other guy with us," she'd mumbled.

Theo had waited until Rosemary had stepped away from her desk before sneaking out of the office, an unnamed dread sending his pulse racing. It hadn't taken him long to find an emergency exit to the rooftop, the demons he'd crossed paths with too busy to pay him much heed.

Theo fisted his hands as he studied the eerie sky.

Everything that had happened in the last twelve hours still felt like some kind of terrible dream. The alleyway and the monsters. The strange light his body had emitted and the presence he'd felt inside him. What Frost had done to him in that hotel suite. Victor coming to his rescue.

Theo flushed. *And what we did in his bedroom, in this very building.*

He still couldn't believe that he'd let Victor touch him that way. That Victor had sucked him and made him come so hard he'd almost fainted.

Never mind that the hottest and most sought-after demon on Earth played with my ass mere hours ago. Theo chewed his lip. *We've only just met. So why did I let him do all that to me?!*

Warmth bloomed inside him. Theo pressed a hand to his belly.

The answer had to do with the weird heat in his body and the being whose voice he'd spoken with yesterday, when that beast had been about to kill him. He was certain of it.

The warmness within him intensified. His gaze swung instinctively to the south. Three winged figures appeared in the distance. They grew rapidly in size, their shapes becoming more defined as they emerged from the gloom.

Theo's eyes widened.

Victor was in the lead. A short distance behind him were two angels. One had black and crimson wings. Theo's breath caught.

They landed a short distance away.

Victor lowered his brows when he clocked Theo's presence.

He made his way over. "I told you to stay put."

"I'm still technically in the building," Theo said distractedly.

He couldn't take his eyes off Cassius Black. Like everyone else in the world, he'd known of the angel since he was a child. It was only in the past few weeks that he and the rest of humanity and the Fallen had learned that their collective contempt and loathing for the angel had been misplaced and that he had saved them from countless disasters in the past.

Not that Theo had held any particularly strong feelings toward the angel. He hadn't had much interaction with magic users and the otherworldly in his day-to-day life and job.

Yet, he couldn't look away from Cassius.

The dark-winged angel watched him steadily, his gray eyes full of a nameless emotion. Heat thumped through Theo's core. He could sense another presence rising within him. It was the one he'd felt before, in the alleyway. Except this time, the unearthly manifestation was accompanied by a wealth of feelings that made his breath catch all over again.

Something hot trickled down his cheek.

Victor startled. "Theo?!"

Theo blinked. He wiped away the trace of wetness on his face and stared at the radiant teardrop on his fingertip, his heart beating so hard and fast he thought he would faint.

Brightness bloomed on the rooftop.

Theo looked up. His pulse stuttered.

Cassius Black had transformed into a dazzling being of light, his white wings snapping wide open around him before he folded them, his fair hair and luminous eyes full of power. A tear that shone like a star spilled over and tracked down his cheek.

"*Rohengar,*" he whispered brokenly, his voice full of agony.

Theo found himself moving. He closed the distance to Cassius in a few swift strides and threw his arms around his neck. Cassius shuddered and hugged him back just as tightly.

Theo couldn't explain the storm of emotions threatening to overwhelm him. Sorrow. Happiness. Regret. Love.

They filled his heart and mind to bursting. They were his own, but at the same time they were not.

A singular truth resonated inside him. He knew this man. Had known him in some past life. They were brothers, linked by a bond forged in blood, fated to protect all the realms.

Theo didn't know why he knew all this or how a normal human like him could have made a blood pact with an otherworldly. He just knew it to be true.

He buried his face in Cassius's neck and inhaled his achingly familiar scent. The name that tumbled from his lips should have shocked him. Yet it didn't.

"Icarus!"

CHAPTER TWENTY-SEVEN

Morgan studied Theo and Cassius where they sat next to each other on a couch in Victor's office, faces positively beaming and eyes bright with happiness.

"So, you officially out of love with Cassius?" he asked Victor gruffly where they were making hot drinks.

Victor stiffened. "What makes you say that?"

Morgan smirked at his brother's defensive tone. "Because you made out with Theo. I can smell your scent on him."

"Stop sniffing people!" Victor ground out.

"Everything okay over there?" Cassius said a tad sharply.

Morgan looked over and met his lover's shrewd gaze. "Yeah."

He had no doubt Cassius had already detected that Victor and Theo had been intimate. Somehow, the demigod appeared to have taken that fact in his stride.

Morgan and Victor took the drinks over.

Considering the dire circumstances they currently found themselves in, it was strange to be having a meeting and coffee but he knew they couldn't rush this moment.

Cassius and Theo needed to talk.

The silence between them lengthened as they sipped their drinks. Theo finally put his cup down, his expression growing determined.

"Okay, spill." His gaze swung from Cassius to Victor and back. "Is Rohengar the being I can sense inside me?"

Cassius hesitated before nodding. "Yes. Your body harbors Rohengar's soul."

Theo paled a little. He blew out a sigh and ran a hand through his hair. "So, all the weird stuff that's been happening to me lately is because of him, huh? Who is this guy, exactly?"

"Rohengar is—" Cassius started.

"Wait." Victor lowered his brows. "What weird stuff?"

Theo told them about his strange experiences since he'd come to London. The monstrous visions he'd had. His eyes radiating a bright light. The unexplained fevers that often gripped him.

Morgan straightened when Theo related the incident in Spitalfields the night before. He could see his disquiet reflected on Cassius and Victor's faces upon hearing of the portals, and the monsters and hellbeasts that had emerged from them.

"Those flashes of light I saw from the hotel," Victor said, stunned. "That was you?!"

Theo grimaced and shrugged. "I guess so. I don't remember much after Rohengar manifested inside me. The next thing I knew, I was in that hotel suite with—" he scowled and fisted his hands, "with that asshole!"

"The poison he slipped you last night," Victor asked in an urgent tone. "Do you think he might have been giving it to you in another form?"

Morgan shot Victor a surprised look.

Cassius narrowed his eyes at the demon. "What makes you say that?"

Victor propped his elbows on his knees and linked his fists together, knuckles white as he stared at Theo. "Elios said he'd forced Theo to embrace who he really is. By that, I think he meant his status as a demigod." He glanced at Cassius and Morgan, his expression perturbed. "I believe he hastened Theo's awakening."

Theo blanched.

"Demigod?" he mumbled. "What do you mean?!"

A muscle twitched in Victor's jawline. "The light coming from your eyes? That's divine power. And the brightness coming from your flesh? That's divine power too. You were probably not aware of it at the time, but you manifested white wings just like Cassius in his demigod form last night, in that hotel suite."

Cassius blinked, surprised. A fraught silence filled the room, so tense it felt like the smallest noise would fracture it.

Theo jumped a little as Cassius took his hand. "Victor is right, Theo. You are a demigod, like us. Morgan and I felt it too, when you awakened last night and sent that bright beam of light into the sky."

"Bright beam?" Theo said numbly. "*Us?*" His wild-eyed gaze swept over them. "Wait. Are you saying you're *demigods?!*"

Cassius told him then. Of all they had learned since his and Morgan's encounter with Chester Moran and Lucille Hartman in San Francisco a few months ago. Of his own awakening and that of Morgan. Of the battle in the Spirit Realm that had unlocked a crucial part of their forgotten memories and caused Victor's demigod powers to manifest. Of his status as an Awakener and the North Star, and of the other Guardians of the Nether.

Theo swallowed convulsively in the hush that followed.

Morgan masked a grimace. *Poor kid looks like he's gonna bolt.*

A strange expression flitted in Theo's eyes as he stared at Victor. "That's why I called you by that name. Coraos. That's what drew Rohengar to the hotel. He knew you were there." He paused, his face growing haunted, as if he'd just realized something momentous. "Rohengar loved you, didn't he?"

His whispered words made Cassius's eyes bulge and Morgan's jaw drop open.

"*What?!*" Cassius turned an accusing glare on Victor. "Wait. Please tell me you didn't defile Rohengar in our past life?!"

Theo groaned, mortified.

Victor rolled his eyes. "No, we were never intimate."

Morgan smirked at the way Theo flushed. *They have been now, though.*

Cassius stared at Victor, pale-faced. "Did you know Rohengar had feelings for you?"

Victor's expression grew evasive. "I only found out last night."

It was Theo's turn to look stunned.

"What?" he gasped. "How?!"

Victor sighed. "You don't remember?"

"No!"

"You kept saying my demigod name when you—" Victor arched an eyebrow, "you know?"

"When I what?" Theo mumbled.

Victor pinched the bridge of his nose. "Whenever you climaxed, Theo. Both of you kept calling my names."

Theo sucked in air and went beetroot red.

Cassius dropped his head in his hands.

"My poor, sweet, innocent Rohengar is going to take a demonic demigod's cock up his ass," he mumbled, ashen faced.

"Cassius!" Theo squeaked, aghast.

Morgan muffled a snort. Cassius glared at him.

"Oh, come on!" Morgan protested. "It's funny."

The way Victor's shoulders quivered as he studiously inspected the floor indicated he was trying not to burst out laughing at Cassius's reaction. It was clear to both of them Icarus had been a protective brother in their past life.

"I have a question," Theo said haltingly. "Isn't—isn't it just because Rohengar is inside me that I have these powers?" He looked at his hands and flexed his fingers, distressed. "I'm just an ordinary human. I don't have any special abili—"

"You do, Theo," Cassius said firmly.

Morgan knew his lover was speaking the truth. Cassius's gifts as the Awakener meant he could detect someone's soul core and the powers it contained.

"Your soul core is unlike anything I've ever sensed before," Cassius continued. "Rohengar chose to reincarnate in you for a reason. Merging his soul with yours was crucial to your awakening. You're special, Theo." His face softened. He lifted a tender hand to Theo's cheek. "More special than you know."

Theo blinked back sudden tears.

He cleared his throat to hide his embarrassment and turned to Victor. "Coming back to your original question, Frost did insist on having tea with me every afternoon. He made me drink his favorite brand from the Far East. He told me he had it imported. Now that I think about it, it always had a strange bitterness to it."

They all sobered at that.

"What was Elios hoping to achieve by hastening Rohengar and Theo's awakening?" Cassius said, puzzled.

Hellish corruption drenched the office before anyone could come up with a suggestion. They jumped to their feet just as Delphine burst inside the room.

"We have incoming to the north and south!" the demon barked.

CHAPTER TWENTY-EIGHT

An updraft danced under Julia and Zach's wings as they glided effortlessly above the stormy Atlantic, the wind whistling at supersonic speed in their ears. A thrill shot through Julia.

It had been a long time since either of them had flown this fast.

She could tell from Zach's exhilarated expression that he was relishing the rare experience, just as she was. It was easy to forget that they had been born to spread their wings in the sky when they spent so much of their time on the ground.

They'd stayed high enough above the water to avoid the salt spray coating their feathers but low enough to take advantage of the air currents Zach created by churning the surface of the ocean with his Aqueous powers. It had been four hours since they'd left San Francisco. Impatience twisted Julia's gut.

We should be there soon!

"Look!" Zach shouted.

Julia stared where he pointed. A low-lying landmass appeared on the distant horizon. It grew rapidly in size and breadth. Relief loosened the tightness in Julia's chest.

It was short-lived.

Two dots had appeared in the sky above England.

Julia stiffened and slowed a fraction. "Are those fighter jets?"

"Shit!" Zach frowned. "I hope they know we're friendlies!"

The aircrafts zoomed past them moments later. They veered around smoothly and came level with where they flew. One of the pilots waved from the cockpit before giving them a thumbs up and pointing toward the looming landmass.

Zach relaxed. "Looks like they intend to escort us."

The fighter jets kept pace with them as they made for the English coastline. They headed up the Bristol Channel and were soon soaring over the rolling, green landscape of the Cotswolds. A dark spot became visible in the distance after they passed Oxford and the Chiltern Hills. It grew into a dome-shaped structure when they approached the outskirts of London.

Julia's pulse quickened as they drew closer to the barrier. It was even more daunting in reality than on a screen. Flashes of red light lit up the inky billows, the crimson flares lending an ominous appearance to the already eerie phenomenon.

Zach stared. "Just how big is this thing?!"

Julia spotted a group of angels and demons hovering about midway up the west wall of the structure. They were keeping the media helicopters swarming around it at bay. She started heading over to them.

Zach grabbed her arm. "Wait!"

He indicated the fighter jet to their left. The pilot was stabbing his finger at the sky above where Inner London should have been. Julia and Zach followed the direction he was pointing at.

Their eyes widened.

Two bright dots flashed at the top of the sphere. The clouds rippled in expanding circles above them as they attacked the barrier repeatedly, their weapons too far away to discern. Faint booms accompanied the vibrations that fluttered across Julia's wings as she and Zach rocked to a halt in mid-air.

Zach had unleashed his Stark Steel blade, his pupils crimson with demonic energy. "What the hell are those?!"

Julia shared his dread. Whatever those beings were, they were immensely powerful. She could taste it on the wind.

Movement ahead drew her gaze as the fighter jets peeled away and disappeared. Two of the otherworldly poised outside the barrier were arrowing rapidly toward them.

A female angel slowed to a hover next to them seconds later. "Are you the Argonaut agents we've been expecting?!"

"Yes." Julia indicated the dazzling spots above the dome, tension humming through her limbs. "What's happening up there?"

"We don't know," the demon who'd accompanied the angel said. "Those two turned up an hour ago through some kind of—black hole! They've been attacking the barrier since and have been hostile to anyone who's approached them!"

"We don't know what they are," the angel added worriedly.

Zach lowered his brows. "What do you mean?"

"They have white wings and colored armor," the demon explained. "One of them is wielding some kind of giant war hammer. The other guy has a bow and arrows that look like they're made of stars."

Zach cursed.

Shock reverberated through Julia. *Shit! Could it be—?!*

"Do they look like Cassius Black in his demigod form?!" she asked the angel and demon in an urgent tone.

They exchanged a startled look.

"Now that you mention it, they do," the angel said, pale-faced.

"Goddammit!" Julia spread her wings and shot up, Zach on her tail. "Tell everyone to stay back!" she yelled at the surprised angel and demon as they shrank beneath them. "Those guys are demigods!"

"I can't believe those two are here!" Zach shouted as they ascended swiftly. "I thought no one's been able to leave or enter the Nether since the Fall!"

"Yeah, well, they're here and we're gonna have to deal with them!" Julia retorted.

Cassius and Morgan had told them what they'd

recalled about the War in the Nether during their fight with Elios in the Spirit Realm. The descriptions of the two beings who had just appeared on Earth fitted those of the West and East Stars.

Archon and Nildar.

Their names rang through Julia's mind, bringing with them a faint echo of blurry memories. Frustration gnawed at her. Her past had slowly been emerging from the darkness inside her mind in the last couple of months, just as it had started to do for every otherworldly on Earth since Cassius and Morgan's demigod powers had awakened. The process seemed to have accelerated following Victor's revival as Coraos in the Spirit Realm.

Zach glanced over. "You scared?"

Julia made a face. "Not so much scared as worried what they might do to us when they find out we're Cassius's friends."

"I'd rather they stop trying to smash through this thing until we know exactly what we're dealing with." Zach studied the seething, crimson-tinted darkness to their right. "Hell only knows what's beyond it!"

The radiant figures became clearer as they neared the summit of the dome.

One was a beast of a demigod dressed from the neck down in a rust-colored battlesuit that failed to mask his bulging muscles, his formidable war hammer as long as Julia was tall and his long, red hair fluttering wildly in the wind. Though the demigod in the green armor with the brown ponytail was slender and more civilized looking, he wore a ferocious expression and was letting loose arrows shimmering like stars at the barrier, the bow in his hands crackling with divine light.

"Better put your sword away," Julia told Zach grimly. "We don't want to come over as aggressive."

The two demigods paused their assault as Julia and Zach drew level with them seconds later.

Archon's brows met in a heavy scowl. *"I thought we made it clear we have no interest in conversing with—!"*

"Wait." Nildar lowered his bow. Recognition brightened his gaze. *"Breenelle and Orramgauth. It has been a long time."*

The names he spoke sent heat flaring through Julia. Zach startled beside her.

Archon squinted. *"Well, wonders never cease."* He swung his hammer onto his shoulder, his animosity fading to an amicable glower. *"We did not know you two were on Earth."*

"Are those—" Zach swallowed and licked his lips. "Are those our true names?!"

Nildar looked puzzled. *"Of course. Those have always been your names."* He indicated Julia. *"Breenelle, the angel who could raise mountains. And you, Orramgauth, the demon who loved the seas more than anyone."*

Breenelle. Julia's heart pounded against her ribs as she savored the name she had lost five hundred years ago. The name of the angel she had once been. She could tell from the way Zach's eyes glistened slightly that having his true name revealed meant as much to him as it did her.

"Why do you act as if you do not recall your own identities?" Nildar said.

Julia registered the demigod's bewildered expression with a sinking feeling. *They don't know.*

"We lost our memories," Zach said, his haunted tone reflecting Julia's own unease. "All of us who fell to Earth. We do not remember anything before five hundred years ago."

Archon and Nildar recoiled.

"What?!" Nildar mumbled.

"How is that possible?" Archon snarled.

"Hypnos," Julia said stiffly. "Pan believes it was Hypnos who caused our memory loss. No one knows his whereabouts since the Fall."

"You are friends with the Wild God?" Archon growled.

"Friends is pushing it," Zach muttered. "We're amicable allies."

"Demetrius would be sad to hear that," Julia observed.

"Demetrius can stay." The demon narrowed his eyes. "It's his asshole of a boyfriend I object to."

Julia blinked. "Wait. Did he make a pass at Suzie?!"

Zach clenched his jaw.

Julia swallowed a sigh and focused on the matter at hand. "Victor believes Elios may have manipulated Hypnos into erasing our memories, just like he used him," she told the two demigods. "Cassius and Morgan agree."

Archon's face darkened. The air vibrated violently around him. *"Elios! Is Elios on Earth too?!"*

"Oh boy," Zach mumbled.

"*Calm down, brother.*" Nildar frowned. "*We do not recognize the other names you mentioned.*"

Julia and Zach traded a tense glance.

"You do it." Zach grimaced. "They're less likely to punch you."

"Thanks," Julia muttered. She steeled herself and met the stares of the demigods watching her closely. "The name Coraos goes by these days is Victor Sloan. He is one of Earth's most powerful and well-respected demons. Morgan King is the name Ivmir assumed after the Fall. As for Cassius Black, his true name is one you know well. He is your brother and fellow Guardian, Icarus. The North Star and Awakener."

Julia gasped as the storm of divine power that exploded around Archon drove her and Zach back some dozen feet. She choked on her next breath.

Archon had his hand locked around her throat.

Julia blinked. *Shit! I didn't even see him move!*

"*You are acquainted with the Oathbreaker and that treacherous snake Coraos?!*" Archon roared inches from her face. "*Where are they right now?! Speak, Breenelle, or I shall crush your windpipe!*"

"*Stop, Archon!*" Nildar barked.

Zach unleashed his Stark Steel blade, his pupils burning a violent crimson. "Let her go!"

Archon pointed his war hammer at him, his eyes bright with seraphic energy and a rage that would not be quenched. "*Back off, Orramgauth!*"

Zach grunted as divine power blasted out of the weapon and smashed into his gut, sending him flying some fifty feet. The demon recovered and darted toward the demigod, his intent clear as his Aqueous powers erupted in his hands and along his blade.

"Wait!" Julia wheezed.

She lifted a hand to stop Zach. He slowed to a hover a short distance away, frustration clashing with anger on his face.

Julia met Archon's incandescent gaze, air whistling painfully through her throat. "Listen to what we have to say before you pass judgement!"

Archon flexed his fingers and squeezed tighter. Nildar grabbed his wrist and tried to yank his hand from her neck. The demigod might as well have tried to move a mountain.

"Please, just listen to what they have to—!"

Something shifted inside Julia's armor. Loki scrambled out of the space between her shoulder blades, darted onto her head, and transformed as he launched himself at Archon.

"Will you calm down and just listen, you damn beast of a demigod!"

The imp grabbed Archon's temples and headbutted him violently.

CHAPTER TWENTY-NINE

THE TEMPORARY HEADQUARTERS OF THE TASKFORCE THE British armed forces, the agencies that governed the otherworldly and magic users, and what remained of the British government had set up to deal with the unprecedented disaster that had struck the capital was located at an air base northwest of London, some four miles from the barrier.

After hearing what had happened atop the dome, the station chief had loaned Julia a conference room in the giant hangar where a command center had been hastily put together. Even though thick, metal walls and a bulletproof, blackout window separated them from the main area, Julia could still hear an agitated buzz coming from the makeshift operations area and see the tense glances aimed at the conference chamber.

It wasn't every day two demigods burst through a portal to reach Earth.

Archon rubbed the spot on his forehead where Loki

had hit him, his expression disgruntled. *"That was uncalled for, imp."*

The cuts and swellings the imp's horns had inflicted had already healed, courtesy of his divine powers.

"You deserved it, asshole," Loki grumbled, arms crossed and arrowhead-tipped tail swinging with contempt where he sulked in a chair.

Nildar pinched the bridge of his nose. *"The two of you need to calm down."* He narrowed his eyes at Archon. *"And you! I cannot believe you attempted to kill Breenelle!"*

Remorse darted across Archon's face.

"I was not going to kill her," he said defensively. *"It was in the heat of the moment."* He scratched his cheek and flashed a contrite look at Julia. *"I apologize, Breenelle."*

Julia sighed. "Apology accepted. And it's Julia."

Archon blinked, confused.

"That's the name I've gone by these past five centuries," Julia explained.

"And I'm Zach," Zach muttered.

Horror filled Archon's tawny eyes. *"Why, those are almost as ugly as the name Icarus gave the imp."*

Loki jumped to his feet. "Take that back, you buffoon!"

Julia and Nildar rolled their eyes. Zach rubbed a tired hand down his face.

"Come, tell us what you intended to reveal to us," Nildar said wearily, ignoring the demigod and the imp glowering at one another.

An urgent knock came at the door before Julia or Zach could reply. It barged open to reveal Adrianne, Bailey, and Charlie. Julia stared.

"You guys weren't meant to be here for several hours yet," Zach blurted out.

"Bostrof found us a portal to Greenland," Adrianne said with a dismissive wave. She rocked to a halt when she saw Archon and Nildar. "Who the hell are these guys?"

It took several minutes to explain what had happened when Julia and Zach had reached London and who Archon and Nildar were.

Adrianne paled as she studied their armor and weapons. "So, you are the West and East Stars?"

Nildar raised an eyebrow. *"I am surprised you know our titles."*

"Pan told Cassius and Morgan about you," Julia said.

Nildar and Archon traded a guarded look.

"Please start at the beginning and tell us what has happened since you fell to Earth," Nildar said carefully.

It took over an hour for Julia and Zach to explain the events following the Fall, including the Hundred Year War that the otherworldly had been forced to wage against mankind after the disaster that destroyed their cities, and the truce forged in part by Victor that had been upheld to this day. They spoke of how human magic had flourished as a consequence of people's proximity to the otherworldly and how humans, angels, and demons now worked together to maintain peace around the world.

Nildar's brow furrowed when Julia mentioned all Victor had done to improve relationships between humans and the otherworldly. Archon scowled while

Zach talked about the incidents with Tania Lancaster and Chester Moran. The West Star swore when Julia related the details of Eden Monroe's unique magic and her awakening as the wielder of the Bloodcursed Devilwood Summoning Staff.

Both demigods visibly stiffened at the news of what had happened in Ivory Peaks and the Spirit Realm a few weeks back.

"Elios imprisoned Boreas and Demetrius and attempted to destroy the nexus of those realms to tear open a passageway to the Abyss?!" Nildar said, shocked.

"You say his goal is still to free Chaos?" Archon growled. *"Has that foolish God not learned his lesson from the War in the Nether?!"*

A taut silence befell them.

"What about you?" Zach asked the demigods curiously. "The Nether was cut off from all the realms after the Fall. What happened to you and how did you get to Earth?"

A hush followed. Nildar's eyes took on a faraway look.

"We have been virtual prisoners in our own home for most of the past five hundred years," he said finally.

Julia's belly clenched. Adrianne drew a sharp breath.

"It is true that the portals the Nether shared with the other realms were destroyed by the tear that ripped it open," Archon said in a hard voice. *"But there were small, unstable rifts that appeared from time to time that showed us glimpses into the other worlds. We were even able to travel*

through a few of them, though most led to places that had been separated from their original realms."

"*One was a black hole,*" Nildar added. "*It took us several attempts and a lot of divine energy to find Earth through it. We almost reached our intended destination last night but the doorway became unstable and closed before we could exit the interdimensional rift.*"

A savage smile curved Archon's mouth. "*But we did catch a glimpse of Icarus. I was glad to see he is still cursed.*" His gaze swept them, his expression turning morbidly gleeful while Nildar's became pained. "*Tell me, does he still suffer when he kills someone with a soul?*"

Julia's breath froze. Zach straightened in his seat. Adrianne, Bailey, and Charlie frowned.

"What do you mean?" Loki said quietly.

Julia's gaze shifted. The imp had gone deathly still, his pupils wide and the crimson light burning within them full of shock.

"*Archon, please, we should not talk of this,*" Nildar said awkwardly.

Archon's brow knitted. "*Why not? It is good for them to know what that traitor earned as punishment for his sins.*" He stared challengingly at the rest of them. "*We cursed Icarus when he fell. We wished for his wings, coated with the blood and ash of our fallen comrades, to stay forever stained. And we prayed that he would experience excruciating pain whenever he felled a being with a soul, be it an otherworldly or a human.*"

Agony squeezed Julia's heart at the enormity of the demigod's confession, drawing a gasp from her lips. Zach shot to his feet, his face darkening and his pupils flaring crimson. Adrianne pressed a trembling hand to her mouth, tears overspilling her eyes and tumbling down her pale cheeks.

"He experiences pain whenever he takes a life?" Bailey asked numbly.

"But he—he never told us!" Charlie mumbled, ashen faced. He looked at them wildly. "He never said it caused him pain!"

"It's probably because he's gotten used to it," Zach said in a dead voice. "Fuck!"

The demon twisted on his heels and walked over to the window, his knuckles whitening at his sides.

Archon frowned at their expressions, clearly confused. *"Icarus deserves what he got. Besides, it is not as if he would have had much opportunity to kill otherworldly beings and humans—"*

"Thousands," Julia whispered hoarsely. She looked at her hands, nausea churning her stomach as she recalled all Cassius had done to defend Earth and the other realms for the last five centuries. "His hands are stained with the blood of thousands!"

"What do you mean?" Nildar whispered, shock rounding his eyes.

Archon scowled. *"So you are saying he went rogue and is a criminal? That does not surprise me in the—"*

"—kill you."

Julia's skin prickled at the blast of divine energy that washed over her and rattled the windows. Loki was gritting his teeth, his face wet with tears and his eyes full of wrath.

"I will kill you!" the imp snarled.

Golden light flared on his belly. He reached inside his body, ripped out the Eternity Key, and leapt across the table, all fangs and claws and hate.

THE ARTIFACT BLOOMED INTO A GOLDEN BROADSWORD brimming with divine power even as the imp's shape continued to grow. Julia jumped to her feet, her chair crashing to the floor. Adrianne, Bailey, and Charlie similarly stumbled back from the table, eyes rounding as they stared at the creature Loki was transforming into.

Loki grabbed the neckline of Archon's armor and pressed the blade to the demigod's throat, seemingly oblivious to his new form and his curved horns, or the way his claws scratched the metal as he lifted the demigod off his feet.

"How could you?!" he screeched. The ceiling creaked as he kept getting bigger, his horns piercing it with ease. "Cassius has had to kill since he fell to Earth. And he did it to defend this realm and many others! While you were lamenting your fate in the Nether like fools, he was doing the job he had been born to do. *He protected everyone!"*

The ceiling ripped away from its supports, the sound of shearing metal partly drowning out the imp's enraged bellow. It brought him to his senses.

A shocked silence descended on the hangar as Loki startled and straightened to his full twenty-foot-giant-imp height, the roof of the conference room a makeshift hat crowning his head comically while he blinked at the mass of humans and otherworldly gaping up at him from the main floor.

"*Great,*" Nildar told Archon morosely. "*You had to anger the Gargantua.*"

"What—what's wrong with me?!" Loki whined.

He stared in horror at his colossal shape, the Eternity Key looking like a paltry toy in his hand.

"*It is just your full Gargantua form.*" Nildar paused at everyone's confused expressions and Loki's blank stare. "*You did not know you were a Gargantua?*"

Julia blinked as a dim memory resurfaced. "Wait. Isn't that a rare race of imps? The ones who are said to be descended from the Gods?!"

Zach startled. "You're right!"

"Wow," Adrianne mumbled, gawping at Loki. "And to think I scratched your belly."

Archon swallowed. "*Is it the truth?!*" His gaze swept over Julia and the others where Loki held him aloft, his fair wings limp and his face haunted. "*Is what the imp said the truth? That—that Icarus has had to take many lives since the Fall?*"

Loki's face darkened with fury once more. His grip tightened on the Eternity Key. "That's right, asshole! That curse you guys wished on him?! It must have broken his heart every single time he had to take another life! Give me one good reason why I should not slice your head off, you monster!"

Julia's heart thumped as the golden sword carved a thin, red line across Archon's neck.

"Let him go, Loki," someone said calmly behind them. "Cassius would not want you to harm his brothers."

Loki froze. Julia spun around.

A heavily pregnant Lilaia and a pale-faced Bostrof were standing in the doorway of the conference chamber.

Loki's lower lip trembled when he saw the Nymph, the fight draining out of him. "Lilaia!"

He shrank back down to his small imp form and leapt into the Nymph's arms, the Eternity Key vanishing inside him. The roof crashed back down upon its supports, sending everyone jumping and the windows rattling.

"There, there, little one," Lilaia crooned as she petted the whimpering imp clinging to her. "It's gonna be okay."

"Little, my ass," Bostrof muttered.

"I don't want to be a giant oaf like them!" Loki indicated Bostrof and Archon. "I want to stay small and cute so Cassius will like me!"

He started bawling his eyes out.

"*Impertinent imp!*" Archon growled, touching his throat.

Bostrof scowled. "Why you—!"

Lilaia cut her eyes to her husband.

"Cassius will love you whatever shape you take, Loki," she told the imp.

Loki sniffed. "Promise?"

Lilaia smiled. "I promise."

The imp promptly turned back into a cat.

"Are we good here?" someone said in a strained voice.

Everyone turned. The station chief was standing in the corridor, two soldiers, a magic user, and an angel framing her.

Julia grimaced. "Yes. I'm sorry about the, er—"

She pointed awkwardly at the damaged ceiling.

"Don't worry," the station chief muttered. "I'll add it to Argonaut's bill."

She scanned the room, her frowning gaze lingering on the two demigods amidst them before she left with her escort.

"Kazmi is gonna kill us," Adrianne said numbly.

Zach grimaced. "Not if Strickland gets to us first."

They straightened their upended chairs and sat down, the demigods reluctantly joining them.

"What are you doing here?" Julia asked Lilaia and Bostrof curiously.

"I felt drawn to the east," the Nymph explained with a faraway look. "Now that I am here, I can sense the pull of something…familiar close by."

Julia traded a mystified look with the others.

Bostrof's expression was guarded as he observed Archon and Nildar. "So, you are the West Star and the East Star?"

"*We are,*" Nildar replied. "*You are far from your home,*"

King of the Shadow Empire." He frowned faintly at Lilaia. "*So are you, Nymph.*"

"That we are." Lilaia sighed. "I'm afraid thousands of Lucifugous demons and a few Nymphs got stuck here after the Nether tore. We have been unable to find a way back to Rain Vale." She looked at Bostrof and squeezed his hand. "As for the Shadow Empire, it is no longer my husband's kingdom."

Archon raised an eyebrow. "*You are wed?*"

Nildar's gaze dropped briefly to Lilaia's pregnancy bump. "*You should give birth in Rain Vale.*"

Bostrof tensed at his cautionary tone.

Lilaia patted the Lucifugous's hand reassuringly. "I'll be fine." She studied the demigods shrewdly. "What of you? Why are you on Earth and how did you get here?"

Nildar recounted what he had told Julia and the others.

"A black hole?" Bostrof's brow furrowed. "Wasn't that dangerous?"

"*Not for beings like us,*" Archon grunted.

"Why now, though?" Julia asked stiffly. "Why did you try so hard to reach Earth all of a sudden?"

Suspicion tightened Adrianne's jaw. "Does it have to do with that barrier?"

"It does seem like a strange coincidence that you two turned up once Inner London vanished off the face of the Earth," Zach said coolly.

Archon frowned. "*Inner London?*"

Nildar straightened, his expression clearing. "*That must be the city I saw in my vision and the one we glimpsed last night.*" He turned to Archon, his pupils flashing with seraphic radiance. "*That is where Icarus and Rohengar are right now. Beyond that barrier.*"

"Vision?" Lilaia repeated, perplexed.

"Rohengar?" Julia's pulse quickened. "Pan told us the South Star died during the War in the Nether!"

"*He did.*" Nildar dipped his chin solemnly. "*His soul has reincarnated inside another.*"

Lilaia gasped and pressed a trembling hand to her mouth. "The South Star lives once more?!"

Loki stirred in her arms, the demon cat's ochre eyes locked unblinkingly on the two demigods.

"*Yes.*" Nildar lowered his brows. "*There is a sacred pool inside the palace of every Guardian of the Nether. It holds the tears of the First God and a fragment of the soul of each Guardian. One that is meant for the future Guardian who will take on their role. The fragment that belongs to Icarus still burns, which is why we knew he was still alive.*"

"*We heard rumors from the rare few otherworldly whose paths we crossed after the War and came to realize he was likely in this realm,*" Archon said brusquely.

"*The soul fragment in the palace of the South Star disappeared on the day the Nether tore,*" Nildar explained. "*It revived a day or so ago.*"

"*We came to Earth to meet the new Guardian and return him to where he belongs,*" Archon said. "*The Nether.*"

Julia's heart pounded wildly at the demigods' words, her shock reflected on everyone's faces. *Who did Rohengar's reincarnate inside?!*

Adrianne recovered first. She stared at the

demigods with a focused expression. "You said you saw them. Icarus and Rohengar. Tell us about your vision."

Dread traced icy fingers down Julia's spine as Nildar explained what he had witnessed when he had touched the soul fragment in Rohengar's palace.

"There are monsters and hellbeasts in London?!" Adrianne gasped.

"There will be if they are not already there," Nildar replied matter-of-factly. He rubbed his chin, faint lines marring his brow. *"Whatever that barrier is, it is unnatural. We should have been able to pierce it with our weapons. It feels more like an interdimensional fracture."*

Loki hopped onto the table and transformed with a poof of air. "The only object with a chance of getting through that thing is the Eternity Key." He turned to Julia. "Your instincts were correct."

Julia heaved a tremulous sigh. The first thing she'd thought of when she'd seen the images of the void engulfing Inner London had been the Eternity Key. She and Zach had witnessed what Cassius had been able to do with it during their battle with Elios in San Francisco.

Loki narrowed his eyes at Archon and Nildar. "I will need your divine power to attempt to carve a path through it though."

Archon grimaced and traced the place on his neck where the cut the imp had inflicted had already healed. *"You seem to have your fair share of that, imp."*

Loki shook his head. "It's still not enough. I am not the Awakener."

A somber silence descended upon the room.

Lilaia's knuckles whitened as she looked at Julia and the others, her dread plain to see. "So, you guys are determined to go through that barrier?"

"We don't have any other option," Adrianne said grimly. "By the sounds of it, Cassius, Morgan, and Victor are going to need all the help they can get."

"But you don't even know where they are." A muscle jumped in Bostrof's jawline. "If Nildar is right, then London is not simply on the other side of that barrier. You could end up anywhere if you go through an interdimensional fracture."

"I know where they are," Loki muttered.

Everyone stared at the imp.

Loki shuddered, his pupils brightening to a blood-red glow for a moment. "I can smell my old home from here. I don't know how all those humans are still alive, considering their current location. It must be that barrier keeping them from suffocating and their bodies from liquefying from the noxious gases."

"Wait." Horror widened Bostrof's eyes. "You mean they're—?!"

Loki dipped his chin, his expression brittle. "The Seventh Hell. Inner London is somewhere in the Seventh Hell right now."

CHAPTER THIRTY-ONE

"Shit!" Victor carved through three monsters in one fell swoop, his black flames rendering their bodies to ash in seconds. "There is no end to them!"

A giant hellboar pounded the street toward him, its tusks stained with the blood of those it had already gored.

Cassius cut it down before it could reach the demigod, his holy sword brightening the gloom as he wielded it at dizzying speeds, his white wings flaring above him.

The hellboar squealed as it landed on severed stumps. It fell on its side, its monstrous body rattling the ground. Blood pooled rapidly beneath it.

Cassius ended its misery with a single stab to its soul core, the pain of taking a life searing his belly for an agonizing moment. He took a ragged breath and shook it off like he always did before turning to face the mob of monsters converging on their location from the north.

They were at a junction in the center of Camden Town, not far from one of two places where the strange barrier surrounding the city had torn open.

The creatures charging toward them slowed when they saw the divine radiance emanating from Cassius and his blade, their gimlet eyes full of hate. They stopped and clawed the ground a safe distance from the light, heads snapping around as they bit and snarled at one other, their drool burning holes in the asphalt.

Dryad magic fluttered across Cassius's skin from where Morgan and a group of otherworldly engaged the lesser demons high above them. Though the Sword of Wind had helped diminish their numbers considerably, more were making their way over, their wings darkening an already lightless sky.

The angels and demons beside Morgan kept glancing worriedly at Victor's demigod form. It was their first time seeing it.

Cassius ignored their stares and frowned at the growing masses of monsters on land and in the air.

"I need to get to where they've breached the barrier," he told Victor urgently. "I should be able to close it, like I did at the hotel. It's the only way we're going to be able to keep the city safe."

Victor dipped his head grimly. "I'll help clear a path."

His black flames intensified, the fire licking at his wings and engulfing his armor and sword crackling with power.

Cassius shot up in the sky to Morgan's side. "Victor and I are going to find where they're coming from!"

Morgan glanced at his brother, who stood watching them from the ground.

"Okay." He curled a hand around Cassius's nape and pulled him in for a swift kiss. "Be careful."

Cassius nodded, his lips tingling. He rejoined Victor and cast a final glance at his lover.

"You ready?" Victor said grimly.

Cassius focused on the sea of crimson eyes glaring at them. His hands tightened on his holy blade. "Yes."

They moved as one, light and darkness carving seamlessly through the horde as they attacked and countered. Blood and gore dripped heavily from their swords as they felled their enemy yard by yard and street by street, the blasts of Heaven's Light Cassius released blinding the creatures and gaining them the upper hand.

By the time they reached the barrier, they were both panting and a fine sheen of perspiration covered their faces.

Victor pointed at a jagged, glowing, crimson fracture some two hundred feet up the curved wall of storm clouds. "There!"

Hellbeasts and monsters were pouring through it, those unable to fly aided by their winged companions.

Cassius's heart thundered against his ribs as he and Victor ascended swiftly, their feathers forming turbulent streams in the sulfurous miasma corrupting the atmosphere. It took many precious minutes to fell the creatures in their path.

Cassius clenched his teeth as more kept on appearing. *They'll keep getting through before we reach that opening!*

He drew on the unearthly power within him. Heat flooded his veins. His flesh grew warm and his teeth rattled as divine energy streamed out of him and sparked the air.

"Victor, shield your eyes!" he barked.

The demigod squeezed his eyes closed a heartbeat before Cassius released a violent burst of Heaven's Light. Screams rent the sky as the creatures recoiled in pain, those too close scorched by the blistering blaze. They started to retreat.

Cassius and Victor followed.

The monsters snarled and spat at them over their shoulders as they darted back through the twenty-foot-wide crack they had materialized from. The power of the Hells washed across Cassius as he and Victor finally drew level with the opening. Darkness roiled within the jagged breach. A crimson flash lit it seconds later.

It offered a horrifying view of what lay beyond the barrier.

The sweat coating Cassius's skin turned to ice. Victor swore.

The Seventh Hell? Cassius stared at the dreadful landscape of lava pits and erupting volcanic peaks shimmering in the distance, his mouth dry. *We're in the Seventh Hell?! But how?!*

Another wave of monsters appeared at the far end of the opening.

"Cassius!" Victor yelled. "*Now!*"

Cassius flinched. He took a deep breath, charged his sword with Heaven's Light, stabbed the center of the fracture, and let loose an explosion of divine energy.

Victor braced his wings as the detonation washed over him and sent violent ripples across the surface of the barrier.

The fissure screeched and started to distort, the sound setting Cassius's teeth on edge. It imploded from the inside out in a savage, spinning maelstrom that tore through the horde trying to make their way through, ripping them to shreds.

The breach closed with an anticlimactic whoosh that made Cassius's ears pop. The stink of sulfur abated.

Their heavy breaths filled the silence that followed.

Victor pressed his comms device. "Delphine, can you see some kind of opening in the south wall of the barrier? It'll be a few hundred feet up and where the monsters are thickest!" His pupils flared a moment later. "We're coming to you!" He ended the communication and met Cassius's gaze. "Crystal Palace Park!"

"Let's go!"

They picked up Morgan en route, leaving the otherworldly with him to dispose of what remained of the lesser demons and monsters who'd invaded the north of the city.

It took them less than a minute to reach the dark mass concentrated at the barrier enclosing the southern end of Inner London. Relief lightened the knot in Cassius's belly.

Delphine, Jacob Marsh, and the troops of otherworldly with them had been successful in keeping the invaders from spilling into the suburbs, although it appeared to have cost them dearly in terms of injuries.

"Delphine!" Victor shouted as they approached.

Delphine turned in mid-air, her left wing askew. Crimson stained her feathers where something had torn into it. Jacob wiped blood from a fresh cut on his cheek where he hovered beside her, the wound already partly healed.

They recoiled when they saw Victor's new form.

"Are you guys okay?" Victor asked, disregarding their brittle stares.

"Victor?" Delphine mumbled. Her gaze swept his dark flames and black wings. "What is—?"

"I don't have time to explain right now," Victor said briskly. "I'll do so later, I swear. Tell us where you saw the opening!"

Delphine swallowed and indicated a spot on the barrier. "That's where Jacob saw an opening earlier."

Cassius narrowed his eyes at the living cloud of monsters masking it from view. He looked at Morgan and Victor. "You guys watch my six!"

The demigods dipped their heads.

Just like the time before, they cut through their enemy as one, black flames merging with dark wind and Dryad magic, Heaven's Light a bright beacon at their head that blinded and scorched the winged monsters and lesser demons in their path. Cassius's heart raced with the same fierce feelings he'd experienced in the hotel suite as he glanced at the two men beside him.

This is how we'll defeat Elios! I am certain of it now!

They reached the breach moments later.

Morgan's eyes rounded when he caught a glimpse of what lay on the far side. "Is that—?!"

"Yeah, we forgot to tell you earlier," Cassius said darkly. "We're in the Seventh Hell!"

He drew on Heaven's Light, pierced the crack, and closed it.

Screeches and shrieks rose from the ground and the sky as the otherworldly protecting the city disposed of the remaining monsters and lesser demons.

Cassius, Morgan, and Victor were making their way across to Delphine and Jacob when a monstrous bellow echoed in the distance, bringing them and everyone else up short. The sound was followed by a bright flash that lit the gloom above the center of the capital.

Divine energy washed across their bodies in a powerful wave. The barrier throbbed violently in response to it, startling them.

Victor's gaze found the fading glow above the city. He paled. "Theo!"

He arrowed toward the Cabalista headquarters.

Fear tightened Cassius's chest as he and Morgan followed in a burst of speed. *Please be okay!*

His soul core thumped. Cassius blinked. A second source of light flared at the summit of the barrier.

Something had just come through.

Something that fell toward the city like a blazing star.

CHAPTER THIRTY-TWO

A FAINT NOISE REACHED THEO'S EARS. HE LIFTED HIS head from his knees, his legs pressed to his chest where he sat in the dark in an armchair in Victor's apartment.

The noise came again. Theo's pulse stuttered.

That was definitely a scream!

He unfolded his legs and rose, heading barefoot down the corridor that led to Victor's office. The tiled floor cooled his feet when he stopped before the door. He hesitated, his hand hovering a hairbreadth above the knob. He'd promised Victor he wouldn't leave his apartment.

A shriek full of horror and pain rose somewhere in the building.

Theo scowled and grabbed the doorknob. *I can't just stay put!*

Something heavy landed atop the building, causing him to jump and making the chandeliers in the apartment tremble. A fine shower of plaster dust rained down on him. Glass cracked ominously somewhere above.

Theo was in the office and through the outer door before he knew it. The screams punctuating the air grew clearer as he approached the marble staircase that formed the central axis of the building. He paused, one foot hovering above the first step, his heart in his throat.

Warmth burst through his belly.

Do not be afraid...

Theo blinked back sudden tears at the comforting words that came from the other half of him. He fisted his hands, determination overcoming the terror locking his limbs in place.

That's right. Rohengar is with me!

He started down the stairs. The stench of sulfur soon flooded his nostrils and burned his eyes. Corruption prickled his skin when he reached the third landing, raising goosebumps on his flesh. The sound of heavy fighting rose from somewhere below.

His soul core thumped.

He could feel Rohengar stirring.

Theo skidded to a halt, grabbed the main banister, and leaned over. Nausea churned his gut at the glimpse he caught of the front vestibule.

A grotesque creature was dragging the convulsing torso of a dying woman across the floor. Blood and gore stained the marble as it bit down on her head and severed it from her body.

Horror drew an incoherent mumble from Theo's lips. The beast's head snapped up. It froze mid-chew, the crimson third eye in the middle of its forehead locking on him.

Theo gasped and shot back from the banister, dizzy with fear.

"Quick, hide!" someone whispered fiercely to his right. "They'll find you if you stay out there!"

He looked around wildly. A man in a business suit was peering out of a crack in the door of a conference room, his face glistening with perspiration. Panicked faces loomed in the gloom behind him. The chamber was crowded with people, their terror so thick it clogged the air.

Theo saw another door crack open farther down the hallway and realized every room in the building was likely harboring citizens of Inner London who had come to Cabalista to seek shelter and protection.

For a second, he was tempted to join them.

The path he should take blazed through his soul, filling him with a conviction that could not be denied. The Theo he had been yesterday might have run away from the disaster unfolding before him. The Theo he was now could not.

He swallowed and met the frightened man's stare. "Stay low and don't make a sound." He paused, surprised at how calm he sounded considering he could barely feel his own legs. "And try to stay calm. Your heartbeats will draw them if you panic."

Theo turned and started down the staircase without a backward glance. His belly clenched when he heard Rosemary's voice seconds later.

"Levi, look out!"

He hurried down the steps to the second landing and finally saw the main foyer. His flesh turned to ice at the sight that met his eyes. It wasn't just one hellbeast that had breached the building's defenses.

Several monsters and a second hellbeast had managed to get through the squad of otherworldly protecting the entrance. A fierce battle still raged outside, the Cabalista demons doing their best to keep the main horde threatening to overrun them at bay.

A smaller crew of six agents was holding the final line of defense in the vestibule. Two were attacking the three-eyed beast that had managed to decapitate the woman. Three had engaged the monsters.

The sixth demon faced down a creature similar to the giant hound who'd attacked Theo in the alley in Spitalfields. It was one of the guys Rosemary had been speaking to earlier, outside Victor's office.

That must be Levi!

Levi ducked beneath a giant paw, carved through a tendon in the beast's front left leg with his Stark Steel blade, and blasted it with a violent explosion of wind as he rose from under it.

The hellbeast grunted, claws raising sparks on the marble as the demon's Aerial powers sent it skidding some ten feet across the ground. It bellowed in rage and charged again.

Levi took flight. He wasn't fast enough to avoid the giant paw that swatted him from the air and pinned him to the floor. Bile flooded Theo's throat as the hellbeast lowered its massive head and tore into the demon's right wing. It lifted him in its jaws and tossed him aside violently.

Levi crashed into a marble column, the impact sending a crack all the way up it even as he slid to the floor. He shook his head dazedly, gripped his blade, and climbed awkwardly to his feet, mangled wing askew and crimson pupils full of resolve.

"*Levi!*" Rosemary screamed.

Theo's heart stuttered. The secretary dashed into view from beneath the landing. The hellbeast turned toward her.

Levi's eyes widened. "No! *Run, Rosemary!*"

The heat that seared Theo's belly flushed the fear from his mind. He moved, his hands finding the banister, his legs swinging smoothly up and over.

A wild thought darted through him as he fell. *I'm gonna crack my skull open!*

Rohengar whispered through his heart. *You will not…*

The ground caved beneath Theo's feet as he landed in a low crouch between the hellbeast and Rosemary. Rosemary fell back with a startled cry.

Levi's jaw dropped open.

The hellbeast stopped.

Theo straightened, stunned that he was still in one piece. His soul core throbbed. The scent of summer washed across the foyer, along with a pulse of divine energy that filled him with an otherworldly strength.

Rohengar's presence flooded his body. *This is both my power and yours, Theo. Embrace it…*

Theo stared in wonder at his glowing skin. He

flexed and unflexed his fingers, blood thumping in his skull. *I can feel it! I can feel how to control it now!*

"Theo?!" Rosemary mumbled.

"I'm okay." Theo narrowed his eyes at the hellbeast as it took a step toward him. The words Rohengar had spoken in the alleyway came to him. He raised a hand, palm out. "Suspend!"

Light bloomed around his fingers.

CHAPTER THIRTY-THREE

THE HELLBEAST'S EYES FLARED AS IT FOUND ITS LIMBS locked in place by the time spell. Its pupils crossed when Theo drew a fist back and punched it in the solar plexus.

The creature smashed into a monster and carried it out the front doors and straight over the heads of the Cabalista agents into the monstrous mob, crushing several lesser demons beneath its body when it crashed down.

One of the agents whirled around. "What the hell was—?!"

She stopped and gaped at the sight of Theo.

The three-eyed hellbeast and the remaining monsters turned to him, their garish faces filling with hate when they registered his demigod radiance, their battle with the Cabalista demons all but forgotten.

"I'll draw them outside!" Theo told Levi. "Barricade those doors with anything you can find!"

The demon nodded shakily.

Theo realized the demon was staring at something above his head. He looked over his shoulder and froze. Blazing white wings rose from his back.

He'd felt a slight itch between his shoulder blades a moment ago but hadn't realized it was because he'd suddenly sprouted wings.

Wow. I have wings!

He flushed sensing Rohengar's faint amusement. Theo moved his new appendages a little and gasped when he shot up and nearly cracked his head on the vaulted ceiling.

"Whoa!"

"Theo, Victor will be upset if—!" Rosemary called out.

She faltered when Theo turned and pinned her with a seraphic stare.

"He will understand. For this is my duty."

Theo dropped to the ground and advanced across the vestibule. The Cabalista agents parted as he moved through them, leading the hellbeast and monsters who couldn't seem to tear their gazes from him outside.

He found himself in the midst of the horde that had amassed in front of the Cabalista headquarters. The creatures closed in around him, jaws dripping with drool as they snarled and pawed the ground, their loathing thickening the air.

Theo's heart raced as he gazed into their hateful eyes, the folly of what he was doing hitting him once more. *I'm going to die!*

A soft sigh danced through him. *No, you shall not perish...*

Theo swallowed. *That's great and all, but I could really do with some kind of weapon right now!*

Rohengar's voice fluttered in his ears. *Draw the Spear of Light, Theo. It is but a trace of the real thing, but it shall do for now...*

The horde charged.

"Suspend!" Theo barked.

Most of the monsters and hellbeasts stilled in their tracks. He lowered his brows at the few still moving at the back of the mob, albeit sluggishly.

So, this time spell doesn't work on a huge crowd. Good to know!

Theo closed his eyes to the talons and fangs frozen a couple of feet from him and the ones creeping closer.

He focused on the source of power within him. *So, how do I draw this thing?!*

Call to it...

Theo took a deep breath. *Come to me, Spear of Light!*

Fire flooded his veins. Something warm filled his hands.

He opened his eyes and stared at the translucent weapon of pure brilliance he now held. His fingers flexed around it, its shape hauntingly familiar.

Theo shifted his body in a stance that stemmed from Rohengar's memories and his own instincts. He ended the time spell and moved, the gossamer weapon guiding his fingers as if it were alive, the seraphic beams shooting from his eyes blinding his enemy.

Razor-thin slashes of light carved through the

monsters and hellbeasts, their lower bodies still moving fractionally even as their torsos and heads tumbled to the ground, to be crushed beneath their stampeding paws and feet.

Blood splattered Theo's face and body as he attacked, the Spear of Light humming in his grip, Rohengar's commands to duck and stab and weave and slash ringing in his ears. He ignored the sticky gore staining his glowing flesh as he dealt deadly strikes upon his foe, his focus unbroken, the brightness throbbing from his body lighting up the street in dazzling pulses.

The last monsters fell around him moments later. Theo stopped and slowly straightened. He raised his face to the dark sky and let out a shaky breath, his limbs trembling and his heart racing as the adrenaline from the fight finally caught up with him. He looked over his shoulder and flinched at the sight of the trail of death he'd left in his wake. Resolve hardened his jaw.

It was a necessary evil. One he would be forced to endure again in future.

An eerie boom reached him. The ground shuddered beneath his feet. Theo turned, an unnamed dread knotting his stomach. His gaze landed on the building at the end of the road.

Tremors shook the Cabalista headquarters where it straddled the corner of the junction, each judder accompanied by the mysterious booming noise. A shadow moved against the sky.

The hairs rose on Theo's nape.

A giant, one-eyed monster was scaling down the

flank of the building from where it had perched on the cupola crowning it.

Cyclops!

Theo's mouth grew dry, the creature's identity and deadliness as much borne from his newly awakened preternatural instincts as it was from human folklore.

It was likely the creature that had landed on the rooftop earlier.

"Can I defeat it?!" he half mumbled to himself.

Yes...if you believe in yourself and our brothers...

Theo startled at Rohengar's calm words. "Brothers?!"

They draw near. Listen to how our weapon sings in delight and our heart throbs with joy...

Theo blinked.

He pressed a hand to his belly and stared at the Spear of Light. *Rohengar's right! I can feel my heart growing lighter and the spear's happiness!*

The Cabalista agents protecting the entrance of the headquarters fell back with horrified cries as the Cyclops stepped down in front of them. The monster turned and observed the demons. It raised a giant foot to crush them.

Fly, Theo...

Theo was in the air in one heartbeat and in front of the monster with the next. He punched the creature in the jaw and slashed it across the chest with the spear.

The Cyclops stumbled back a step, its foot skimming the demons it meant to crush. A thin, red line some one inch deep bloomed on its body from its left shoulder to its right waist.

Theo scowled, knuckles tingling. *Shit! That punch barely made a dent in him and nearly broke my bones!*

"Stay back! He's too strong for you!" he yelled at the Cabalista agents cowering under the porch.

"You sure he's not too strong for *you?!*" the female demon from before shouted.

She stared at the Cyclops, pale-faced. Theo swallowed. He couldn't really deny the truth in her words.

"I'm a demigod," he said, sounding far more confident than he felt. "He can't kill me." *I think!*

Nothing is stronger in this universe than a newly awakened demigod other than the Awakener...

Theo puzzled at Rohengar's words. Then, there was no more time to think. For the Cyclops's eye had just flared. Theo's skin prickled as the crimson glow within it grew brighter.

That's not good!

"Suspend!" Theo barked.

The scarlet light in the Cyclops's eye kept growing.

Theo's heart pounded heavily. *Does the spell not work on him because he's too big?!* His nails scored his palms. *Time to try the other thing!*

"Dimensional Gate!"

A portal burst into existence in front of his outstretched hand just as a scarlet beam detonated from the Cyclops's pupil. The gate swallowed it inches before it could strike him.

Sweat beaded Theo's forehead when the portal snapped out. He was pretty certain that red light would have pierced straight through him and the building at his back.

I've got to draw him away from here!

He looked around wildly and shot off toward a junction to his right. The Cyclops followed him with its gaze before turning and lumbering after him.

Theo whirled around at the intersection. He gripped the ethereal spear, rose until he was above the rooftops of the surrounding buildings, folded his wings back, and dropped. He arrowed toward the Cyclops as its pupil brightened once more.

The red beam exploded into life. Theo twisted around its axis as it carved the empty air above London.

He slashed the monster's face, kicked off its shoulder, and darted around it at a lightning-fast speed, the Spear of Light unleashing attack after attack that carved shallow wounds upon its flesh.

The monster growled in irritation and tried to swat him from the air with a gigantic hand.

Theo sucked in air and bent back sharply at the waist. Massive knuckles sent his clothes and hair fluttering as they missed him by a scant inch. He somersaulted onto the monster's hand, scaled his arm in the blink of an eye, and sliced his left ear off in a burst of power before shooting away to a safe distance.

The Cyclops bellowed in rage and raised his fingers to the bleeding hole in his head.

Blood hammered at Theo's temples as he hovered in place and studied his enemy with a frown. The cuts he'd inflicted upon it were hardly going to slow it, let alone make it bleed to death. And he couldn't keep using those explosive bursts of energy to defeat it. He could feel them draining him of strength.

Shit! What's it gonna take to bring this thing down?!

The Cyclops's hateful gaze locked on Theo's position. It opened its mouth.

The sound that left its throat almost burst Theo's eardrums. He gasped as the monster's scream immobilized his body and froze his wings. Theo fell, the Spear of Light scattering into vanishing light motes in his hands.

The Cyclops snatched him from the air, its fingers locking so tightly around him Theo was surprised he wasn't immediately squashed to a pulp. His bones ground together as the monster started to squeeze.

Theo scowled and drew on the sphere of heat inside his belly. He had no choice but to let loose another discharge of his divine power.

Let's make this a big one, Rohengar!

A blaze streamed through his veins and flooded his flesh. He roared as an incandescent radiance detonated from within him and lit up several blocks.

The Cyclops squinted and released him.

Theo fell to the ground, shuddering. A shadow engulfed him. He lifted his head and saw the Cyclops's foot descending toward him, an unstoppable mountain of wrath wrapped in living flesh.

Theo raised a trembling hand, his heart in his throat. "Dimensional Ga—!"

"*Ooof!*"

Theo blinked as something stopped the giant some

dozen feet above his head. His gaze shifted from the enormous war hammer holding the monster's leg off the ground as if it weighed nothing to the white-winged beast of a man in rust-colored armor who stood holding the weapon.

The guy grinned at him. *"That was close, little one."*

CHAPTER THIRTY-FOUR

Theo narrowed his eyes. *Little one?*

Rohengar's tone sounded a smidge irritated as it rang through Theo's mind, as if he wanted to ding a sibling's ear. *Do not mind him. Archon likes to show off his brute strength.*

Theo's pulse stuttered at the name. *That's Archon? The West Star?!*

The Cyclops grunted in pain and stumbled back a couple of steps.

Theo saw the cause an instant later. Arrows of dazzling light had pierced its chest. Another volley followed, the shafts multiplying five-fold before punching into the Cyclops's thigh and making it screech.

Theo's gaze found the demigod archer in the sky. Nildar's eyes flashed with seraphic light as he met Theo's gaze, his features softening into an expression of such pure love Theo's heart throbbed. Movement drew their attention.

"*Move, Rohengar, Archon!*" Nildar barked.

Theo's legs responded to the demigod's command. Archon smashed his war hammer into the Cyclops's ankle as it attempted to crush them once more. Bone cracked. The monster shrieked.

Theo and Archon rolled out of the way of its foot and darted up to Nildar's position. The Cyclops turned its hateful gaze upon them and opened its jaws once more.

This time, Theo was ready. "Dimensional Gate!"

The Cyclops's paralyzing bellow was swallowed by the portal he generated before its face.

"*Time to finish this, brother.*" Nildar cast a fierce look at Theo. "*We will lend you our strength.*"

He hooked his bow onto his back. Light bloomed on his palms.

"*Go get him, little one,*" Archon grunted.

Radiance erupted on his fingertips.

Theo gasped as bright arcs of divine energy shot from Nildar and Archon's hands and struck his belly. Power filled him, so bright and pure and righteous he felt he could destroy entire worlds. The Spear of Light exploded into being once more, the weapon more solid than it had been before.

"Theo!"

Theo looked over his shoulder. Victor, Morgan, and Cassius were winging their way rapidly toward them.

Cassius transformed into Icarus and cast his holy sword and a divine beam at him. "*Use it well, brother!*"

Theo shuddered as Icarus's energy entered his soul core at the same time his fingers closed on the hilt of the Awakener's sword. He rose, gripped the spear and blade, and dropped toward the Cyclops.

Light flooded London as he poured the power of four into the weapons he wielded. He roared and slashed the Cyclops clean in half from the head down.

The blacktop caved beneath him when he landed on the street, sending cracks shooting off hundreds of feet in every direction and up the closest buildings. A lamp post creaked and smashed onto the ground at the same time the Cyclops fell. Broken chunks of asphalt levitated briefly from the second impact before smashing back down to form even smaller fragments.

Theo panted and slowly straightened on trembling legs.

He turned and stared at the giant he had felled, blood thumping in his skull. "Did I really do that?!"

Archon landed beside him and slapped him heartily on the back. *"You did."*

Theo stumbled forward with a wince. He would have fallen had Nildar not caught his arm.

"Will you stop being such an oaf?!" the demigod snapped at a suddenly sheepish looking Archon. *"He does not have his armor on!"*

Archon blinked, as if registering Theo's bloodied human clothes for the first time. *"You are right. Where is his armor?"*

"Theo!"

Theo whirled around. Victor had alighted a short distance away and was hurrying over toward them. Power exploded around Archon. His hammer vibrated in his hand.

"*Cora—!*" the demigod snarled.

He froze when he saw the figure behind Victor. His bellow made Theo jump.

"*OATHBREAKER!*"

"*Archon, no!*" Nildar yelled.

Theo blinked as a gust of wind buffeted him. Archon had vanished from his side.

"*Cassius!*" Morgan shouted.

"Let him go!" Victor growled.

Theo's stomach plummeted.

Archon had grabbed Cassius by the throat and smashed him into the facade of a building some fifty feet away. Black flames and inky wind wreathed with a dazzling, green light washed over the demigod's rust-colored armor as Morgan and Victor aimed their blades squarely at his neck.

Archon ignored the weapons, his features distorted with rage.

Theo swallowed as he and Nildar rushed over to the four demigods. It wasn't just rage he was reading on Archon's face.

"He said let him go, asshole!" Morgan ground out.

Victor's pupils flashed crimson.

"It's okay." Cassius's gaze remained locked on Archon's crunched-up face. "I deserve this."

Archon blinked. His lips curled back. He let go of his hammer, fisted his hand, and raised it to strike Cassius.

Theo's soul throbbed with a wave of such intense sorrow it brought tears to his eyes.

"Suspend!" he cried out.

Archon froze. He turned his head and met Theo's wild-eyed gaze. *"Your spells do not work on other Guardians, little one."* He glared at Cassius. *"Give me one good reason why I should not knock your teeth out, Awakener!"*

A sad smile tilted Cassius's lips.

His pupils glowed. *"I have none, brother."*

Archon studied Icarus for a timeless moment, the emotions racing across his face making Theo's heart ache all over again. The demigod shuddered and closed his eyes briefly. His head drooped. He lowered his fist.

"If it were not for what the imp said, I would have turned you into the Toothless Awakener just now," he mumbled.

Cassius's lips twitched.

Archon narrowed his eyes at him. *"Are you laughing?!"*

"The Toothless Awakener has a certain ring to it," Cassius said lightly.

Archon smirked. He recovered and scowled again.

Cassius sobered. "Also, did you say something about an imp?"

The ground shook before Archon could reply. Theo stiffened, alarmed. Something heavy was navigating the adjacent street.

"It is alright," Nildar said as Morgan and Victor reached for their swords. *"They are friends."*

Theo's eyes widened at the mismatched group that rounded the corner. A giant, squishy, black-winged creature with curved horns, red eyes, an arrowhead-tipped tail, and the softest fur he had ever seen lumbered rapidly toward them. He was carrying three figures in Hazmat suits in his arms and was framed by an armored, female angel and a male demon, both wielding Stark Steel blades.

"*Why you—!*" the giant furball hissed. He dumped his load unceremoniously on the ground, grabbed Archon by the shoulder, and sent him flying across the road. "I didn't bring you here so you could kill him, asshole!"

Archon crashed into a lamp post and bent it clean in two. The demigod groaned and shook his head dazedly as he climbed to his feet.

"*Ow.*" He rubbed a spot on the back of his skull and glared at the creature. "*I was only greeting him, you stupid imp!*"

Nildar sighed. "*You were not, you liar.*"

The furball's scowl melted when he looked down at a stunned Cassius. He lifted the demigod gently and hugged him to his chest. "Are you okay? Did that beast hurt you?!"

"No, but your fur is kinda suffocating me," Cassius protested in a muffled voice, his face buried in a luscious fleece Theo itched to sink his fingers into.

"Oh! Sorry!"

Cassius gasped when the creature loosened his hold. He drew back and stared into the crimson eyes above him.

"Loki?!"

The creature's face fell. His lower lip wobbled. "I'm ugly, right? Lilaia said you would love me whatever shape I took, but no one could possibly like a Gargantua!"

He sniffed, giant tears glimmering in his eyes. One fat drop splattered onto Cassius's head and drenched his hair through.

"What the hell is going on?!" Morgan hissed at Victor.

The demon shrugged, equally flummoxed.

He turned to Nildar. "Is that really the imp?"

The demigod scratched his head. *"Yeah. It seems he did not know he was a Gargantua. They do not usually manifest their full form unless they are heavily provoked and possess enough divine energy to shapeshift."*

He gave Archon a jaundiced look as the redhaired demigod joined them.

"What?" Archon said defensively.

Theo startled as the furry giant shrank down into a smaller version of himself before shapeshifting into a black cat with ochre irises. He sat on the ground and meowed forlornly at Cassius.

Cassius picked him up. "Lilaia is right. Your new form just surprised me." He tickled the cat under the chin. "I will love you whatever shape you're in, you stupid imp."

The cat's pupils dilated. He purred, closed his eyes, and headbutted Cassius's chest lovingly.

One of the Hazmatted figures peeled their respirator off their head with a gasp. It was a pretty blonde with hazel eyes. She shook out her hair and ran a hand through the messy strands, her face somewhat pale.

"Not that all of this isn't incredibly touching, but how about we go somewhere else and have this chat?"

She glanced around nervously. Her gaze landed on the remains of the Cyclops. Her mouth rounded on a shocked O. She pointed a trembling finger. *"What the hell is that?!"*

"It is a Cyclops," Nildar said calmly. *"One of the most fearsome monsters in the Seventh Hell."* He gave Theo an admiring look that made him flush. *"There are not many even among demigods who can hold their own against one for so long."*

Morgan gaped at the blonde.

"Adrianne?!" he spluttered. He swore when the other two figures removed their respirators, revealing a blond guy with blue eyes and an ashen faced young man about the same age as Theo with dark hair and gray eyes. His gaze shifted to the angel and demon who landed beside them. "How—*how did you guys get here?!*"

Adrianne cocked a thumb at the black cat. "We hitched a ride on the imp."

The dark-haired guy went distinctly green. He gagged, turned around, and threw up.

"Is Charlie okay?" Cassius asked worriedly as the blond guy squatted and patted the other man's back.

Blond Guy grimaced. "We saw a glimpse of the Seventh Hell on the way here, so, no." Lines wrinkled his brow as he studied Theo. "Who's the kid?"

"I think that's the new Guardian," the female angel said guardedly.

The demon observed Theo with similar caution.

Theo chewed his lip and stared at Loki, his heart pounding for a whole other reason.

"Can I, er, hold him?" he asked Cassius.

Loki blinked his eyes open.

Cassius's face softened. "Sure."

Loki stayed limp while Cassius handed him to Theo. Theo gently hugged the cat to his chest and buried his face in his fur.

"So soft," he whispered.

Loki's eyes rounded. He licked Theo's cheek tentatively, a purr rumbling from his chest.

Morgan dug an elbow in Victor's ribs and smirked. "Looks like it's love at first sight. That imp sure has a way with those Guardians, huh?"

Victor cast an irritated glance at his brother and lowered his brows at Loki. "That imp should learn his place."

"Now you know how I feel," Morgan grunted.

CHAPTER THIRTY-FIVE

"*Do I have something on my face?*" Nildar asked.

"No," Cassius replied.

Nildar blinked. "*Then why do you keep staring at me?*"

"You're much prettier than what I saw of you in Icarus's memories," Cassius said bluntly.

Color painted pink flags on the East Star's cheeks. Morgan curled his lips in disgust.

"Christ," Victor grunted. "They might as well start a fan club."

He glowered at the four Guardians as he went about straightening up various items in his office. All he wanted to do was drag Theo into his apartment, strip him naked, and check him over for wounds. Intimately. Alas, he knew the chances of that happening any time soon were close to zero.

Theo was currently holding Loki and looked like he never intended to let the damn cat go. Loki was purring and swinging his tail with the languid pride of a king atop a throne where he lay curled up on Theo's lap, his ochre gaze mocking as he blinked innocently at Victor. Archon was watching the pair with an expression that flitted from big brotherly love to murderous irritation at the intruder in their midst.

"*You have changed, Icarus,*" Nildar said sourly. "*And I know exactly who is to blame.*" The demigod narrowed his eyes at Morgan. "*You were never this shameless before Ivmir seduced you.*"

"Why do I feel like we're in some kind of soap drama?" Adrianne muttered.

"That's because we are," Bailey said drily.

The door opened. Zach, Julia, and Charlie returned from where they'd been helping assess the damage to the Cabalista headquarters, Delphine and Levi in their wake.

"The building will hold," Julia said confidently. "I've reinforced the foundations just in case."

Zach dipped his chin curtly at Victor. "Your team did a great job keeping everyone safe. Bar the woman who tried to run out of the building, there were no fatalities among the humans."

"How's Rosemary?" Victor asked Levi.

The demon made a face. "She's holding up well considering she faced up to a hellbeast."

"And your wings?"

Delphine smiled. "Already healed."

Levi flexed a pinion.

They regrouped around the seating area in the office.

Victor's gaze swept over Nildar, Archon, and Morgan's team. "We heard a little about how you came to be here." He glanced at Loki. "Care to tell us how you managed to force your way into the Seventh Hell?"

Delphine and Levi shifted uneasily where they stood by a bookcase. Rumors were already spreading through the agencies and the British government about their current location. Not that there was much anyone could do about it right now. Panicking was not going to get them out of the Seventh Hell.

Nildar started by recounting what he and Archon had discovered in the Nether a day or so ago and the vision he had had when he'd touched the soul fragment in Rohengar's palace. Theo's face grew dazed when he described the two fused souls he'd felt in the fragment.

Archon related how they'd left the Nether and skirted abandoned sections of other realms using temporary rifts. It had taken several attempts through an unstable black hole, including the one where they'd caught a glimpse of Cassius, Morgan, and London the night before, before they'd reached Earth.

Julia took over and gave them a curtailed account of their encounter with Nildar and Archon, and the discussions that had led to Loki's assertion about what he could feel through the barrier.

Cassius's eyes widened. "Loki used the Eternity Key to tear a path through to the Seventh Hell?"

He stared at the imp. Loki let out a pleased meow.

Cassius swallowed. "I mean, I knew he could detect the location of realms, but I didn't know he could create a doorway between them."

"He needs a lot of divine energy to tear open a portal," Nildar explained. *"We gave him some of ours."*

Cassius faltered. "His Gargantua shape. He's never manifested it before. Why now?"

Loki stiffened, his gaze turning to Nildar and Archon. Theo stroked him reassuringly.

"Bree—I mean, Julia told us he has been living with you for some time," Archon said gruffly. *"You have probably been feeding him your divine energy without your knowledge."*

Everyone stared at Loki. His tail stopped swinging.

Bailey squinted. "So, he's like some kind of divine energy sucking vampire kitty?"

Loki's tail drooped.

"He doesn't mean it," Cassius told the imp hurriedly.

"There, there," Theo crooned.

He patted Loki's head gently and narrowed his eyes at Bailey.

Victor resisted the urge to go over, wrench the imp from Theo's arms, and march the newly awakened demigod into the apartment to teach him exactly whom he belonged to. He blinked, shocked by the direction his thoughts had just taken.

Shit. This soulmate bond is something else. No wonder Morgan always looked like he wanted to rip my heart out!

He glanced at his younger brother with newfound respect. Morgan gave him a puzzled look.

"Lilaia said something drew her east too?" Cassius said uneasily.

Adrianne dipped her chin.

Nildar frowned. *"Now, tell us what happened in this city."*

Theo spoke of how he had been recruited out of the

blue by the man who would turn out to be Elios in human guise and the strange experiences he'd undergone since he'd come to London. Nildar stiffened when he described the attack in the alley that had preceded his first awareness of Rohengar.

Archon clenched his jaw as Victor took over and recounted his encounter with Elios and Theo at the hotel and how his instincts had driven him to seek them out. Divine energy pulsed from the West Star when Victor described what he'd found when he'd broken inside the suite.

"*Elios tried to violate you?!*" the West Star growled at Theo.

Theo flushed. "He—he wasn't successful. Victor saved me."

Theo's expression as he looked over at Victor had his blood stirring. Suspicion dawned on Nildar's face. His narrowed gaze swung between the two of them.

"Wait," Delphine mumbled, pale-faced. She was staring at Victor. "You're a demigod too?! Is that why you manifested those black flames and wings?!"

Levi frowned. "What black flames and wings?"

Victor steeled himself. This was the moment he'd been dreading ever since he'd recalled who he truly was. He stood up and unleashed his demigod form.

Levi gasped and stumbled back. A muscle jumped in Delphine's jawline as she drew herself to her full height, her fingers twitching at her sides.

"I am Coraos, half-brother to Ivmir, Elios, and Hypnos," Victor said quietly. "I fought by Elios's side during the War in the Nether."

Demonic power surged around Delphine and Levi. Their pupils flared crimson as they manifested their armor and weapons.

"*Coraos?!*" Levi spat out. "You're *Coraos?!*"

Theo jumped to his feet, divine power brightening his skin.

Another's radiance bloomed across the room, overtaking his.

CHAPTER THIRTY-SIX

DELPHINE AND LEVI FROZE AS THEY BEHELD ICARUS'S divine form.

"*Hear me well, sister and brother who fought alongside me. Though Coraos did indeed side with Elios, know that he was duped into it. Elios knew that if Coraos joined our ranks, he would lose the War. That is why he spent centuries cajoling him and lying to him. He convinced Coraos that he would win my heart if he killed my lover Ivmir.*" Cassius glanced at Morgan before he shifted his seraphic gaze to Theo, his expression poignant. "*And he disposed of Rohengar, the South Star, because he knew it would hurt the Guardians of the Nether and break our spirit.*"

Cassius shuddered as he retracted his powers. His gray gaze locked on a stunned Delphine and Levi. Nildar and Archon fisted their hands, their faces equally wretched.

"So, do not blame Victor. I have long forgiven him and so has Morgan."

Delphine closed her eyes briefly. Levi visibly deflated. Their armor and weapons vanished.

"If it's any consolation, we made bets on who would be the first one to punch him when we found out who he was," Julia told them wryly, indicating Zach.

Victor made a face. "You did?"

"Yup," Zach grunted. "Unfortunately, Cassius overheard us and said he would tan our hides if we did anything to you."

Cassius sighed.

He explained how he'd sensed Rohengar's soul and been drawn to London. He and Morgan described the beam of light they had witnessed, how they'd helped Victor fight off the monsters and hellbeasts that had invaded the hotel, and how Cassius had subsequently closed the dozen portals that had opened around the city.

Archon and Nildar traded a tense look in the lull that followed. Victor stiffened at the dread growing in the depths of their eyes.

"What's wrong?" Cassius said, his tone reflecting Victor's unease.

"*I think I understand why Elios fed Theo that poison to hasten his soul awakening,*" Nildar said in a brittle voice.

A fraught silence filled the room.

"Tell me," Theo whispered, seraphic light flashing in his pupils.

Nildar took a shallow breath and gazed at Cassius and Theo. "*You have likely lost your memories of this and it seems Rohengar does not remember either. New Guardians must awaken in the Nether.*"

Victor's skin prickled.

"New Guardians have to undergo intensive training before they awaken," Archon explained. *"The Nether is the only realm that can sustain the violent outbursts of power their soul cores release while they are still maturing. The only beings stronger in Heaven and all the Hells than a newly awakened Guardian is the Awakener themself and the First God who breathed life into all the realms."*

"Legend has it that the Nether was once a single floating continent," Nildar said. *"The first generation of Guardians who trained there wrecked the place so much they smashed it into thousands of airborne isles."*

"Unlike us, who are simply demigods, they were Primordial Gods," Archon grunted. *"They were the ones who created the Nether after they banished Chaos to the Abyss."*

Victor's pulse raced. Though he didn't like it one bit, he could tell where this was going. Judging from Cassius and Morgan's frozen expressions, they'd guessed the truth of the matter already.

"What happens if a Guardian awakens in another realm?" Theo mumbled.

Nildar faltered.

"At best, it can cause an interdimensional fracture that will open it up to the Abyss," he said quietly. *"At worst, it will destroy it."*

Cassius flinched. Morgan swore.

The blood drained from Theo's face. Victor finally surrendered to his instincts and went over to him. Eyebrows shot up around the room as he laid a proprietary hand on the new demigod's shoulder. Theo shuddered and clasped his fingers, his own trembling.

Archon and Nildar narrowed their eyes at their interlinked hands.

Victor ignored their disapproving looks, his pulse racing. *So, that was Elios's plan all along? To force Theo to tear open the Abyss with his awakening powers?!*

"Those explosions of light I kept having," Theo said in a frail voice. "That was my soul core being forced to awaken? You're saying I'm—" he swallowed and indicated the gloom outside the windows with a vague wave, "I'm the one responsible for this disaster?!"

His tone rose to a panicked shrill.

Cassius shook his head vehemently. "No, Theo." He left his seat, knelt by Theo's chair, and gently touched his leg. "It's Elios who's responsible for what happened. You did nothing wrong."

Loki meowed worriedly. He sat up and carefully licked Theo's chin. Theo trembled and hugged the cat to his chest.

"Then those portals that opened last night and the barrier around the city are all the same phenomena?" Morgan frowned. "They're interdimensional fractures?"

"But you ended up in the Seventh Hell," Julia said, confused. She looked around the room. "Shouldn't London have relocated to the Abyss or imploded?"

Nildar rubbed his chin, equally puzzled. *"I do not understand either. You should all be dead, either way."*

"Jeez, thanks," Delphine mumbled.

Cassius drew a sharp breath. His gaze locked on Theo's ashen face.

"That's why Rohengar merged his soul with yours!" he said dazedly. "He tempered your awakening. He knew you were the next South Star, so he bound himself to you and stayed cognizant so he could control your outbursts to an extent!"

Theo's mouth rounded.

Nildar blinked. He slammed his fist in his palm. *"You are right!"*

An electric buzz filled the room.

"This barrier, though." Archon furrowed his brow. *"It is more than an interdimensional fracture."* This earned him a battery of puzzled stares. He ignored them and turned to Nildar. *"You felt it too, when we breached it with the imp, did you not?"*

Nildar hesitated. He looked at Theo, a muscle jumping in his jawline.

Victor tensed. "What is it?"

"What Archon is alluding to is the fact that the barrier that formed when this city was ripped from Earth should not be there," Nildar said. *"It is a shield. One that is meant to protect what is within it from external forces. In this case, that is Elios and the Seventh Hell."*

"Our titles represent our powers," Archon explained to the stunned room. *"Icarus, the North Star. Awakener and wielder of the Light of Heaven or the first Primordial Light. Nildar, the East Star. Seer and wielder of the divine bow Sky Piercer. Archon, the West Star. Beast and wielder of the war hammer Echo."* He turned to Theo, a crooked smile curving his lips. *"And last but not least, Rohengar, the*

South Star. Master of Time Spells, Dimensional Portals, and Shields, and wielder of the Spear of Light."

"You are the reason everyone did not die, Theo," Nildar said quietly. *"You moved London from its intended location in the Abyss to the closest realm you could find in that moment and you shielded it even as you ripped open the fracture. Both you and Rohengar saved the people of this city."*

Tears tumbled down Theo's face.

Victor came around his chair and squatted beside him. He wiped Theo's cheeks tenderly with his thumbs and crushed him to his chest, his heart twisting at the way the young demigod trembled in his arms.

He wished he could take him away from the living nightmare they currently found themselves in. But he couldn't do that. So, instead, Victor told Theo the words he needed to hear.

"It's okay. It's gonna be okay, Theo."

Theo clung to him, his tears soaking into his shirt.

"Hey, are Victor and the new guy—?" Levi muttered to Delphine.

"Don't rock that boat," Delphine mumbled as a turbulent, seraphic glow erupted around Archon and Nildar. "Two pissed-off demigods might go off like a bomb."

"Ten bucks says Archon loses it first," Bailey wagered.

CHAPTER THIRTY-SEVEN

CASSIUS SHIVERED SLIGHTLY WHERE HE STOOD ON THE rooftop of Cabalista. The scarlet lightning rippling through the dark clouds above had intensified and the stench of sulfur drenching the air was strong once more. He stared worriedly at the churning firmament, Nildar's words from earlier echoing in his skull.

"*I do not know how long the barrier Theo created will hold,*" the East Star had told them. "*It is unstable and will likely fall soon. When it does, there is an equal chance this city will end up in the Seventh Hell or the Abyss.*"

"*What of the humans?*" Archon had said as everyone exchanged troubled looks. "*Your streets are empty of life. Where have they all gone?*"

"We decided the safest place for them for now was underground," Victor had replied. "We have teams of otherworldly and magic users guarding the entrances and exits to all tube stations in Inner London."

"*They will not survive when the city truly ends up in the Hells,*" Archon had said gruffly in the face of their growing dismay. "*Only the otherworldly will have a fighting chance of escaping that disaster.*" He waved a vague hand. "*Of course, if it is the Abyss it falls into, no one will survive.*"

Cassius's soul core throbbed. Strong arms slipped around his waist. A familiar scent filled his senses and soothed his unsettled heart.

"What are you thinking about?" Morgan said quietly.

Cassius leaned his back against Morgan's chest and clutched his arms closer. "What can we do to save them?" His tone turned brittle. "What can we do to save this city, Morgan? Nildar said we couldn't move all those people in time even if Loki tore another route through to Earth. And we don't have enough Hazmat suits for everyone."

"I don't know," Morgan murmured. "But we'll come up with something. We always do."

He pressed a kiss to Cassius's hair.

"I'm not sure about that," Cassius said bitterly. "I get the feeling we won't be able to save the day this time."

Morgan turned him around and cradled his face in his hands. "What can I do to make you feel better?" His gaze grew heated. He glanced around the empty rooftop. "How about we—?"

"We are *not* having sex on the rooftop of Cabalista!" Cassius snapped.

Morgan made a face. "You sure know how to ruin the mood, Awakener."

The heavy mantle that had weighed Cassius down lifted a little. He pressed his mouth impulsively to

Morgan's. Morgan yanked him closer and proceeded to deepen the kiss until Cassius's senses fairly swam.

The air rippled with a faint pulse of power.

They froze and stared into each other's eyes before wrenching their lips apart and gazing stiffly in the direction it had come from.

Cassius's pulse quickened. The river was glowing with a pale light.

Morgan lowered his brows. "What the hell is that?!"

They transformed into their demigod forms and grasped their blades. The rooftop door slammed open behind them as everyone else headed up top.

"Is it another breach in the barrier?" Theo asked anxiously, Victor at his side.

Loki leapt from Theo's arms and darted to the edge of the roof. He braced his front paws on the lower ledge, transformed into his small imp form, and glanced at them over his shoulder, his eyes bright with excitement.

"That's a portal to another realm!" He sniffed the air. "That's—!"

"Rain Vale," Cassius whispered, his heart hammering against his ribs.

Morgan looked at him, confused.

Cassius swallowed. He didn't know why or how he knew this. He just did. Because a singular word was resonating through the very core of him at what he could taste on the wind.

Home!

"*Something is coming,*" Nildar warned.

He and Archon took to the sky as metal glinted in the distance.

The being that grew closer smelled of the earth and an unspoiled forest. Though she was dressed in armor from the neck down and had a broadsword strapped to her back and a battle helmet on her head, Cassius recognized her nature.

A lush carpet of greenery exploded under the Nymph's boots as she landed on the rooftop, the water dripping down her armor soaking into it. Her eyes rounded behind her visor when she saw Cassius. She removed her helmet hastily and dropped to one knee, her rich, wet, auburn hair tumbling down her back.

"It is good to see you again, Awakener." The Nymph pressed her fist to her chest and bowed respectfully. She raised her head slightly, her green eyes glittering as her gaze hungrily roamed his face. "It is good to see you, Prince Icarus!"

Cassius's breath caught at the title she'd called him. He flinched, pain gripping his temples as Hypnos's spell activated to suppress another memory when it tried to resurface. He gritted his teeth.

Morgan clasped his hand, apprehension dawning on his face.

"*Galatea?!*" Nildar gasped.

He and Archon dropped down before the warrior Nymph.

Her eyes widened. "East Star? West Star?!" She bolted to her feet. "You are here too?!"

"Did she just call Cassius Prince Icarus?!" Julia hissed at Zach.

The demon nodded numbly.

"How did you get here?" Nildar's gaze shifted dazedly to the glowing river.

"We have tried to find a route to Rain Vale for eons but never could," Archon said stiffly.

"I don't have time to go into the details," Galatea said curtly. "Suffice to say a portal opened to guide me to the Awakener and the new South Star. Or, more precisely, to guide the remnant of the Spear of Light." She reached inside her armor and removed a thick, velvet pouch. A shard of dazzling light tumbled into her palm as she upended it. "It was roused two days ago," she explained at their stunned expressions. "That's how we knew a new South Star had likely been born!"

"How? How is it that you have that in your possession?!" Nildar asked, shocked. *"We thought it lost during the War!"*

Archon was staring at the radiant shard as if he'd seen a ghost.

Theo approached Galatea in a daze, his gaze locked on the fragment. Light flared in his pupils and around his body. The shard responded to his divine power, its pulses of brightness matching the beat of Theo's heart and souls.

Galatea stared.

"Are you the new South Star?" she said breathlessly.

Cassius startled as Theo's irises shifted from green to a hauntingly familiar sapphire. His heart thudded painfully against his ribs. Nildar and Archon paled.

"*Hello, Galatea,*" Rohengar said gently through Theo's lips.

Cassius's belly twisted. Sorrow and wonder washed across Nildar and Archon's faces.

Galatea gaped. "Ro—*Rohengar?!*"

Tears bloomed in her beautiful eyes and tumbled down her cheeks. She launched herself at Theo and almost took him to the ground. Theo laughed in Rohengar's voice and hugged her back.

"My Queen will be so happy to see you!" Galatea whispered, her voice breaking.

"*So will I.*" Theo blinked, his irises returning to their usual shade. He squeezed Galatea closer. "So will we."

Galatea cleared her throat and stepped back. "This is yours." She slipped the shard of light back in its velvet pouch, pressed it into Theo's hands, and studied him and Cassius with a fierce expression. "We must make haste and return to Rain Vale before the portal closes." She glanced at Nildar and Archon. "You will accompany us, East and West Stars!"

"What?" Morgan snapped.

"We're coming with you," Victor growled.

Galatea made a face at Morgan. "I see you're still your truculent self, Ivmir." She squinted at Victor. "Wait." Her jaw hardened. "Is that Coraos?!"

Her hand rose menacingly to the pommel of her sword.

"It's okay!" Cassius said hastily. "He's on our side."

Galatea hesitated, still suspicious. "Are you sure, my prince? That dark demigod has fooled us before."

Victor's brows drew together.

"Everybody kinda hates you on sight, huh?" Loki told Victor sympathetically.

"Shut up," the demigod muttered.

A violent shimmer rippled above the river.

Galatea startled, her head swinging around to stare at it. "It's closing! We must go, *now!*"

She rose on a burst of wind. Cassius unleashed his wings and took to the air with Theo, Nildar, and Archon. He knew without asking that they were all feeling the same thing right now.

Something was calling them to the river.

Is this what Lilaia felt? Did she somehow sense Rain Vale close by, through the broken borders that separate our realms?!

"Hold the fort while we're gone!" Cassius called down to Morgan and Victor as they followed Galatea to the river.

"The barrier will hold for a while yet!" Nildar yelled. *"The imp should be able to close any breaches from the Seventh Hell with the Eternity Key if you feed him your powers!"*

Frustration tightened Morgan's face as he watched them leave. He shrank to a dim shadow that soon vanished in the gloom atop the Cabalista headquarters.

Cassius's heart throbbed at the separation. He steeled himself and turned to face forward. Rain Vale held the answers he wanted right now. And that was where he needed to be.

CHAPTER THIRTY-EIGHT

"*That was disgusting!*" Archon said with a shudder as he walked out of the lake.

"Tell me about it," Galatea grumbled. She stopped in the shallows and squatted to douse her head and face with the crystal-clear lake water. "I had to go through that damn cesspit twice. What do humans put in their rivers to make them so foul?!"

"You don't wanna know," Theo mumbled, wiping his wet hair back with a hand.

Nildar removed the reeds that had clung to his armor at the bottom of the lake, upended his quiver, and shook water from his wings.

They'd emerged upon the lakeshore outside a magnificent, walled city. Pale towers rose beyond the tall ramparts to a clear, blue sky where colorful birds whirled and danced on thermals. The hustle and bustle of a busy metropolis drifted on a faint breeze that carried the rich smell of the verdant realm that stretched out around them as far as the eye could see.

Galatea's face softened at the sight of Cassius's expression. "Welcome back to Rain Vale, Prince Icarus."

Cassius stared unblinkingly at the landscape before him, his heart in his throat. Though he could not recall the time he had spent here, he knew it was the place of his birth and the kingdom he had once called his home. The sheer joy swelling inside his soul and the power of the land beneath his feet were telling him so.

He looked over at Nildar and Archon, his pulse racing. "Did you know?"

"*That you were a prince of this land?*" Archon scratched his cheek awkwardly. "*We did.*"

Nildar's face grew contrite. "*I am sorry, Icarus. It never even dawned on us to tell you about your past.*"

Theo's bedazzled gaze shifted to a low hill to the right. It rose on the edge of the forest that encircled the shallow valley the city of Isyanore stood in. Some kind of monument crowned its summit.

One of the guards monitoring the checkpoint at the city gates spotted them. He signaled to a soldier atop the wall. A horn sounded a moment later.

"Better brace yourself, Prince." Galatea patted Cassius on the shoulder and started making her way toward the capital. "She's going to cry enough tears to fill a lake."

Cassius stared before following, Theo, Nildar, and Archon falling in step. "Who's gonna—?"

More horns exploded across the city, drowning out the rest of his words.

Theo kept glancing at the hill as they approached the gates. Cassius couldn't help but look at it too. He could feel something drawing him there. It was the same sensation he'd experienced when he'd been on the other side of the river portal, in London. Nildar and Archon frowned faintly, their expressions reflecting the same confusion as they stared at the distant monument.

A faint vibration shook the ground. Cassius slowed, startled. He looked to the gates. A grand avenue was visible beyond them. It seemed to lead straight to the palace at the center of the city.

A cavalry was charging down it at full gallop, the hooves of their mounts raising sparks as they struck the paved boulevard.

Leading the guards, her red cape flowing behind her, her dress riding high on her booted legs, was a beautiful Nymph with long, blonde hair that flowed like a field of wheat behind her. A gold crown glittered on her head as she urged her stallion forward, a focused frown on her brow.

Cassius's mouth grew dry. Icarus's presence bloomed inside him.

I know her!

The guards manning the gates bowed as she shot past them. The Nymph drew up sharply some dozen feet from where Cassius and the others stood. Galatea winced as she jumped down from her rearing horse and rushed ahead of the cavalry coming to a stamping stop behind her. The guards, a mix of Nymphs and Potamois, dismounted and lined up rigidly in file.

"Welcome back, Captain!" a Nymph at the front shouted.

Galatea dipped her head. "At ease."

The guards relaxed slightly, their gazes sweeping the Guardians with awe. Many froze when they saw Cassius. Frenzied murmurs broke out among the troop.

"It's the prince! *Prince Icarus has returned to us!*"

Galatea narrowed her eyes. The guards flinched and went silent.

The Nymph with the crown had stopped a short distance from Cassius, her deep blue gaze roaming his face as if she could not quite believe he was truly there. Her face crumpled. Her eyes took on a wet sheen.

"Here come the tears," Galatea warned in a low mumble.

"Icarus!"

The Nymph threw herself at Cassius and almost took him to the ground. Cassius stumbled back a step, steadied them both, and closed his arms around her as she sobbed violently, her face buried in his chest.

Her scent filled his nostrils, so familiar it choked his breath. His soul core throbbed at what he sensed. Sorrow squeezed his heart, drawing a tortured gasp from his lips. Cassius tightened his hold on the crying Nymph, not wanting to let go either.

She was of his bloodline. She was kin.

She was the sister he had lost.

Memories flashed before his eyes for precious seconds, before the agony of Hypnos's spell gripped his mind and made him clench his jaw.

He saw a small girl with ash-blonde hair and a little boy with dark blond locks playing in an orchard behind the castle, their laughter loud and their faces beaming as they chased one another beneath trees that dappled them with shadows. He saw them sharing meals and baths and even a bed on the nights thunder and lightning drove the little girl to seek the boy's warmth and the comforting words that would allay her fear of the storm until she fell asleep. He saw them as older children studying in a vast hall of books, making faces and throwing paper birds at each other behind the backs of their tutors. He saw them as teenagers clashing swords in a drill hall and competing with each other in hunting contests.

Cassius's pulse stuttered at the final glimpse he caught of the pair. They were now adults and were strolling the corridors of the palace while they debated something with animated expressions, thin, gold crowns on their heads and their attendants trailing a short distance behind them.

It was him and the Nymph in his arms.

The pair of them stopped and grinned when another figure with a crown drifted into view. Cassius stiffened. Though he had his back to him in the vision, he recognized the man's rich, black hair. The stranger turned slightly, offering Cassius a heartrending view of a sapphire-blue eye and a dazzling smile.

Rohengar?!

The Nymph lifted her head and gazed at him, her cheeks flushed.

"Carus!" She raised trembling fingers to his cheeks. "My Carus! Oh how I have missed you, brother!"

Cassius shuddered at the hauntingly familiar pet name.

Something broke through Hypnos's spell. Letters that strained to form a name. He willed them on despite the pain tearing through his skull.

"Kalli," Cassius mumbled hoarsely. "Kallis…te…"

The Nymph's features crumpled once more. She locked her arms around his neck and squeezed tighter. "You remember!"

Nildar sighed. *"You are going to choke your brother to death, Kalliste."*

Kalliste peered over Cassius's shoulder. "Nildar! Archon!"

Archon grinned. *"Hello, little mouse."*

Kalliste stepped out of Cassius's arms and went over to hug them. "It has been too long, Guardians!"

"I see you have become a fine queen, Kalliste," Nildar said warmly. *"Rain Vale thrives under your rule."*

Galatea indicated Theo solemnly. "My Queen, this is the new South Star."

Kalliste froze. She stared at Theo, the color staining her cheekbones bright as she paled a little.

She recovered her composure and curtseyed. "Welcome to Rain Vale, South Star. I am sure you have many questions."

Seraphic light bloomed in Theo's pupils. His irises shifted to sapphire.

"It has been a long time, Kalliste," Rohengar said, his voice quavering slightly.

Kalliste's head jerked up. Her mouth rounded to a shocked O.

Galatea sniffed, her own eyes wet again.

Kalliste brought a trembling hand to her mouth. "Rohengar!" Another sob left her. *"Rohengar!"*

She flung herself at Theo. He closed his eyes and held her close, radiant tears glimmering on his lashes.

Archon coughed a little and turned around, his shoulders quivering.

"Are you crying?" Nildar asked.

"Shut up," Archon mumbled.

CHAPTER THIRTY-NINE

"So, that is what happened after the Nether tore." Kalliste sat back heavily in her chair, her tone numb and her features drawn.

Galatea looked similarly stunned where she stood by Kalliste's chair, her hand unconsciously gripping the backrest. They were in Kalliste's private chambers, in the palace of Isyanore.

A dull clamor reached them on the breeze that fluttered the curtains on the balcony. News of Icarus's return and the Guardians' arrival had spread through the capital.

Cassius had just given Kalliste and Galatea an abbreviated account of the aftermath of the War in the Nether and the Fall, the memory loss all those who had tumbled to Earth and the affected otherworldly in other realms had suffered due to Hypnos's powers, and the machinations he and Morgan had subsequently uncovered by the God of Darkness at the source of it all.

"The human city we just traveled from is currently suspended in the Seventh Hell?!" Galatea gasped.

"*Yes.*" Nildar frowned. "*And it will soon either fall there completely or tumble into the Abyss.*"

Kalliste tapped a finger on the armrest of her chair, a thoughtful frown creasing her brow. "I think there might be a way to save it."

Cassius's stomach clenched at her words. "There is?!"

"Yes." Kalliste dipped her head firmly. "It will take you and Theo to do it."

Cassius and Theo exchanged a surprised look.

Kalliste's expression grew determined. "But first, I need to tell you about your past. Our grandmother was Nephele, the first Queen and Goddess of the Nymphs. Arielle, our mother, was a demigod who bore three children. The eldest was Rohengar, sired with Adohr, a Primordial God of Summer. The middle child is you, Icarus. Your sire was Aether, the elusive Primordial God of Light." She pressed a hand to her chest. "And I am the youngest, sired by Ismene, the demigod Potamoi our mother finally married and made her royal consort."

Cassius's mouth went dry. He blinked, dazed.

Our grandmother was the first Queen of the Nymphs?!

"Rohengar was to inherit the throne as eldest. He spent a lot of his time traveling in and outside our kingdom to learn to be the kind of ruler our grandmother and mother were, and to reinforce our existing alliances in other realms, as well as form fresh ones." Kalliste smiled faintly. "Did you know the two of you were the most sought-after bachelors in all the realms? Grandmother and mother had to beat off many princesses and queens who asked for your hands in marriage after you came of age." A low chuckle left her. "There were even kings seeking to take you as consorts, so besotted were they with your beauty."

Theo bit his lip. Cassius grimaced.

Kalliste laughed. "Those are the exact expressions you and Rohengar had when one of Arielle's attendants let that fact slip!"

"We should tell Ivmir and Coraos this story," Archon told Nildar with a hint of glee.

Cassius rolled his eyes. Theo sighed.

Kalliste's smile faded to a small frown. "Alas, all of Rohengar's carefully laid plans came to an end the day his demigod soul core awakened and he became a Guardian candidate."

Cassius's pulse quickened. "So, we aren't born Guardians?!"

It was Nildar who answered. *"No. Guardian candidates are very rare. They only come about every few millennia, when it is time for an existing Guardian to retire. They can originate in any realm—"* Nildar glanced at Theo, *"although I must admit it is the first time a human has been chosen to be a Guardian."*

"I am from a desert realm of nomadic deities, whereas Nildar comes from a realm of forest Gods," Archon explained.

"A Guardian normally awakens after they come of age," Kalliste explained. "We found that out when your soul core was roused too. Grandmother said two

Guardians awakening in the same realm within a few years of one another, *and* related by blood, was unheard of. Needless to say, she and Mother were pissed at losing both you and Rohengar to the Guardians who came to claim you as their successors."

Galatea shifted where she stood beside Kalliste's chair.

Guilt flashed on Kalliste's face at the captain's slightly disapproving look. "I mean, Grandmother and Mother were terribly upset." She squinted at Galatea. "There, happy now?"

"Mother would be ecstatic," Galatea murmured.

"Galatea's mother was my etiquette tutor," Kalliste explained morosely at Cassius and Theo's puzzled looks.

"If the portal to the Astrea Sea is ever fixed, your potential fiancé shall be visiting with a delegation," Galatea said coolly. "We cannot have you speaking so crudely in front of them, my Queen."

Kalliste lowered her brows. "Prince Astrid and his delegation can stick their offer of marriage where the sun does not shine, Galatea. I told you four hundred years ago that I wanted you as my consort. My resolve has never faltered since and neither will it do so in the future."

Archon's jaw dropped open. Nildar and Theo's eyes rounded.

Cassius found himself swallowing a grin. *Morgan would definitely like her.*

Galatea glanced at the Guardians and flushed. "My Queen, we are in company!"

"And the right kind," Kalliste snapped. "I care about these four as much as I care about you and our kingdom."

Galatea clenched her jaw and straightened to her full height. "I am not of royal blood. And I cannot give you an heir."

Kalliste fisted her hands, her expression stormy. "Are you saying all those nights you have spent in my bed mean nothing to you, Galatea?"

Theo sucked in air.

"Hmm," Cassius mumbled.

"*Maybe you two should talk about this in private,*" Nildar muttered awkwardly.

"*Hush, this is getting interesting!*" Archon hissed.

Kalliste ignored them. "I care little for royal bloodlines, Galatea. You know this more than most. If it is an heir you are concerned about, we can ask the Dryads if we can eat the fruit of Esnant and birth a child in their kingdom once we fix the portal to Ivory Peaks."

Cassius's heart thumped heavily in his chest. *The fruit of Esnant?!*

Galatea stared at her queen for long seconds. The fight visibly drained out of her. "You are *so* stubborn."

Kalliste beamed.

"Can you tell me more about Rohengar and the Spear of Light?" Theo said.

Kalliste's face softened at his hesitant expression. "Yes, I shall. Let's go somewhere first."

CHAPTER FORTY

A SOFT BREEZE TICKLED THEO'S CHEEKS WHEN THEY came out of the city moments later.

He inhaled deeply, the sweet scent of Rain Vale filling his lungs to bursting. Though he had been born on Earth, he could not help but feel that this was his home too.

"Both Rohengar and Icarus were identified as potential Awakeners?!" Cassius said, shocked.

Kalliste nodded as they headed briskly for the hill in the distance. "Yes. You both carried the Awakener seed within you. Yours was stronger than Rohengar's, which is why you were finally chosen for that role and Rohengar granted the seat of South Star. Rohengar's weapon, the Spear of Light, is the fifth divine pillar of the Book of Rain."

Warmth flared through Theo's belly and in his hand, where he held the pouch containing the dazzling shard Galatea had given him.

"The Book of Rain?" Cassius repeated.

Kalliste's expression hardened. "It is an elemental weapon that can draw on the very power of the universe itself. It is one of many artifacts that were used when the Gods of Heaven and the Hells and Chaos's own children fought to bring down the father of the Primordial Gods. From how our grandmother described it, the Book of Rain is the most powerful shield in the known universe and was used to protect all the realms from the destruction that was wreaked during the Holy War." She looked at Theo. "The Spear of Light, its fifth pillar, chose Rohengar as its liege before he left for the Nether. It granted him the gift of—"

"Master of Shields," Theo mumbled hoarsely.

Kalliste's eyes sparkled. "Yes."

"*Where are you taking us, Kalliste?*" Nildar asked guardedly.

Kalliste's expression grew sad. "To Rohengar's grave."

Theo's pulse stuttered. Cassius stopped in his tracks, the blood draining from his face just as it did Nildar and Archon's. Their gazes locked on the hill they were approaching and the monument atop it. Now that they were closer, they could see it was the figure of a man.

Theo's heart beat wildly in his chest as he scaled the slope with his newfound brothers and Kalliste.

"Rohengar," Cassius mumbled.

Tears glittered in his eyes as he stared at the statue growing before them. Made of marble with veins of colored quartz, it depicted a hauntingly beautiful man garbed in armor and holding a spear, his long hair falling to his waist.

Theo's gaze roamed the features of the one who should have been king of everything he could see. The one chosen by the Gods themselves for a most sacred role. A demigod who had dedicated and sacrificed his life to a cause greater than himself, for the brothers he loved, and the man he secretly cherished.

The weight of the unrequited feelings Rohengar had harbored for Coraos almost brought Theo to his knees as he stopped before the twenty-foot statue looking over Isyanore. He could not help the shame that twisted his gut at the thorn of doubt that had prickled his heart ever since Victor had realized where Rohengar's affections had lain.

Had Victor seen him, Theo the human, when they'd made love? Or had the passion he had shown him been for Rohengar, the demigod who had loved him in the past?

All the uncertainty he'd experienced faded as he gazed at Rohengar's statue, his face wet with tears. *I'm sorry, Rohengar. I'm sorry I took your place!*

A wind coursed through Rain Vale then. It stirred the forest around him and the grass beneath his feet, bringing with it a faint whisper.

He was always meant to be yours, Theo. Thank you for giving me the chance to meet him again...

"Are those graves?" Archon asked in a strained voice.

Theo looked down. His breath caught.

Hundreds of marble headstones were spread out across the hill beyond Rohengar's statue.

"Yes," Kalliste replied quietly. "They represent all those we lost when the Nether tore. Nymphs. Potamois. The angels and demons who did not survive their wounds from the War. They are all here."

"This is where Rohengar ended up when he fell?!" Cassius said shakily.

Nildar and Archon stared at Kalliste, similarly stunned.

Kalliste dipped her chin. "The Book of Rain drew Rohengar and what was left of the Spear of Light when I activated the artifact to protect Rain Vale."

Footsteps sounded behind them. They turned. Galatea was climbing the hill, a small, metal chest in hand.

Theo's soul core throbbed as he stared at it. A glow pierced the pouch containing the last remaining fragment of the Spear of Light.

Galatea handed the box to Kalliste. Divine light bloomed on Kalliste's fingers. She touched the lock. It opened with a soft click. She lifted the lid to reveal a glowing, blue book wrapped in an elaborate lattice of silver and gold.

"It has been a long time since I have seen this sight," Nildar said reverentially.

Kalliste removed the artifact from the chest and walked over to Rohengar's statue. "Come."

Theo exchanged a puzzled look with Cassius and the other Guardians before following.

A rectangular depression had been carved in the plinth, between Rohengar's feet. It was the exact size of the artifact Kalliste held. She placed the Book of Rain inside it and turned to Theo.

"Take out the fragment of the spear."

Theo blinked, confused. His belly thumped on a flare of heat. Light exploded in his hand. The shard within the pouch had grown incandescent and was shuddering as if it were in the grip of a violent fever. His pulse raced as he drew it out of the bag with trembling fingers.

It lit up the hill, making them squint.

The Book of Rain quivered. The clasp holding it shut came undone soundlessly. The tome opened, exposing the divine energy it contained.

Theo's body knew what he had to do before his mind did. He walked over and put the shard inside the book. For a moment, nothing happened.

Power rippled from the artifact in a sudden wave that boomed across the hill. It came again and again, shaking the ground beneath their feet and the trees in the forest. Rohengar's statue trembled. A radiance that threatened to sear the senses started emanating from the tome, accompanying each violent pulse of energy bursting from it.

"Draw the spear, Theo!" Kalliste shouted from where she and everybody else had been shoved back several feet by the unearthly force exploding from the artifact. "It is yours to wield!"

Theo swallowed, scared all of a sudden.

Rohengar's voice reached him. *Do not be afraid. The spear belongs to you as much as you belong to it...*

Theo clenched his jaw. Fire filled his veins as he

reached inside the Book of Rain. His fingers closed on something solid. Something that hummed and sang and roared with happiness when it felt his touch.

Theo's soul core went supernova. He shuddered as divine light poured out of him and lit the valley and forest beyond.

In that moment, he felt akin to a God.

A bellow left his throat as he drew the newly reborn Spear of Light. Wings sprouted on his back. Turquoise armor exploded on his body.

The Book of Rain closed with a snap, the divine brilliance pouring out of it flashing down to a simmering glow. Theo stared at the dazzling weapon in his hands where he now floated some dozen feet off the ground.

Unlike the ghostly spear he'd manifested when he'd fought the monsters and hellbeasts attacking Cabalista and the Cyclops who'd almost killed him, this one looked like it could carve a path through worlds.

A singular truth resonated inside him then. Each Guardian of the Nether bore a weapon that was intrinsically linked to their soul. If they died, so would the weapon. Yet a fragment of the spear had survived. And now he knew why.

Rohengar had bound the piece of his soul that had resided in his palace to his weapon as he fell to Rain Vale, to keep it alive. Theo could see this in the memories coursing through him from the reborn spear.

All that Rohengar had been and experienced and lived since the moment of his birth to his gruesome death flooded Theo's mind and heart. Radiant tears slipped down his face, awe and love and fury filling him in equal measure.

I will avenge you, Rohengar. As the new South Star, I will avenge you and honor all that you stood for!

"*Theo?!*"

Theo registered Cassius's presence where he floated before him in his demigod form. He looked beyond him to the ashen faces of Nildar and Archon.

"*Your eyes,*" Nildar mumbled.

"*What is the matter with—?*" Theo startled. His voice had the same musical inflection as Nildar's and the other Guardians'. He touched his face. "*Is something wrong with my eyes?*"

Archon shook his head and swallowed convulsively. "*No.*"

Cassius came over and hugged him. "*They are beautiful.*"

Theo closed his arms around the North Star. A storm of bittersweet feelings squeezed his heart. "*Brother!*"

Nildar and Archon joined them. A shudder shook Theo as he felt the embrace of the three demigods who shared his fate. They stayed like that for a long time, arms and wings wrapping them in a cocoon of love and warmth that replenished their starving souls.

They wiped glittering tears from their cheeks and smiled tremulously at one another when they finally let go.

Kalliste was blubbering in Galatea's chest when they landed on the ground. She rubbed her face on the sleeve of her dress and focused a fierce stare upon them.

"You must return to the Seventh Hell and save that city and your friends. *This* is what you have to do!"

Theo's heart thumped heavily while Kalliste described her plan. Nildar and Archon traded a startled look.

"Will that work?" Cassius asked, shocked.

Kalliste shrugged. "I can't see why not. Besides, you'll have Nildar and Archon's divine energy to draw upon. And there's the Eternity Key and the imp if you need them too."

Theo frowned. "But how do we open a doorway to the Seventh Hell?"

Kalliste smiled. "What do you think you're holding in your hand? You are the Master of Dimensional Portals and you wield the Spear of Light. If you can't open a doorway to where you wish to go, no one can."

Theo's stomach flipflopped. "Oh."

Kalliste pressed the Book of Rain into Cassius's hands. "Only those of Nephele's direct bloodline can wield this artifact. You must pour your power into it to manifest the shield. Use it well, brother. I shall entrust it to you for now."

Cassius nodded shakily. He faltered. "Will I see you again?"

Kalliste tilted her head to the side, a half-smile on her lips. "I don't see why not. Theo should be able to open a portal to any realm. And, if my suspicions are correct, the doorways between the realms may start to right themselves now that the Spear of Light and its master live again. I don't know if we will ever get to the stage of how things were before the Nether tore, but it should be a vast improvement on the current state of affairs."

Cassius's eyes rounded. "You mean—there might come a time when the Fallen could return to their realms?!"

Kalliste bobbed her head. "Possibly. And if they so wish."

Nildar and Archon looked at each other dazedly.

"We will be able to leave the Nether at will," Nildar mumbled.

"Yes." Archon sighed. *"Black holes are vastly overrated."*

Theo's fingers tightened on the Spear of Light. *Let's test Kalliste's theory!*

He took a shallow breath, drew on the new power pulsing through his core, and raised a hand. *"Dimensional Gate!"*

A shimmering, golden portal whispered to life in front of him. Inner London became visible through it. Theo's gut twisted in horror. Cassius swore.

They could see flames above the rooftops and monsters roaming the sky.

"Now go, Guardians!" Kalliste's mouth thinned as she observed the war being fought in the trapped city. "And if you see Elios, I hope you kick that God's ass so hard you give him a Stark Steel enema!"

"My Queen," Galatea groaned.

CHAPTER FORTY-ONE

"Watch out!" Morgan shouted.

Victor and Julia shot back. An enormous stone mace skimmed the space where they'd been a heartbeat ago, the slipstreams tugging at their wings. Morgan regrouped with them as they twisted around to face the Nephil.

It was the last of three giants who had invaded the city through a fracture in Theo's barrier.

The first one they had felled lay dead in the grounds of the Tower of London. The remains of the second floated in the River Thames, its blood slowly turning the waters a dark crimson.

Julia's breaths came in shallow pants as she observed the combat zone Inner London had become with a heavy scowl. "This place really has the worst luck, huh?!"

Explosions rocked the city as far as the eye could see. Despite the devastation, the army of otherworldly and magic users defending it appeared to be holding their own against the troop of beasts and monsters of the Seventh Hell that had breached its defenses.

Morgan glared at the blank-faced, crimson-eyed colossus before them. "First the Cyclops, now Nephilim. It's like those bastards were waiting for Cassius and the other Guardians to leave before attacking."

"It must be Elios." Julia gritted her teeth. "He must still be here, somewhere!"

Victor grasped his black-flame-wreathed broadsword tighter, pulse racing and dread a living thing eating at his insides.

"Cassius would have sensed him if he were in London." He glanced at the grotesque creatures clashing with angels, demons, and magic users in the avenues around them and the aerial battle taking place under the domed barrier. "Nildar was right. This shield is failing. I don't know how much longer we'll have before London falls into the Seventh Hell."

"Or the Abyss," Julia said glumly. "In which case, we'll never know. The lights will go out and that'll be that."

"Here he comes," Morgan warned.

The Nephil crushed a bus beneath his foot as he advanced toward them.

Considering how much it had taken out of Morgan, Bostrof, and him when they'd fought the Nephilim in the Sixth Hell, Victor was surprised they'd managed to slay the first two monsters before the latter could inflict catastrophic damage upon the city. He knew their success had to do with how well Morgan's team and his own worked together.

Lassoes of water slashed the air. They locked around the Nephil's left leg. Delphine, Zach, and four more Aqueous demons and angels grunted and braced their wings where they hovered behind the giant, their armor stained with the blood of the Nephilim they had helped slay.

Adrianne's offensive spellbombs smashed into the partly immobilized Nephil next, Bailey's defensive magic shielding her and Charlie from the monsters trying to attack them on the ground. Sweat beaded the enchanter's face as he weaved a dark spell. Thorns exploded into life around the Nephil's head, wrapping his eyes in a band of barbed foliage.

Wind locked the giant's stone mace in place as Levi and another Aerial demon attacked next.

"Now!" Victor barked.

The Sword of Wind hummed furiously as Morgan dove alongside him, Julia at their side. The Terrene angel raised the asphalt and the ground beneath the giant to entrap his other leg as she swooped low along the street. Alas, the soil was clay and held him for mere seconds before he smashed the manacle with the sheer momentum of his motion.

The Nephil ripped Charlie's enchantment from his eyes and freed himself of his aqueous and aerial shackles, his face still expressionless.

The distraction gave Morgan and Victor enough time to carve a cut in the side of his neck and slash his right Achilles tendon, Victor's black flames scorching a red track of burnt flesh across his calf.

Victor, Morgan, and Julia regrouped at a safe distance in the air and inspected the damage they had caused.

Julia scowled. "That's not gonna be enough to slow him down!"

She cast an anxious glance over her shoulder, a bead of perspiration dripping down her temple.

Charing Cross Station was a mere five hundred feet behind them along the Strand. A group of otherworldly and magic users were defending the barricade in front of its entrance.

If the Nephil reached them, thousands would die.

Adrianne's shout startled Victor. "Zach! Delphine!"

"Shit!" Morgan cursed.

The Nephil had focused his attention on the Aqueous demons.

Victor folded his wings and dove with Morgan and Julia.

The Nephil swung his mace, his motion lightning quick. Spellbombs and a violent windstorm bloomed as Adrianne, Bailey, and the Aerial demons launched a combined assault, Charlie's dark enchantment joining them to lock the Nephil's wrist in concrete.

The giant smashed through all their attacks.

Victor's gut clenched as he and Morgan accelerated, the wind whistling in his ears. *We're too late!*

Something big and black soared from an adjacent rooftop and snatched the two Aqueous demons from the air before the stone club could strike them. Victor rocked to a halt and stared, Morgan similarly drawing to a stop beside him.

Loki landed on the opposite building in his Gargantua form and deposited the stunned demons on the rooftop. He rose and bared his teeth at the Nephil.

"That little shit!" Morgan swore. "We told him to stay at the Cabalista headquarters!"

Horror widened Julia's eyes.

"Loki, no!" Adrianne yelled.

Redness detonated in the Gargantua's pupils. He leapt, the Eternity Key growing into a golden broadsword in his hands. The Nephil squinted at the divine light flaring from it.

Loki landed on the giant's head and drove the weapon into his skull with a roar. Bone cracked. The Nephil froze. The light in his eyes started to dim.

"Did he do it?!" Julia mumbled.

The Nephil's hand flashed up. He grasped the Gargantua and wrenched him from his head. Loki grunted as he found himself in the monster's grasp. The Nephil started squeezing.

Morgan, Victor, and Julia swooped, Zach and Delphine similarly arrowing toward the Nephil from the opposite side of the road.

Blood burst from Loki's lips.

"*LOKI!*" Morgan screamed.

Black wind and Dryad magic detonated around him.

Victor drew on all his demigod powers and prepared to swing his blade as they closed in on the monster.

Someone else reached the giant first.

A golden portal exploded into existence some hundred feet above them. Radiance flooded London as four beings brimming with divine energy came through the opening.

"Let go of my cat, asshole!"

Heaven's Light seared the Nephil's vision and half blinded Victor and the others. Victor blinked through the black spots dotting his vision and saw Cassius carve the monster's arm clean off at the elbow. The Nephil's head followed next, the slash of light that sliced his neck coming from behind it.

Time slowed. Victor's heart thudded painfully against his ribs as the demigod who had dealt the killing blow came into view beyond the spurting stump rising from the Nephil's torso, its skull tumbling over upon itself before gravity took effect.

It was Theo. Dazzling, white wings framed his armored body, the metal a beautiful turquoise that complemented his fearless eyes, one sage green and one sapphire blue. The Spear of Light hummed in his grasp, the weapon as solid as the one Victor wielded.

"Theo," he mumbled.

The demigod that was Theophile Serrano met his gaze and flashed him a breathtaking smile that was as fierce as it was beautiful.

CHAPTER FORTY-TWO

CASSIUS CAUGHT LOKI AS HE FELL FROM THE NEPHIL'S plummeting arm. By the time the giant's decapitated body struck the ground, the imp had shrunk right back down to his cat form.

Cassius clutched him gently to his chest. "You idiot!"

His belly twisted as he checked the limp cat over for injuries. Loki's left front leg was all smashed up and his tail was crooked.

The imp shuddered, the Eternity Key glowing with every beat of his heart where it had been reabsorbed by his body. He opened an ochre eye and licked Cassius's hand with a weak meow.

"*That Nephil was over three times your size,*" Nildar said admiringly as he landed lightly beside them.

Archon smashed down next to the East Star. "*You did well to fight him, Gargantua!*"

Cassius's soul core throbbed. Morgan almost tumbled him to the ground as he took them in his arms. Cassius shuddered and hugged him back just as tightly, Loki making a small sound of protest between them.

"Next time, I'm coming with you!" Morgan said heatedly.

Cassius nodded tremulously.

Theo alighted next to them.

"Is Loki okay?" he asked anxiously.

"He will be."

Cassius swallowed and stepped out of Morgan's hold, relief coursing through him as he looked upon his lover and down at the shivering imp. Morgan was safe. And though he was badly hurt, Loki's soul core was still intact.

Adrianne, Bailey, and Charlie jogged across the street toward them while Julia alighted with Victor and Zach.

"We'll go help them out!" Delphine shouted.

She indicated Charing Cross. Victor nodded. Delphine and Levi headed toward the barricade along with the other angels and demons.

"What happened to Theo?!" Julia asked, wide-eyed.

"This is his ultimate demigod form," Cassius explained.

Victor started toward Theo. "You look—" He stopped and swallowed, a storm of emotions dancing across his face as his gaze roamed the demigod from head to toe. "You look good."

A teasing light brightened Theo's eyes. He smirked. *"Good enough to eat?"*

Archon blinked. *"Eh?"*

Nildar lowered his brows.

"*I have been meaning to ask, but is there something going on between you?*" he said stiffly, his suspicious gaze swinging between Theo and Victor. "*You seem incredibly intimate for two people who just met.*"

"Yes," Theo said bluntly. "*Rohengar loves Coraos. And I love Victor.*"

Julia sucked in air. Zach gaped. Charlie pressed a hand to his mouth.

Victor's pupils flared crimson. "You—you love me?!"

"This kid's got balls of steel," Morgan mumbled.

Cassius sighed.

Theo ignored Archon and Nildar's thunderous expressions and walked over to Victor. He pressed a soft kiss to the stunned demigod's mouth and trailed a hand down his chest, his lips tilting in a seductive smile.

"*So, how about it? Fancy deflowering two demigods after this is over?*"

"*What?!*' Nildar barked.

"*Over our dead, rotting corpses!*" Archon growled.

"Wow," Adrianne whispered. "Just. Wow."

"You said it," Bailey muttered.

Cassius stifled a snort. For the first time since he'd met him, Victor looked like a rabbit caught in headlights.

"Sure," the demigod finally croaked.

Theo grinned.

Morgan shook his head at his brother with a look of pity. "That kid is gonna eat him up and spit him out."

A loud crack boomed across the sky, making them

jump. Crimson lightning tore through the clouds above.

Cassius's pulse quickened.

The dark mantle forming the barrier was starting to thin.

"Shit!" Victor cursed. "The shield is about to fall!'

"There's a way to save the city!" Cassius said urgently. "You guys take care of the remaining monsters and hellbeasts. Theo and I are going to return us to Earth! Here, look after Loki!"

He passed the imp to Morgan.

Morgan frowned, confused. "Return us to Earth? How?!"

"*I shall explain.*" Nildar dipped his head curtly at Cassius and Theo. "*Go!*"

Theo shot up beside Cassius. They rose rapidly above London, the slipstreams they passed through drenched with the stench of sulfur.

They reached the summit of the dark dome in time to see the fire of the Seventh Hell pierce through a section of clouds to the east. It started to burn the oxygen in the air, a growing fireball that would soon consume everything in its path.

"*Shield!*" Theo barked.

Divine light exploded from his outstretched palm.

A golden guard formed over the flames and breach a mile away, freezing them out.

Cassius's chest tightened with dread as he removed the Book of Rain from inside his armor. He sheathed his holy blade, touched the clasp, and released a burst of divine power. It popped open.

Another fracture tore the barrier to the south.

"*Shield!*" Theo shouted.

More cracks appeared in the sky. Cassius took a deep breath, reached for the divine energy within him, and poured it into the artifact he held.

Time slowed. Guard after golden guard exploded around London as Theo sealed shut all the breaches that started to materialize as the barrier failed, his eyes blazing with seraphic light and the weapon in his hand roaring with power.

The Book of Rain throbbed in Cassius's hands. It exploded into life a heartbeat later, the detonation so powerful he feared it would tear the city apart. He hung on grimly as the artifact shuddered violently in his grasp.

Pillars of light flashed into existence at the cardinal points of Inner London. The barrier that had shielded the city finally started to collapse all around them.

"*Shit,*" Theo muttered.

Fear knotted Cassius's belly. The armies of the Seventh Hell waited beyond the crumbling dome. Dozens of Cyclops and Nephilim were among them.

There was a moment of breathless stillness.

It was broken by savage roars as the troops charged toward the soon-to-be-unprotected city.

Cassius clenched his jaw so tight he almost cracked a tooth. Elios floated above the hellish wave coming at them from the north. Even from this distance, he could see the dark God grinning.

"*Smug fucker,*" Theo ground out. Something caught

his eye. A savage smile lit his face. *"Asshole won't see* this *coming."*

The tightness in Cassius's chest started to ease.

"This" was the semi-lucent veil that was rising to engulf London in a protective bubble even as the barrier Theo had first manifested rippled into nothingness. Elios screeched in fury when he registered the four pillars generating the shield of the Book of Rain.

The sphere closed, sealing off the crimson sky and noxious atmosphere of the Seventh Hell.

The troops at Elios's command smashed into its sheer wall, those at the front rapidly crushed by the ones behind them. Their bodies started piling up all around the new shield.

Theo looked at the city below, where Morgan, Victor, Nildar, Archon, and all the otherworldly and magic users in London still fought a desperate battle.

"I'm going to try something!"

Cassius met his gaze and dipped his chin, his pulse racing. *"Okay."*

A focused look brightened Theo's eyes. He frowned and raised his hand. *"Dimensional Portals!"*

Dozens of golden gateways opened across London.

Cassius's breath stilled as they sucked in the inhabitants of the Seventh Hell who did not belong. Even the corpses of their dead vanished inside the doorways, the remains of the Nephilim and other monsters and beasts twisting at impossible angles as they were siphoned back through to the realm on the other side of the shield of the Book of Rain.

Morgan and Victor soon joined them in the sky, Nildar and Archon at their side.

Victor pointed at the last portal as it whooshed closed above the river. "What was that?!"

Theo grinned. *"A parting gift for Elios."*

An outraged shriek reached them, the sound muffled by the barrier.

Cassius blinked. A portal had appeared above Elios. The dead Nephilim and hellbeasts were raining down upon him.

Archon squinted. *"What is that brown stuff?"*

Theo's smile turned vengeful. *"I opened a portal in the sewers."*

Cassius and Nildar snorted. Victor chuckled.

Morgan grinned and patted Theo on the back. "Attaboy!"

Cassius slowly sobered. He met Theo's gaze. "Ready for the next step?"

Theo grew serious. He nodded. Cassius, Nildar, and Archon took up position around him and laid a hand on his chest and back. Theo inhaled and exhaled. His pupils lit up.

The air trembled and brightened as he started to radiate divine energy.

Cassius poured his own essence into the new demigod's soul core, Nildar and Archon's powers fusing alongside his in a maelstrom of explosive energies.

They braced their wings at the detonation that rocked the South Star.

Theo clenched his jaw and focused all their powers into the Spear of Light. *"DIMENSIONAL PORTAL!"*

A dazzling beam erupted from his weapon as he raised it above his head. It pierced the shield of the Book of Rain and tore open a twenty-mile-wide, golden gateway in the crimson sky above it. Earth and Outer London shimmered into view through the interdimensional space beyond.

Sweat beaded Theo's forehead.

Cassius grasped the Book of Rain tighter and transferred some of its incredible power through his own soul core to Theo's.

Inner London trembled and started to rise inside its translucent bubble.

"Now, that is something you do not see every day!" Archon shouted in admiration.

Victor's gaze shifted to Theo, his eyes bright with emotion. "No, you don't."

Cassius swallowed a smile. *Hook, line, and sinker.*

Elios tried to smash through the barrier as the city entered the portal, his screams of rage faint.

Theo glared at the God of Darkness as they continued to ascend. *"You and your job can kiss my butt, assface!"*

Nildar frowned a little. *"I have been meaning to say this, Theophile, but you are somewhat foul mouthed compared to the last South Star."*

Then they were inside the portal and everything went a pure gold-white.

EPILOGUE

Cassius grimaced and tugged at his bow tie.

"God, I hate tuxedos," he muttered to himself.

Morgan approached through the crowd, a champagne flute in each hand and seemingly oblivious to how everyone parted to make way for him.

"Don't they have anything stronger?" Cassius said sourly.

Morgan made a face. "Victor told them to keep the good stuff away from us. He knew you would ask for it, apparently."

Cassius narrowed his eyes at Victor where he stood chatting with the prime minister on the other side of the vaulted hall. The demon noted his grumpy stare and raised his champagne glass with the smile of a born politician, his expression knowing.

They were at the National History Museum, in London. A week had passed since Theo had returned the inner city to Earth. Though the world was still in uproar about what had happened in England and the capital would not recover from the disaster that had struck it for months if not years to come, the mayor and the prime minister had insisted on holding a reception to thank everyone who had helped save them from a worse fate. News of the incredible feats the four agencies and the public services in Inner London had achieved was still making headlines across the globe, each day uncovering dozens more tales of acts of bravery. Dominating the reports were the four demigods who had ultimately saved London.

The Guardians of the Nether the Earth had never known existed, let alone seen before. Victor and Morgan's demigod status had equally stunned the world, the agencies forced to reveal who they truly were. Though humans had gotten used to co-existing with the otherworldly, the same could not be said of Gods and demigods.

Adrianne, Julia, Zach, Bailey, and Charlie had already left for San Francisco at Strickland's behest. As for Loki, Cassius had dispatched the reluctant imp with them to get the rest and care he sorely needed.

Adriane had sent them a picture of the recuperating imp yesterday. A harassed Bailey and Charlie were chasing Loki in his demon cat form around Cassius's apartment to give him his medicine.

The attached message had read: **The imp has officially gone feral!**

Cassius's cell buzzed with an incoming text. He removed the phone from his pocket and smiled faintly.

It was from Theo. **Help!**

Cassius looked to the grand staircase and the

landing where Theo, Nildar, and Archon were playing host to a group of world leaders. Archon looked as uncomfortable in his monkey suit as Cassius felt in his own, his long, red hair tamed into a slick ponytail by Nildar. Nildar, on the other hand, fit into his surroundings with the ease of a diplomat, his stunning good looks and smile drawing dozens of admiring stares. Theo was sweating buckets.

Even though he was nearly as powerful as an Awakener in his newly roused demigod form, Cassius knew he was still coming to terms with all the incredible changes he had gone through over a matter of days, not least his awareness that his body housed two souls.

Theo mouthed, "Seriously! Help me!" with a panicked look.

Morgan saw the exchange, narrowed his eyes, and took Cassius's phone. He fired back a message that had Cassius sighing.

How about you ask your own boyfriend for help and leave mine alone.

Theo's expression grew pinched. Affection flooded Cassius's heart. When Theo had told them how Rohengar had bound the last piece of his soul to the Spear of Light to keep it alive, Cassius had cried. But it wasn't just sorrow he had felt at Theo's trembling words.

His memories of Rohengar were returning. All their memories were coming back. Hypnos's spell was slowly coming apart and the Fallen had begun to recollect their past. For some, the agony of what they had lost almost drove them insane and it was left to the companions they had found on Earth to soothe their broken hearts and ravaged minds.

Cassius hoped they would all be whole again soon. Because the war wasn't over. He frowned.

Elios will come back. And the final battle will be fought here, on Earth.

"A penny for your thoughts," Morgan said.

Cassius grimaced. "Sorry. My mind was—"

"Miles away, I know." Morgan pouted. "Is it that hard to focus on your hot demigod boyfriend for one night?"

Cassius's lips twitched. He studied Morgan sternly. "Considering said demigod boyfriend has pretty much fucked me senseless every single night since our return from the Seventh Hell, I think I could do with the break."

Morgan had the grace to look a bit guilty. "Speaking of which, I don't think your bed will last another night of, er, passion."

Cassius narrowed his eyes. "I told you to slow it down."

Morgan brightened. "We've still got the couch."

Cassius punched him on the arm.

"Ow." Morgan chuckled. His expression slowly sobered. "Do you think she's given birth yet?"

Cassius's chest lightened a little. "Kalliste said she would try and send us a message when she did."

Theo had opened a portal to Rain Vale for Lilaia and Bostrof a few days ago and the expectant couple was currently in Kalliste's palace, preparing for the birth of their first child. Lilaia had also started to regain her memories before she'd departed.

"Prince Icarus!" she'd sobbed into his chest while he'd gently patted her back.

"Mind yourself, dear," Bostrof had said worriedly where he hovered beside them.

"Do you think it's the pregnancy hormones?" Morgan had muttered to Victor. "I've never seen her this emotional before, except for when she kicked Pan in his balls."

Victor had smiled at that. "Those were good times."

Lilaia had raised her head and glared at Morgan.

"I can't believe we lost you to that cocky fool of a demigod," she'd told Cassius. "How dare he seduce you?!"

"Hey!" Morgan had protested.

Cassius had grimaced. "Well, technically, you lost me to the Nether and the previous Awakener."

Lilaia's face had crumpled at that.

"Great," Bostrof had mumbled morosely as his wife had started sobbing again.

"Excuse me," a voice said presently.

Cassius looked around. A group of women and men in resplendent outfits had approached them. He noted the bodyguards behind them and realized he was likely dealing with the spouses of several of the world leaders around his Guardian brothers.

He smiled politely. "Yes? How may I help you?"

Four of the women and one of the guys looked like they were about to swoon. Morgan narrowed his eyes slightly.

The woman leading the group shoved a napkin and a pen at Cassius. "Could we have your autograph?"

Cassius blinked. "Er, sure."

Five minutes later and he was starting to regret his answer. A queue had formed, hordes of guests vying to get his signature when they realized what was happening. Though he knew Morgan was pleased the world no longer looked at him in fear and loathing, Cassius could tell his lover wasn't happy about the new kind of attention he was garnering from the way he was currently grinding his teeth beside him. A commotion on the staircase caught his gaze. Cassius bit his lip hard.

The entire hall had caught on to the fact that they could get the autographs of all four Guardians and had formed an even bigger crowd around Theo, Nildar, and Archon. Theo and Archon were looking at the avid admirers pressing in on all sides and the sea of napkins and pens they held with mounting horror.

It was Victor who came to their rescue. "I'm sorry, ladies and gentlemen, I'm afraid the Guardians have somewhere to be."

He ushered Theo, Nildar, and Archon up the steps and signaled to Cassius. A bittersweet feeling tightened Cassius's chest as he and Morgan excused themselves and headed up the staircase to join them.

Nildar and Archon were leaving for the Nether tonight.

Though Cassius wished the East and West Stars could stay on Earth, he knew he could not ask that of them. The borders of the Nether were still unstable and needed to be guarded. Nildar and Archon had proposed Cassius and Theo accompany them, but, again, that was not a viable option. The final battle with Elios would take place on Earth and they needed to be there to root out his evil machinations in the meantime.

There's also the fact that if we choose to go to the Nether, Morgan and Victor will insist on following, leaving Earth even more unprotected.

The noise of the party faded behind them as they headed up a corridor and climbed a smaller staircase. They emerged on a rooftop moments later. A cool breeze ruffled their hair and clothes as they walked to the edge and stood gazing silently at the city they had saved.

"Was I the one who tore the Nether?" Cassius said quietly.

Nildar and Archon startled. Victor flinched.

Morgan and Theo stared at Cassius, shocked.

It was Nildar who broke the tense lull. *"You remember?"*

Cassius swallowed, his stomach churning. "Bits of it."

So, it's true.

He recalled Elios's mocking words concerning the tear in the Nether and Pan's statement when they'd first met him in San Francisco that it was not the God of Darkness who had caused the Fall.

Archon's face darkened. He fisted and unfisted his hands. For a moment, Cassius thought he would strike him.

"It was not your fault, Icarus," the West Star ground out. *"It was Elios who provoked you to do that."*

"What?" Morgan mumbled hoarsely.

Cassius turned to meet his lover's gaze, wondering if the affection he had always shown him would turn to hate when he told him the truth. "When Coraos wounded you and Elios killed Rohengar, my rage tore the Nether apart." His breath caught, his voice quivering on his last words.

Morgan froze, horror leaching the color from his face. He moved.

Cassius stiffened as the demigod wrapped him tightly in his arms. He shuddered when their cores resonated and buried his face in Morgan's shoulder, his hands trembling as he wound his arms around his lover's neck.

The feelings he could sense radiating from Morgan through their connected souls remained unchanged. If anything, they felt even stronger than before.

"Elios took advantage of your power as an Awakener," Nildar said. *"And he needed to dispose of Rohengar. It was clear to us afterward that those had been his goals all along. That the War in the Nether was just the prelude to the Abyss opening up to release Chaos and swallow all the realms."*

Cassius's pulse raced as he looked at the East Star.

"All of us who were in the Nether when it tore know what you were going through at the time, Cassius," Victor said leadenly.

Cassius blinked, confused. "What do you mean?"

Victor swallowed. "The pain of your loss? We all experienced it when the Nether cracked under the power of your rage." He pressed a hand to his heart. "I felt it when I remembered what I did to Ivmir. It almost tore my soul in two."

His eyes glittered with a wet sheen. Theo walked over to him and clasped his hand, his lower lip trembling and tears running freely down his cheeks.

"The Nether needs four Guardians."

Nildar's words made Cassius's belly clench all over again.

The East Star frowned faintly. *"When this is over, you will have to return to your duties."* He sighed at Cassius and Theo's distraught expressions. *"You both know it, deep inside. Though Kalliste is confident Theo's awakening and that of the Spear of Light will heal the broken realms, I am certain it is the presence of all four Guardians in the place where they belong that is key to this."*

Cassius and Theo exchanged a tense look.

"Give us time to think about it," Cassius said.

"Yeah," Theo mumbled.

Archon stabbed a finger at them. *"Once we defeat Elios, you are coming with us even if I have to drag you two kicking and screaming."*

Morgan scowled. "We'll see about that."

"Yeah," Victor said in a hard voice.

Nildar pinched the bridge of his nose.

"And this is why Guardians should not have sex," he grumbled. *"The emotions that follow are an unnecessary complication."*

He glanced at Archon with a small frown.

"How about you open that portal?" Cassius told

Theo hurriedly as dark wind and flames erupted around Morgan and Victor.

Theo took one look at Victor's face and bobbed his head jerkily. A golden doorway hissed into life above the building at his command, its glow illuminating the rooftop. Divine light bloomed around Nildar and Archon as they transformed, their suits replaced by armor and their radiant wings dazzling as they sprouted from their backs.

Archon looked at Cassius.

"*Your wings. Can I see them?*" he said gruffly.

Cassius blinked. "Sure."

He unleashed his wings. Morgan sucked in air. Victor's eyes widened.

"What?"

Cassius stared at their stunned expressions before looking anxiously over his shoulder. His heart stuttered.

Gone were his crimson and black feathers. His wings were as white as the other Guardians' once more.

"*Good,*" Archon grunted, his face somewhat flushed. "*Just wanted to check.*"

"*The curse we wished upon you has finally dissipated,*" Nildar told Cassius with a gentle smile. "*The pain you experience when you take the life of another should be gone too.*"

Cassius swallowed and nodded numbly. "Thank—thank you!"

Pain and regret clouded Nildar's eyes.

Archon scowled. "*It is us who should be seeking your forgiveness, you fool!*"

Nildar sighed. "*Can you not just apologize normally?*"

"Oh." Archon blinked. "*I forgot something.*" He pointed at Theo. "*Make sure you teach him the ways of the ass before he is defiled by that demonic beast,*" he told Cassius, shooting Victor a glare.

Theo gasped and scowled. Victor narrowed his eyes at the Guardian. Morgan snorted. Cassius's jaw dropped open.

Nildar dipped his head solemnly. "*Indeed. We would not want our precious Rohengar or Theo to experience pain from the enormous phallus of that lecherous demigod.*"

Cassius groaned.

"Jesus fuck," Theo muttered in disgust.

"Hey, watch it!" Victor growled at the East and West Stars.

Morgan started laughing, tears streaming down his face.

Archon's gaze dropped to Victor's crotch. "*Poor Rohengar. Coraos's weapon looks like it might be mightier than Ivmir's.*"

Morgan stopped laughing.

"*I hear the nectar of the Fenoa flowers makes a good lubricant,*" Nildar informed them briskly as he headed for the portal to the Nether while Morgan glowered at Archon. "*It also has mild analgesic properties. You shall find it in the home of the Naiads.*"

"Will you assholes just leave already?!" Theo snapped, face bright red.

Archon sniffed. "*We are only trying to help, little one.*"

He turned and followed Nildar. *"Hey, Nildar, how do you know about those Fenoa flowers?"*

Nildar gave him a mysterious smile.

Archon paled a little. *"What does that smile mean? Nildar? Talk to me, dam—!"*

The portal closed on them.

THE END

Cassius and Morgan's adventures continue in Harbinger.

AFTERWORD

I hope you enjoyed Oathbreaker, the fourth book in Fallen Messengers. This book is another major turning point in the series, with the introduction of Cassius's Guardian brothers, a look into our favorite demigod's mysterious origins, and an unlikely match for Victor Sloan. I would be grateful if you could leave a review of Oathbreaker on Goodreads or on the store where you purchased it. Reviews help readers like you find my books and I truly appreciate your honest opinions about my stories.

Make sure to sign up to my store newsletter for special deals on my books and new release alerts.

Or you can sign up to my author newsletter instead to get upcoming release notifications, sneak peeks, and giveaways.

BOOKS BY AVA MARIE SALINGER

FALLEN MESSENGERS

Fractured Souls - 1

Spellbound - 2

Edge Lines - 3

Oathbreaker - 4

Harbinger - 5

Crimson Skies - 6

CONTEMPORARY ROMANCE WRITTEN

AS A.M. SALINGER

Nights Series

Twilight Falls Series

ABOUT THE AUTHOR

Ava Marie Salinger is the pen name of an Amazon bestselling urban fantasy author who has always wanted to write MM urban fantasy romance. When she's not dreaming up hotties to write about, you'll find Ava creating kickass music playlists to write to, spying on the wildlife in her garden, drooling over gadgets, and eating Chinese food. She also writes contemporary MM romance as A.M. Salinger.

Visit Shop AD Starrling and buy all of Ava's ebooks, paperbacks, hardbacks, and exclusive special edition print books direct.